I0461063

CHAOS
OF
HARD CLAY

FOR THOSE WHO LOVE A GOOD APOCALYPSE

AND ESPECIALLY FOR GEORGE A. ROMERO

I MISS YOU, BIG MAN

CHAOS
OF
HARD CLAY

Tales of the Apocalypse

Edited by G. Allen Cook and Kathy Cook

BANJAXED Books

Chaos of Hard Clay © 2018 by G. Allen Cook

Back Illustration © 2017 by Jamie Bristol Hampton

Jacket Design © 2017 by Kathy M. Cook

All Rights Reserved

The following page represents all copyrights

Printed in the USA

First **BANJAXED Books** Printing

10 9 8 7 6 5 4 3 2 1

PUBLISHER'S NOTE

This is a work of fiction. Names, characters, places, and incidents either are the product of each author's imagination or are used fictionally. Any resemblance to actual persons, living or dead, events, or locales is coincidental. No part of this book may be transmitted or reproduced in any form or by any electric or mechanical means, including photocopying, recording, or by any information storage or retrieval system, yet invented or otherwise, without written permission of the authors or their representation.

ISBN-13: 978-0-692-05229-7

The name **BANJAXED Books** and the stylized "B" when used in tandem are copywritten and may be used only with permission.

No Tears to Spare © 2017 Crystal Leflar

When the World Fled East © 2017 Daniel Willcocks

A Game of Tag © 2017 David Henderson

Grim Diesel © 2017 G. H. Finn

What's Below the Surface © 2017 Hákon Gunnarsson

A Short History of the Future © 2017 Han Adcock

After © 2017 Jack Stone

Been Here Before © 2017 Jessica Mizell

Hanging, Just Outside the World © by 2017 Jim O'Donnell

The Beginning, Again © 2017 Justin Bloch

What Remains © 2017 Kamron Taylor

Dust and Fingers © 2017 Luke Kondor

Verity © 2017 Megan Manzano

Black Water © 2017 N. J. Reynolds

How Do They Like It © 20017 Ray Prew

Ghost Woman © 2017 Roxanne Dent

Take Me to Your Fucking Leader © 2017 Olin Wish

And to All a Good Night © 2017 Steve Bissonnette

Dead Wrong © 2017 Vonnie Winslow Crist

Endgames and Epilogues © 2017 by G. Allen Cook

If you'd like to learn more about **BANJAXED Books,** please go to:

www.gallencook.com

"And I looked, and behold a pale horse; and his name that sat on him was Death, and Hell followed with him."
—Revelations 6:8

6:12

All clocks display this time after a world-altering catastrophe in Craig Harrison's *book,* The Quiet Earth.

TABLE OF CONTENTS

NO TEARS TO SPARE
by Crystal Leflar

What went into the decision to kick off a post-apocalyptic anthology with a story concerning Climate Change? Well, if I have to answer that question you may be reading the wrong book.—Ed.

THEY SAY THE SAHARA was once a rainforest and even our own country was once a marsh, so no one should have been surprised. Hell, *The Dust Bowl* should have been warning enough. I'd like to say that I saw it coming, but I was just as surprised as anyone. The farmers were maybe the most aware; they said the warm winter would be their downfall. It was warm and dry with no snow, and they said their crops would suffer come spring and wither come summer, but you know farmers. Well, I knew a few and they were always preparing for the worst, even when they believed it was gonna be a good year they would just shrug and say "maybe".

So, after the warm, dry winter the spring came early and warmed things up even more. Flowers blossomed; animals came out of their shelters and the birds, well the birds never left, and that should have been another clue. I can remember being disappointed. There's nothing like a long, cold winter to make you really appreciate spring when it comes around.

Anyway, summer came and never left, it just got hotter and hotter until folk's ponds and pools dried up. Then it seemed the Folks themselves started to dry up. The farmers locked themselves to survive as long as they could at first, didn't take 'em long to realize their livestock needed water just as much as they did. Most of them are gone now. Dead, if they're lucky.

Everyone has their own theories 'bout how and why it happened. The Doc talks about "climate change" and how he ought to have been protected from this existence, since he had gone "green." Dale just laughs and reminds him that he could be dead. "The only way you'd be above this mess is if you died and were lucky enough to get into heaven. You wanna test that theory?" To that Doc would mumble and sit in his chair and read his books and that would be the last of it until the next time Doc tried to get more'n his share of the food or water.

Caleb was the one who brought the CB radio and a bag full of nothing but batteries. He insisted there had to be others out there and if there were he was gonna be able to get in to contact with them. He spent hours every day fiddling with it, trying to get someone on every station. 'Bout a month ago he actually got a response. There was a lot of static and the message itself was short, but it was some woman giving coordinates to water, an "oasis" she called it, and she told us to come. Not that she knew she was talkin' to us, it was more like what used to be emergency broadcasts. You know, the beeps and then the message? It was kinda like that.

Caleb kept trying to get through again to ask questions I guess, or because it was the first connection he'd been able to make with the radio, but we didn't hear anything more. Still, we needed water and needed it soon. I don't know much about navigation, but Dale seemed to know where we were going, always messing with his maps, I think he maybe drove a truck 'round the country when he was younger. I've had my doubts about leaving home, but I guess that maybe drying up on the move is better than sitting still and drying up for sure.

~ ~ ~

The sun setting was our cue to get moving again. We broke camp and loaded up the wagon and hitched it to the horse. We just had one; Dale brought it with him from his farm, along with the wagon and most of the supplies. That's why he was in charge, seeing as how it's all his stuff. We all have our own shotguns and ammo and most of us can hunt if there is anything to hunt, but Dale was old, and he knew he wouldn't get far on his own. He let us all come along with him for two reasons, he said. One, we were alive, and the second reason was different for all of us. For me he said it was because my Daddy was a good friend to him.

With the sun gone, we started out. It was almost habit,

the way we did it. My job was to lead the horse that night. We rotated, two up in front with kerosene lanterns to light the way, two on either side of the wagon with guns ready. I led the horse while Dale followed the wagon, watching our tail. Jason's dog usually ran up front for a few hours before sleeping in the wagon slouched onto whoever happened to be sitting there. We'd thought about killing him a few times (the dog, not Jason), but he was a good hunting dog so after the first few squirrels he chased down for us we figured he was worth the water.

I remember when it took a day or two to travel. We'd been at it for a month now and were just getting "almost there." An old horse with a loaded wagon sure makes for slow travel. Joe suggested that we take a car; he had been living out of an old school bus when we found him, and I guess he got attached to it. Doc was quick to support that suggestion, but Dale shot them down. "And what do you reckon we'll do for gas? It ain't that easy to come by these days. No, we go like we have been." And since Dale said it, it was law. Didn't stop Doc from complaining all the time when he had to walk, but he walked. Joe said complaining was Doc's fuel. Dale didn't seem to mind, and I think he liked the idea of havin' a doctor with us, just in case. Farmers tend to be a cautious lot.

We were getting closer to our destination, out in what Caleb called "Nowhere," but anything that didn't warrant a big star on Dale's map seemed to be "Nowhere" to him. It's true, there wasn't much around, but I think that's mostly 'cause Dale took care to avoid the cities where we could. Once we stopped in a town to see if there was anything to scavenge, but the town's survivors shot us off and Dale said that there likely wasn't anything in there worth dying over, so we kept on our way. I felt their eyes on us as we skirted around the town, but they let us be when they saw that we were just passing through with no intention of poaching.

The town we were approaching was different though. I could see no signs of life, not from the road anyway. Usually they put up signs to let others know there are people around. It's kinda like what Caleb seeks with his radio, proof of life. Surviving can be lonely when you think you're all that there is.

"Stop!" Dale called out over the sound of Caleb's guitar. I pulled the reins and Sweetie slowed to a stop. "Town up ahead. We're too short on time and supplies to go 'round, so keep your guns ready fellas, we're going through." There was a murmur of excitement as they got out of the wagon. They loaded extra guns to have on hand, just in case. "Kid, you hop on sweetie, you're gonna need your hands."

I groaned. "I'ma be a target on the horse, Dale." I tried to keep the whine down. I really didn't mind riding Sweetie, as she was old and easy to lead, but damn. "I ain't been shot yet, and I'd like to keep it that way."

"Don't be a sissy, Kid-o, you're gonna be just fine. Doubt

they'll see you up there in the dark, and you'll make a smaller target than anyone else."

"Hold this for a second." I handed my gun to Joe and then climbed on top of Sweetie. I grumbled when I felt her shift under me. "Dale, there's no saddle!"

I heard him chuckle in the dark. "Just hold on tight with your knees, she ain't gonna be moving that fast. You'll be fine." I gritted my teeth and clenched my knees around the horse. Sweetie tossed her mane back and looked at me disapprovingly.

"Take your gun, girl." I turned to look toward Joe and nearly got hit in the head with my own weapon.

"Geez, just gimmie a second will ya?" I looped the reins around my arm and grabbed the gun. "All right." I took a deep breath and slouched down, trying to make myself as small as possible. They could talk 'bout how safe I'd be on Sweetie, but really I knew that Dale just wanted me to have the high ground. I'm the best shot we've got, not that they'd say it out right.

"Ready?" Dale's voice carried forward as the lights were snuffed out. "All right, let's go."

I dug my knees into Sweetie; she huffed but started moving forward, and we moved toward the town in silence. The clopping of horseshoes—and the racketing of the wagon wheels—seemed louder than they ever had before.

"This time ain't no different than any of the other towns

we've had to go around," I muttered to myself as we entered the small town, moving toward the square. I was nervous despite my attempted logic. "Just a town. A deserted town as like as not, nothing here but dust and bones."

"You scared, Kid?" came a whisper from below me. For a moment I thought it was the horse.

"You ain't?" I shot back at Joe. Whatever reply he was gonna make was lost in a howl from behind me. Jason's dog had caught a scent.

"Keep moving." Dale's voice called out from the rear. "We keep moving and keep steady unless I say otherwise." I could hear breaths being taken and held as we readied our guns. The only other sounds could make out were echoes of the noises we made as we moved down the deserted street. We followed the main road because Dale said it'd go right through. We'd gone maybe fifteen minutes without incident and the end wasn't too far off. I started to relax and put my gun across my lap to untangle my hand from the reins.

The dog howled as I slapped my fingers against my thigh to get the feeling back—a moment later gunfire filled the silence. I grabbed my gun and aimed it at the darkness. I saw movement from the corner of my eye and twisted to shoot, struggling to find a line of sight as Sweetie struggled beneath me. As I was about to shoot, she reared up. I tumbled off of her, rolling to avoid the wagon wheels as she took off. I heard Dale shouting something but couldn't make out what it was over the noise. Gunfire, shouts, and growls, it all seemed to dim as I felt hands moving up my legs.

All I could hear was my heart pounding as I grasped my gun tighter and sat up to look the monster in the eye. Death seeped from its opened mouth and its eyes were a flash of yellow before I fired my gun. The force of the shot sent it flying off me. I scrambled to my feet, unable to keep myself from looking back at it as I ran to the others.

I slowed when I saw them standing where the horse and wagon had been, staring at the bodies around them. Dale was looking off in the direction Sweetie had run, and Jason was kneeling down trying to calm his dog. "Hard to believe that they were once people." Caleb said softly, kicking one of the smaller corpses over onto its back. "Hard to think how close we all have come to this existence."

"We take our victories where we can these days," Doc said, wiping blood from his face.

"Sweetie's gone," Dale said.

"Do you want to go lookin' for her?" Jason asked. "We can catch her scent, follow her trail. She can't have gone too far with that wagon on her."

"We need our supplies. She can't have gone far." He led the way down the street, stepping over bodies as we followed the wagon tracks. We walked in silence with our guns ready in case of another attack. Dale led us off the road as he followed the tracks to a fence. "She tried to jump."

I looked ahead, squinting against the darkness. I could just make out four forms over Sweetie. "Kill them," Dale ordered, aiming his gun. His shot rang out, and three more followed. Two of the figures collapsed. I shot at the other one. I hit it in the leg; it fell and started pulling itself away. I stepped closer, right up over it, and fired. I admit to feeling a sense of satisfaction as its chest opened up like they opened up like poor Sweetie's. I shot it in the head to make sure it was dead.

I heard another shot and turned in time to see Dale kneeling next to his horse, petting her as her breath stopped and her eyes went dim. After a moment, he stood and wiped the back of his hand across his eyes. "Everyone else okay?" he asked. When we nodded, he said, "Then get the gear." Jason and Joe walked back to collect the stuff that had fallen out.

I started to climb up to get what was still in the wagon when I saw Caleb limp closer. "No," he groaned, slumping against the wagon. "One of the damn things bit my leg."

"Doc?" Dale gestured for him to come forward. He handed me a flashlight. "Hold this, kid. Give the doctor some light." The Doc kneeled down beside Caleb and inspected his leg.

"The wound itself isn't serious, but the teeth bit through the flesh."

"What's that mean?" I asked, trying to hold the light steady.

"It means I'm gonna turn into one of them." Caleb pulled his gun into his lap as he stared at the doc.

"Well, the bite itself will heal, or it would." The doc stood and adjusted his glasses. "The thing that bit him very likely infected him."

"Can we do anything?" Dale asked.

The doc shrugged. "I don't know. It seems unlikely that any cure has been discovered, and by the time it is he's likely to become one of them."

"Kid, you go on and help the boys." Dale took the flash light from me. I started to protest, but he cut me off. "You heard me, kid."

"But, Caleb..."

"It's all right," Caleb smiled at me. "Doc probably just needs me to take my pants off so he can see it better."

Dale turned me around by my shoulders and gave me a shove.

I was walking toward Joe and Jason when I heard the gunshot. I kept walking until I got to the edge of town. I could hear them getting things together and talking. When they came nearer to me I wiped my nose on my sleeve before I turned to face them.

"Well, we only got a couple of hours 'til we get to where we're going. We will have to do without making camp. We don't wanna waste time sticking around here. We'll have to risk the morning sun and hope our water lasts until sunrise."

I took the bags that Jason gave me and we carried what we could in silence, following Dale further into the darkness.

It took six hours on foot to get there. "I guess we were closer than we thought," Jason said as we looked around an underground water reserve.

There were several people there, underground, enough to fill a small town. A woman approached us, smiling. "Welcome. We have an area sectioned off as a makeshift hospital, if any of you are in need."

"We aren't in too bad of shape, ma'am. We were lucky to have a doctor with us," Dale said, removing his hat. "But you could give us a check over, just to be sure."

She nodded and pushed her hair back off her face. "Follow me please." She led the way down a damp concrete hallway and pushed a curtain aside. "Some of our beds are full of survivors from a nearby town. We heard them above us the other night scratching at the door like animals. Poor things were so dehydrated they were nearly senseless." We followed her in to a largish room filled with makeshift beds, and I froze when I saw them.

"Why are you keeping those things here?" Joe asked, narrowing his eyes. "Don't you know they're dangerous?"

The woman frowned and looked back at her patients. "I suppose they are as dangerous as anyone fighting for survival. Why do you ask?"

"We ran into a group of them a couple of hours ago,"

Jason said. "It was like in the movies. We were moving through, and they came at us out of nowhere."

"Like in the movies? You mean zombies?" Her frown increased.

"That's what they call them," Doc spoke up. "I tell them it's some sort of disease, a virus, but they persist in using that term."

The woman attempted to smile. "These are people. Not zombies."

"Then how do you explain what's happened to them?" I asked, staring at the one nearest us. Its eyes were yellow and glazed, and its fingers were rotted away. I could see bone peeking out from each knuckle. Its yellow skin was stretched tight across a bloated stomach. Someone pulled a sheet up to cover it. I saw its empty eyes and remembered Caleb. I looked back at the nurse. "It ain't human, what they do. Where there's anything flesh, dead or alive, there they are circling 'round it like vultures. Whatever they were—they ain't anymore."

She considered me a moment before responding. "It's true that they resorted to drinking whatever liquid they could find to stay alive, including blood, but I assure you they're just as human, just as alive, as you and I. Zombies only exist in movies."

I looked at Dale and saw my horror reflected in his face. "If only you would've waited," I tried to say, but my throat closed and went dry as my eyes.

"It's a cruel irony, it is." Doc mumbled. He looked at me funny when I started laughing. It was the only thing I could do, and I couldn't seem to stop.

WHEN THE WORLD FLED EAST
by Daniel Willcocks

Sometimes a snack is as good as a feast, and this brief look into the protagonist's search for what may be the most potent symbol of life before the apocalypse is a feast indeed.—Ed.

HE HAD NEVER SEEN the ocean before. Never smelt the air, never dipped his feet in the frozen washes of the foam as it lapped the shore. Never heard the cry of the gulls as they circled and dived without a splash onto the giant mass of the sea.

There was a time when it had been nothing more than a pipe dream. Garth was a proud Nebraskan. A citizen of the landlock. His father had been a lowtime agricultural farmer—mostly working with pigs and cattle. His mother had spent so much time with her legs open, either popping out babies or receiving the pleasures of her husband (really, both in equal measure), that by the time Garth had reached his sixth birthday, he was one amongst thirteen children. The idea of ever gathering enough cash to be lulled by the gentle hush of any kind of water seemed ludicrous. Life was what life was. Chores, lashings, hollering, and chores.

Garth picked up a pebble, slickened with salt water to a dark sheen. He rubbed his thumb across its smooth surface, measuring for the throw. With a flick of the wrist he sent the stone flying, watching as it bounced once, twice, then stopped with a gentle thud as it hit another mound of flesh. A couple gulls took to the air in shock, quickly circling back to peck at the buoyant mess.

When Garth was seven, his mother had gone into town for a couple days. It was a scorcher of a day, he remembered, as he carried bags of animal food across the fields to the various shacks and sheds that housed the livestock. His older brothers, Duey and Howie, were non-identical twins (not that anybody could tell them apart), and, much to their own satisfaction, kept the siblings on track taking care of the chores in the absence of any higher authority, hardly doing any themselves. Garth had sweated buckets that day, but remembered coming home in the evening to a small bundle hidden under cloth near the fireplace.

"Now, now. Calm down, sweeties." Mother only ever called them 'sweeties' when she was flushed and rosy-cheeked with a slight lilt to her walk. "Mama's got y'all a gift from Aunt Sheridan's town. Take a peep at these."

With an over-dramatic reveal, the package was greeted by a gasp and a dozen or so hands all grabbing at once for the books. Picture books, thick books, books with just words.

"Now now," Mother said again, a wry smile on her face.

Garth had taken ahold of a thin paperback with yellow, dog-eared pages, and a large tear in the front. The book was mostly words—grown-up words that he hadn't understood at the time—but on every few pages was a coloured sketch that told the story.

"Ma...Ma!" Garth had panted as he ran into Mother's room one morning. "Lots of water!"

Mother had smiled, invited Garth into bed where Father snored deeply in a naked doze, and explained all about the sea. That Nebraska was a small part of a large area of land, bordered east and west by thousands of miles of water. More water than Garth could ever have imagined in his life.

"Think of the creek at the bottom of Abigail's hill. Times that by two. Then double that. Then keep on doublin' until your breath runs out and you fall to the floor."

Now, Garth's lips peeled to reveal a dry smile. There was salt in the air, he could taste that for certain. Enough to pull all the moisture out of the otherwise choking air. He scanned the horizon as far as he could see, watching the blood-red sun setting.

He missed people, now. There was no denying it. Thirty years since he had first seen the ocean in a picture book and here he was, on the borders of the Atlantic with no one to enjoy the view. Duey, Howie, Mother, Father, all of Garth's bloodline had collapsed and soaked into the ground along with 99.9% of the population. How long he had been alone now he couldn't remember. But the virus was sickening. The virus did unimaginable things. Affected the brain. Made you forget who you were. Pointed your compass east and set you running like a motorcycle kicked into gear and left to watch as it trailed into the distance.

Humanity had become a herd, focused on a universal mindset. Every single citizen of the brave old USA had turned and began to walk, then jog, then run.

All except Garth.

Could he explain it? By heck he could. But Garth was still a Christian and somewhere in the lunacy was a mighty plan that'd reveal itself soon enough. Of that he was certain. Until then, he figured, he'd maybe just follow the herds of human wildebeest and see where the trail may go. He hadn't expected to end up at the ocean. Truth was, he had no idea how far the ocean would have been. But, at last, as he thumbed another pebble and tossed it out to sea, he took a seat and drank in the view.

It wasn't what he expected. The careful illustration showed a heaving mass of blue water and white foam waves.

But all Garth could see, for as far as his vision could stretch, was the throbbing mass of corpses floating on an endless tide. A makeshift raft of the human population, pecked and pulled by a thousand mobbing seagulls. Maybe they couldn't swim. Maybe the virus told them not to.

Whatever had happened, there was no blue.

Only a deep crimson that foamed and bubbled against the shore, and the stale taste of sun-dried ham lingering in the air.

GAME OF TAG
by David Henderson

No post-apocalyptic anthology would be complete without a zombie story. This one, however, may be the proverbial horse of a different color.—Ed.

MICHAEL JACKSON, NO RELATION to his namesake but named after his mother's favorite artist, sat in the window of his second-story bedroom as he often did these days. He looked down to the lot behind the house where a group of his friends had gathered for a game of tag. The sky, mostly cloudy as it always was these days, scattered the sunlight into various shades of red, orange, and purple. Though he lived in a rural town in southern Arkansas, the effects of the nation's involvement in Nuke War One left its evidence everywhere.

Ten years ago, Nuke War One, so called because no one dared call it "World War III," left the country, hell most of the Earth, scorched and in rubble. Turned out North Korea's missiles could reach American soil and the United States defenses had largely been puffed up with propaganda. The country wasn't as prepared as its citizens were led to believe. By the time retaliation came about, both coasts were essentially destroyed. Turned out North Korea had allies in places most of the world thought were against the ruling regime. Guess the world was wrong about a lot of things before Nuke War One.

Though the coasts were obliterated, the interiors of most continents were left intact. Well, if one can refer to poisonous air "intact." Scientists believed, and thus had always taught the lay people of the world, that fallout from such strikes would render much of the planet inhabitable. They were wrong about that. Granted, venturing outside of one's home meant battling the dust and debris floating and swirling around, but one could breathe with no observable effects. People wore coverings over their mouths, but they did not instantly die of respiratory failure or have their eyes melt when the wind blew dirt in them. No, especially in the midsection of the country, people went on living as best they could.

People would come into town from time to time, looking for work, for food, for a place to live or for people to live with. Strangers were usually met with the open end of a rifle long before any conversation took place, encouraged to move along and keep on looking. To many, the Midwest and Midsouth had reverted back to some kind of "Old West." But in this version, local folks barricaded main roads and used little-known trails for travel around. People took turns keeping guard, rationing food and supplies, and keeping the peace.

For kids in town, life sucked so far as they were concerned. Gone were the days of handheld consoles and computers for gaming. They no longer had apps like SnapChat, Twitter or the other apps teens used to communicate with each other before the end of the world as they knew it. Electricity barely kept the necessities running, let alone being "wasted" on frivolities such as consoles and non-critical computers. The kids were relegated to reading, riding bikes, and generally staying out of the way. Schools were converted into shelters and storage facilities, leaving lots of free time for the youth of the town to cause trouble.

Michael suffered with an asthmatic-like birth defect that was a struggle even before the war. Afterward, time spent outside meant painful coughing fits. Sometimes, friends would come over and join him inside for games of UNO and Monopoly, but they mostly wanted to be outside. On the days he was left alone, Michael sat in the window of his bedroom, watching his friends play.

As he looked down, James Dougan was running away from Amy Sweaster as she lunged out, trying to catch him. Billy Rankin and Jessie Smith stood away from the action, keeping a watchful eye in case Amy suddenly decided to head in their direction. Michael smiled down on his friends. They played this game until the light in the sky turned to the shades of evening - darker blues, deep purples, and angry oranges. The town's curfew dictated that everyone associated with local law enforcement leave the streets until morning. Michael returned to his bed and turned on the 40-watt bulb that served as the main light in his bedroom. He picked up a copy of "From the Corner of His Eye," by Dean Kootnz. The novel was decades old, but he loved reading how the children could "walk where the rain wasn't." He wished he could walk where the dust wasn't.

The next afternoon, Michael watched his friends play tag in the lot again. This time, James was "it," chasing the others around the lot, dodging the trash dumpster, climbing stacks of wooden pallets, and kicking other garbage strewn about. As he watched, though, he noticed something different about the game. It seemed more intense, more aggressive. The friendly "tags" became shoves. The laughter turned to growls and grunts. Smiles seemed more sinister, or so Michael believed. He thought he saw Billy try to bite Jessie. Maybe he was trying to kiss her. It was hard to tell from this angle. When the light in the sky changed, the group disbanded and Michael retreated from the window. His mother, thin from years of eating rationed food and fretting over events which she had no control, came into his room.

"Michael," she said, her voice not of frailty but of defeat and dejection. "I know you don't feel well when you go outside to play, but you should think about joining your friends tomorrow. It will be fun." The suggestion contained no real excitement, it just came out flat and monotone.

"It hurts to go outside, Mom. You know that. Besides…"

Besides what? His friends were getting meaner? His friends were trying to kiss each other, or EAT each other? It didn't matter. His mother paid no attention to it.

"I know it does, but you need to soak in whatever sunshine you can. Not that there's much of it going around these days." She looked at the floor, backed out of the room and turned down the hallway toward the stairs. Michael heard her footsteps land on each step as she trudged downstairs.

The next day, Wednesday, he took a long, ragged breath as he pulled the paper mask over his mouth and nose. He grabbed an old "Steelers" cap that used to belong to his Dad, keeping it tight against his head. The plastic band in the back had been set one size too small, ensuring it would not blow off in the swirls of wind. His dark blue jacket and blue jeans protected his body from the pelting dirt and sticks that blasted against him from time to time. He closed his eyes, opened the back door and stepped outside.

The sun felt warm even though there was very little of it. The winds, it seemed, had given him reprieve and he looked around the lot. In the far corner, the old large oak tree stood defiant against all that had come to it in its lifetime. Leafless, its branches were thick and sprawling. They stretched out as if it say, "Come, children, come and play on me. Build a treehouse in the foundations of my arms." Of course, there would be no treehouse. The materials to construct such a luxury sat in community storage—an old lumberyard and hardware outlet—for use by those in need after a night of severe weather. Michael stepped into the lot, tilting his head toward the sky, taking in the veil of clouds with slits like window blinds, allowing the sun to peek through. He was only three when Nuke War One took place, but he remembered green grass growing where now there was dirt and the different colored leaves on the tree. He remembered little from those days. After all, he was only three. Sometimes, his mind flashed with short snippets of memory. The most vivid featured his father standing behind the wheel of a boat on the water. His dad, who died shortly after the war due to his own respiratory complications, had bright, red curly hair. His pale white body sported blue swim trunks with white piping down the sides. Michael pictured it as though the scene were playing out right in front of him.

A gust of wind flared up and brought Michael back into the day. He sucked in a gulp of air reflexively. He coughed. He coughed and coughed and coughed again. He couldn't stop. He tried an old technique of pressing his lips tightly together, forcing the cough through his nose, but he couldn't hold his mouth together. The air quickly, violently exhaled from within him. He sucked in a huge breath, making the cough even worse. He hacked and wheezed. Turning, he held his heaving chest, lumbering back toward the house. His chest constricted and he grabbed his jacket near his heart with his right hand. He dropped to his knees as the dust and dirt and trash danced around him. He shut his eyes against it all and tried to scream. Nothing came out except the hoarse rasp of a person whose life was leaving quickly and most likely bringing the insides with it. Michael leaned forward and put his hands out to catch himself before he hit the ground. He started crawling slowly toward the back door, wincing with each breath as he pulled himself along.

He collapsed. His face lay to one side, the mask no longer protecting it. Every breath he drew brought more dirt and dust into his mouth, his lungs. He moved his left arm and tried to get it underneath himself to raise up, but the pain in his chest was too much. The world around him closed in, blackness creeping closer and closer.

~ ~ ~

Michael opened his eyes and drew a slow, measured breath. No pain. He exhaled. No pain. "Am I dead," he asked the blurry vision before him.

"Not hardly," his mother responded, almost with a smile in her voice. She came into view as his vision cleared. She was smiling, shaking her head slightly. "I thought I'd lost you. You should have been more careful out there."

"But, you told me to—" he started to speak, but she cut him off.

"You have to recognize your limits. No one else can do that for you. Here." She helped him sit up, offering a glass of water she had taken from the night stand beside his bed.

"What time is it?" he asked, still a bit groggy and not quite returned to the world of the living.

"It's late afternoon," she paused a moment before adding, "on Saturday."

"SATURDAY?" Michael spat the water from his mouth. "When I went outside, it was Wednesday!" His mind raced. How long had he laid there? What had occurred in the days he'd slept? Where were his friends? Was he hungry? He thought he might be. Did he remember what happened? He didn't know. His crazed eyes met his mother's and for a moment she jerked back, startled by it.

"Yes. You were outside for a few minutes before I walked into the kitchen and saw you on the ground. I tell you, you scared the crap out of me, Michael." She placed one hand over her heart as she said this and placed the other over Michael's.

"Well, it scared the crap outta me!" he said, almost laughing. Then he added, as he turned his face toward the window, "I saw Dad."

"Oh?"

"He was driving the boat. In his shorts. No shirt. He was white."

"Well, of course he was white, he—"

"No, I mean pale. Really pale," he said, cutting her off. His mother nodded understandingly and moved her hand to his head, where she gently stroked his hair for a moment.

"I miss him, Mom. I miss," he paused for a moment, "a lot of things. Everything."

"I know, honey. I do, too. Your father. Life. All of it." She drew a deep breath. "But, we are still alive. So, we fight on." Michael thought she sounded more awake and resolute than she had been in years. She withdrew her hand from his hair as he turned back to face her. Her lips softened into a gentle smile that made him understand just how his father must have felt when he looked at her. He smiled back.

"It's so hard, Mom."

"If it were easy, it wouldn't be worth having. Why don't you get some rest?" She started to get up from the bed. As she did, he looked at the window again.

"I think I'll see what my friends are playing," he said, to no one in particular.

"Oh, there are new kids! I almost forgot!"

"New kids?" Michael asked as he got out of bed and walked to the window. Below, his old friends had been joined by some new kids.

"Yeah," his mother interrupted. "But, they don't seem too friendly at all. In fact, I'd say your friends have taken on a bit of mischief. They sure do like to roughhouse lately." So, his mother had also noticed the same thing. And, apparently, it's been getting worse. Michael sat in the window, unmindful that his mother has left the room.

There were three new kids. One was thin, skinny even. He had dusty blond hair and wore little round eyeglasses on a long face with a high forehead. Another kid was almost nondescript. He had brown hair, cut cleanly. He wore a red and white striped shirt and blue jeans. He was about as tall as James. Then, there was the fat girl. She was very round with a matching round face, her thick black hair pulled back into two tight pigtails behind her head.

"Or were they called ponytails?" he asked the window. As if in response, the girl shook her head back and forth as the ponytails swung left then right then left then right. It was hypnotic in a way, and Michael found himself mesmerized by the swaying. Back and forth, left and right. Amy shrieked, breaking the trace Michael had found himself in. He shifted his gaze toward her. She was running away from the dusty-haired boy, laughing as he tried to catch her. The other kids scattered about the lot, trying to keep away from the boy Michael nicknamed "Dusty."

Dusty chased Amy, then he turned quickly, heading for James, who dodged aside. Amy grabbed Billy's hand and they ran away from the pursuit, laughing the whole time. The fat girl didn't run so much as waddle from place to place. Dusty would chase her, but he slowed down as he did, as though he knew she couldn't move as quickly as the others and adjusted his chase accordingly. Perhaps the fat girl was Dusty's sister or cousin or girlfriend. The brown-haired boy, whom Michael had now nicknamed "Ringo" (after a picture of some old rock group his mother had hanging in the living room—The Bugs or Spiders or Beetles or something) climbed the tree and watched the action from a perch on an outstretched branch. Suddenly, Dusty changed directions again and chased after James. Just as Dusty reached out to tag James, the fat girl stepped directly into his path, knocking him onto the ground.

"Hey! What did you do that for!?" James yelled at the girl as he started getting up. Dusty placed his right foot on James's shoulder and knocked him onto his back. "Hey!" James yelled again.

"Quit that!" Amy stepped out from behind the dumpster, Billy close by.

"Yeah, what are you doing?" Billy said, stepping in front of Amy.

Michael felt his heart thud. Things turned an ugly sour in the lot below. He thought about yelling out, but sat frozen, mesmerized. He thought about calling out to his mother. He thought about his Dad. He thought about running downstairs and out into the lot. He knew better than to try that. As he watched, Ringo leapt from the branch, tackling both Amy and Billy at the same time. He sat on them, pinning them to the ground. Michael scanned the lot. Where was Jessie? He suddenly realized he hadn't seen her during any of this.

"Get off me!" Amy yelled, squirming underneath Ringo.

"Yeah, ya punk. Get off me!" Billy echoed. Ringo sat on them, smiling. James made a move to stand and the fat girl took two quick steps, moving like a cheetah in a way Michael thought impossible. She darted left then right then landed hard on James, trapping him beneath her. She lowered her face to his. Michael thought she was going to kiss James on the lips! Instead, she widened her jaws and bit down on his nose and mouth then threw her head back like a lion eating a fresh kill. Blood and flesh and bits of bone covered her face. Before he could react, she leaned in and grabbed another chunk of James's face with her teeth and ripped it off. James rocked back and forth, trying to break free, trying to escape. Michael sat frozen.

Amy and Billy began kicking and thrusting at the same time, trying to get Ringo to throw them off. Ringo brought up his left fist and drove straight into Amy's face. It caved in with a loud gurgling. Before Billy could do anything, Ringo withdrew his hand from the cavity where Amy's face used to be and drove it into Billy's face, giving him the same makeover Amy had just received. Dusty stepped forward and got down on his hands and knees. Ringo slid off Billy and onto Amy. Their bodies still shaking, still trying to escape. Ringo leaned in just as the fat girl had and started eating Amy's face. Dusty did the same to Billy.

"Mom?" Michael whispered. "Mom?" he whispered

again. He couldn't make a sound any louder no matter how he tried. He couldn't get up; he couldn't look away. Below him, his friends were being turned into an evening snack by the other kids. The other kids who looked like any other kids. Kids he might have wanted to play with before today. Kids he MIGHT have played with before today had he not passed out. Where was Jessie? Where was his Mom?

He forced his right hand upward and slapped it flat against the window pane. As soon as he did, Dusty looked up from his evening meal with wild, wide eyes that met Michael's. Dusty's face was smeared with blood and flesh and other bits of Billy. Michael's eyes widened in horror and he tried to look away, but he couldn't. Suddenly, Dusty leapt off his prey and scurried on extended arms and legs on all fours like a dog toward the house. He smashed through the back door. Michael heard his mother scream.

Then, he heard nothing.

GRIM DIESEL
by G. H. Finn

This is one of the few overt horror stories found herein. Then again, aren't all stories that deal with the apocalypse horror stories?—Ed.

THE FUTURE WAS BRIGHT. Or so we were told. It was hard to see anything clearly through the myriad clouds of choking exhaust fumes. The world had become insanely magnificent. And magnificently insane. We lived in a brave new world that had risen like a rusty phoenix from the polluted ashes of our previous civilization. It was a time of machine-hammered steel, gasoline-powered robot production lines, Satanic speakeasys and twisted, towering buildings that rose above the clouds. We called them moonscrapers. The city was filled with cherished hopes, fractured dreams, radioactive petrol, and forgotten ghosts.

Such was New Amsterdome. A place that was home to both Angels of despair and Daemons of delight. It was a place of enchanted titanium cogs, armoured caterpillar tracks, and cybernetic carburetors. More than half of which we'd looted and then hybridized from the ruined remains of the cities destroyed in the Epochalypse War. The war that was supposed to end all wars.

~ ~ ~

Living beneath the spellcast reinforced crystal of the mile-high dome above us, we thought ourselves safe. Until the next war came. Bringing with it suborbital airships that dropped bombs from the upper atmosphere, shattering our defenses. Now the streets were regularly filled with masses of mangled metal, crumbled concrete, and broken bodies. And the inescapable smell of smoke, sweat, blood, cordite. And fear.

When the latest air raid came, I ran. The doorway to an underground shelter loomed suddenly before me through drifting acrid black clouds of oil-filled smoke. Relieved, I hurried inside.

Down in the darkness, I found I was not alone. A figure sat slumped in a corner. Huddled. I'd have taken him to be a homeless vagabond but for the expensive tailoring of the torn gabardine trouser-leg that stuck out from beneath a mud-splattered raincoat. I say trouser-leg, singular, as he'd had at least one limb replaced. I noticed the artificial leg but tried not to make it obvious I was looking. I turned my head away quickly, feeling embarrassed to have caught myself staring. The synthetic limb had been top of the range. Once. No off-the-peg leg, all pig-iron gears and mass-produced clockwork. This had been designed with a series of gas-compression pumps and an internal diesel-driven power-assist mechanism. I know, because my late father had been fitted with something similar, albeit a cheaper model. But the once gleaming limb had seen better days. It was battered and scratched now, and a small puddle of oil had formed on the floor beneath the steel foot-plate, dripping from a faulty knee joint. It didn't look to be fresh damage. I guessed they'd fallen on hard times.

I brushed a long strand of hair out of my eyes, then wiped the dust from my spectacles. I was considering whether to see if I could find a radio in the shelter when I felt myself being watched. The crouched figure looked up at me, with one naturally sparkling blue eye, and one artificial one. It glowed a bright green in the dim light. The effect was strange, but not altogether unattractive. Feeling it would be rude not to say anything, I introduced myself, gabbling. "Hello. I'm Genevieve Ming. I'm a librarian. I was on my way home from work when the sirens began, so I dived in here because it was the nearest shelter."

I paused, expecting my huddled companion to offer at least their name by way of introduction. But he just sat. Quietly. Looking at me. I began to wonder if he spoke English. Then, at last, he answered.

"Call me. . .Diesel. . .Grim Diesel."

That was all he said. I didn't know if it was a real name or an alias. It sounded like the sort of name a gangster might have. But in any case, I smiled, a little nervously, saying,

"Pleased to meet you, Grim. Call me Genny."

Grim Diesel made an indistinct sound that could have been a grunt but which I assumed was meant to be polite. Feeling the already strained conversation was liable to dry up at any moment, I asked, "I was born in the city. How about you? You don't sound like you have a New Amsterdome accent."

Grim Diesel nodded. "I'm not local. Just passing through."

I smiled, and to take my mind off the bombs falling outside, I asked, "You must have important business to be travelling in times like these. If you don't mind me asking, where are you heading?"

Grim Diesel looked away, replying, "Nowhere. Anywhere. Just *away*. As far as possible."

I felt a pang of sympathy. "Is it the bombs?" I asked. "I'd leave too. If I could. But I've nowhere to go, and my mother needs me—"

He laughed. It sounded bitter. "Bombs? No. They don't bother me. There are worse things."

Grim Diesel's voice trailed off. I didn't mean to be nosey, but I suppose I couldn't help myself, so I asked, "Did something happen to you?" I frowned. "Before you came to the city?" I suggested.

He let out a weary sigh and slowly rocked backward and forward, eyes closed. After a few moments, in a quiet, far away tone, Grim Diesel began to speak.

~ ~ ~

"I suppose it might help to tell someone. To put it into words," he said.

I nodded encouragingly. "Go ahead. We've plenty of time and nothing else to do until the bombs stop."

He paused then began speaking again, and having once started he didn't stop, as though his experiences had been dammed up inside him and now came pouring forth in a huge torrent.

"I'd thought things were going well," he said, "Or at least well enough. But I was sick of this so-called new civilization, with its petrol fumes, gasoline guzzling technology, and ever-smoking factory chimneys, endlessly belching out smog. I didn't want to become another cog in the machine of modern society. So, I sold everything I had and went South. I left the Unified States of America and crossed the border into the Confederated States. I went simply to go exploring. Adventuring. I knew little about the CSA, other than that since the civil war ended in stalemate, back in '21, they had apparently been re-industrializing heavily. But I'd also read that despite that, much of the countryside was still wilderness. Left untouched after decades of bloody battle.

"Hoping to make a new life, I travelled across the continent for a little over a year. After a few false starts and misadventures, I found myself in one of the New Alabama cities. It was just as bad as what I'd left behind. Worse in fact. There were no attempts to even slightly control pollution, and what passed for local government was even more corrupt than our own, which I hadn't thought possible. I only stayed just long enough to buy some supplies. Food mainly, and petrol for the traction-driven steed I was riding. There still aren't enough roads down there to make auto-mobiles practical, so most people use robot-horses, if they can afford to. I was lucky to buy a reliable imported model, a Rolls Royce "Silver Stallion" Mk 6. I still had plenty of money then, but it's gone now. It costs a lot, to keep moving. To keep running."

~ ~ ~

"I pointed the Silver Stallion out of town and headed eastwards, towards a range of mountains. I wasn't a fool. I knew there were dangers outside the cities. Outlaws. Mutants. Bears. Wolves. All kinds of beasts. But I was young and cocky and I knew my petrol-driven horse could outrun any animal. Besides which, I had a small semi-automatic machine pistol in case of minor emergencies. And, inside my jacket pocket, one extremely powerful and highly illegal fragmentation grenade, just in case of any *real* emergencies. I thought I was safe from anything."

~ ~ ~

"Of course, no matter how fast my horse, I couldn't outrun my own stupidity. In next to no time I was completely lost.

"I found myself riding through dense woodland. The tall, dark forest made it almost impossible to gauge my way, obscuring landmarks, hiding the mountain peaks and even masking the position of the sun sufficiently that I became unsure of anything beyond my general direction. I had no choice but to head for higher ground in the hope of getting a better view. It looked like I'd be spending the night camped out in the wilderness. Again. Not that I minded. I turned the Silver Stallion uphill and, with its engine turning over nicely, I crossed my fingers in the hope of quickly finding my way.

"Half an hour later the rain began to fall.

"I cursed beneath my breath. A treacherous thought reminded me that I could have been living in luxury in a modern turbo-powered city right now. But I dismissed the idea as I always did. It was a hard life, but I felt free. And that mattered more to me than almost anything. With some difficulty I did my best to ignore the driving rain.

"An hour passed and by that time I knew I was so totally lost that I gave up on trying to find my way and concentrated on seeking some sort of shelter. I hoped I might spot a cave to rest in, if it was free of any dangerous inhabitants, but I'd have settled for some fallen trees. Anything that might help to keep the rain off me.

"I thought the gods must have been smiling on me when, against all odds, I spotted a log cabin. I hadn't expected to find any sign of human inhabitation at all.

"The building was dark and empty looking. It had an air of age about it. The cabin seemed to have been disused for a long time, judging by the state of the roof and the way foliage had crept up around the doorway. It might have even been there since before the War. But I didn't care. It was shelter, and it would be as good as a palace compared to spending a night in the forest.

"I dismounted, unsaddled, and tethered the Silver Stallion, making sure the old wood cabin gave it as much protection as possible from the elements. I grabbed my pack, then I wetly made my way to the cabin's entrance.

"Even though I could see no one had lived here in years I still called out 'Hello' when I forced open the almost-jammed door. There was no answer. Perhaps the cabin had once been used by a trapper? A hunter? A mutant? I really had no idea. I was simply glad to have found somewhere dry to rest.

"Once inside, I pulled a heavy chair across the floor and sat wearily. Yawning. I was soaked. Wet and cold and weary. All I wanted now was sleep.

"I took my pack and opened the door to the cabin's only bedroom. The double-bed covered in a moth-eaten patchwork quilt looked inviting. Opposite the bed was a built-in closet with a wooden door. I'd probably have missed it but for the keyhole. I tried the door. The closet was empty. I dumped the pack inside and shut it

"Then I heard a slow creaking. I opened the door, but the cupboard was empty, apart from my backpack. I went and lay on the bed and was asleep the moment I closed my eyes."

~ ~ ~

"I woke with a start. It must've been midnight, or later. I rolled off the bed. Alert. Listening. What had woken me?"

Creak.

"It was the sound I heard earlier. Louder now. What the hell was it? I told myself to calm down."

Creak.

"During my travels I'd spent some time on a fishing boat. Not one of the new many-funnelled motorized ships, spewing out smoke across the water and powerful enough to cross an ocean. Just an old wooden sailing vessel. The masts and rigging of the ship would pull and strain every time there was a wind. These creaking noises reminded me of that. Something hanging. Swinging.

"I was sure the sound came from the closet. I crossed the room then yanked open the door. It was empty. I sighed with relief and shut the door. I was about to get back into bed when I heard it again."

Creak.

"It still sounded like the noise came from the closet. I shrugged. It was late. Far too late. I wanted to sleep. I settled back on the bed and began to snore.

"Five minutes later, I was awake again. This time the

noise was louder."

Creak.

"I got up, my fingers felt their way to the dynamo-powered flashlight I'd brought with me, I flicked the switch and turned it on. The noise stopped. I opened the closet door. My backpack sat where I'd left it. There was nothing else. I closed the door, turned out the light, and got back into bed.

"I was on the cusp of sleep when I heard it."

Creak.

"The noise was definitely coming from the closet.

"I didn't bother with the light, I jumped out of bed, ran to the cupboard, opened the door. It was utterly dark inside. I couldn't see anything. For a moment I thought I heard another creaking sound. Then it stopped. I tried to turn on the flashlight, but the dynamo had run down. I still had matches in my pocket, and I took one, striking it alight. The flickering flame cast eerie shadows. I shook my head. It was just a noise. This time I was going back to bed and get some sleep even if I did hear things.

"I blew out the match and closed the cupboard."

Creak.

"I ignored the sound and lay on the bed. I closed my eyes, screwing them shut. For the first time I actually wished I was back in a smoke-filled city. Surrounded by people. Not out here in the wilderness. Alone.

Creak.

"I opened my eyes and lay in the dark. I knew I'd never get to sleep like this.

"Then I noticed it. A thin beam of light. Shining into the room. Through the keyhole of the closet."

Creak.

"The light shining through the keyhole didn't waver. I crossed to the door and opened it. The noises stopped.

"Inside the closet there was darkness.

"I slammed the door shut and was about to go back to bed when I saw the light through the keyhole again."

Creak.

"I could only think of one thing to do. I knelt on the floor. Carefully I put my eye to the keyhole and looked through.

"I saw it.

"The light was cast by a flickering candle, illuminating the scene before me.

"Another room. Wooden walls. A table on which stood a candle and a book, perhaps a diary. From the ceiling hung a rope. Hanging from the rope was a corpse. Rotted. Little more than a skeleton held together by dried sinews and scraps of clothing. The cadaver swung gently from side-to-side.

"I heard the noise. *The creak of the wooden beam in the ceiling. The creak of the rope rubbing against the wood. The creak as the noose was pulled tight by the weight of the body. The creak made by the corpse swinging like a deathly pendulum.*

"I almost fell back from the keyhole, scrabbling to stand. I yanked open the closet. It was dark. Empty. I stood. Silent. I didn't understand this.

"I closed the closet. Candlelight shone through the keyhole."

Creak.

"I shuddered."

Creak.

"The sound set my teeth on edge.

"The noise stopped. Candlelight still came through the keyhole. Why was it quiet? I bent down, resting on one knee, and peered through.

"It was there. Hanging. A skeletal corpse."

Creak.

"Suspended from the rope, the hanged man swung around to face me. I saw its tattered clothes and mummified skin. I saw a weirdly bestial stone amulet, curiously carved from obsidian, hanging around the corpse's neck. The black jewel seemed to glow in the candlelight. And then the cadaver's skull-like leathery head turned. A shriveled eye looked at me. It saw me. And grinned."

~ ~ ~

"I fell back from the keyhole and clambered frantically to my feet.

"As I watched, the keyhole became dark.

"I had to look. I bent down, pressing my eye against the

keyhole, squinting.

"I couldn't see the hanging corpse. But I could see something.

"A bed. With an old patchwork quilt. Like the one in the bedroom. *Exactly* like it.

"But. . .If I was looking out through the keyhole into the bedroom, that meant. . .

"I was in the closet.

"I reached out desperately to open the door but I couldn't turn the handle on the inside.

"I was trapped.

"I felt around. My fingers closed on a candle-stump. I grabbed it, pulled out my matches, lit it and put it on the table.

"I heard a noise. Behind me. Before I could turn, a noose was thrust over my head. It tightened around my neck, choking me. I felt cold, spectral hands grasp me, pulling me upright. Then further up. My feet left the ground. I kicked. Wildly. Strangling. I saw only darkness. But I could hear. . ."

Creak. Creak.

Choke. Gasp. Creak.

"In shock, all I could think was, 'I didn't expect to die here.'

"I kicked wildly, my legs swinging madly. I felt myself choking and new I would lose consciousness at any moment. But my hands were free and I reached up, grabbing the rope. My arms were strong, well-muscled, and I was able to support enough of my weight to take a little tension off the noose that was strangling me. That was when I had a stroke of good luck. The rope was old and worn. It had been supporting the skeletal cadaver for who knows how long, but I was a lot heavier that than uncanny spectral skeleton. As I hung there, trying to support my own bodyweight by fiercely gripping the rough rope, I felt strands of the cord begin to give way. Suddenly the rope snapped and I fell to land in a breathless heap on the floor. I was stunned, but I frantically clawed the noose away from my throat, gasping with relief as I gulped air into my lungs and felt the blood hammering inside my head once the pressure was removed from my carotid arteries.

"I struggled into a sitting position, pulling the remains of the rope away from my throat. I nearly jumped out of my skin when I saw the desiccated skeletal corpse standing in front of me. I instinctively dropped a hand inside my jacket and pulled out my gun. I'm not a great shot, and I wasn't sure that bullets could kill the dead man any deader than he already was, but it was all I could think of to protect myself. But then I realized that the cadaver wasn't moving. It was dead. Had I only imagined I'd seen the body move? I doubted my own eyes and my memory. Blatantly the man was *dead*. Perhaps I'd hallucinated the whole thing? I felt the raw skin at my neck, burnt by the noose. That was real enough. . .all too real for my liking.

"My eye caught the book I'd seen earlier. A journal. Perhaps it had belonged to the dead man? Had he taken his own life? I shuddered, thinking of him, alone in the cabin, deciding to end his existence amid black despair. I flicked the book open, glancing at the last page. The spidery writing was cramped and hard to make out in the dim candlelight, but I read:

'...I've sealed this room with the strongest binding wards I know, warping its dimensions, and then hidden it behind a glamour, but I dinna ken if it will be strong enough. I cannae take off the stone. The cold burns me. But it will not let me tak it off. I have a rope. There is but one thing left for me to do, that might yet save my soul. If ye are reading this, then god have mercy on yours.'

~ ~ ~

"I stared at the amulet. It was completely black. Carved with odd twisting patterns and what I took to be weird, stylized animals. It seemed ancient. I'd never seen anything like it before. The carving, the style was...strange. No native tribe I'd ever heard of depicted animals in *that* way. I couldn't even tell what they were meant to be. This was far more bizarre than anything I'd seen, it looked...*evil*. I'd spent time in the ruins of museums, but I'd never seen anything like this. It had qualities that reminded me of Viking knotwork. And other aspects that looked a little like bizarre, twisted, African carvings. There was something about it that brought to mind the ornately carved, almost woven decorations chiseled on Celtic monuments. But also something of the curious geometry depicted in Tibetan mandalas. I stared at the interlaced bestial depictions that seemed to grow from the talisman. One looked something like a ravenous, three-eyes bear, or perhaps a rabid wolverine. Another had a serrated beak, and I guessed it might, in its rather twisted way, represent an angry pterodactyl or a mad albatross. A further face looked octopoid, perhaps that of a vicious squid, but with scaled tentacles that instead of suckers bore mouths. Others...well...I couldn't even *guess* at what they might be. Then I saw the top-most face. I shuddered. It was *hideous*. Monstrous. It didn't look like an animal. It certainly didn't look human either. The face had an insectoid quality. Yet it had fur. And eight eyes. Seven were placed in the shape of a septagram—a seven-pointed star, arranged around an oversized eye in the centre of them. It glowed, burning between the nightmarish creature's brows. It's five ears were tusked. Armoured. Reptilian. Its huge jaws bulged forward, displaying both mandibles and fangs. But from its mouth there came a three-forked-tongue which dissolved into a countless number of writhing tentacles, like those of some kind of cuttlefish. They spiraled and squirmed their way down from the awful mouth of the horrendous *thing*, interweaving themselves into the rest of the carvings on the talisman, like spectral fingers inserting themselves into the fabric of reality. Weaving a wormlike path through complicated knots and swirls. Something about the shapes they formed sickened me. The coils reminded me of a mass of maggots, writhing in rotting meat, or spider-silk wrapping and trapping some poor doomed prey. The tongue's fleshy tendrils seemed to enfold the jewel wherever they were carved, strangling it, like a parasitic plant throttling the very tree it lives upon. As foolish as it seemed, the whole thing made me feel nauseous. I'd thought the amulet was carved from jet, but it almost looked like it was made from metal, covered in a thin film of oil. That was when I heard the slithering. Insipid and insidious. A hollow sound. Sibilant, snakelike, as of something sliding slowly over wet stone. I heard a serpentine hiss and then a sickening sucking. Slickly sticky. The sound was somehow ichorous.

"I took a step back in horror.

"The carved swirls and spirals that covered the amulet were all slowly moving. The knotwork twisted and coiled before my eyes. The engraved lines, etched into the dark, metallic, stone-like artifact were moving over and beneath and *through* each other. I knew what I was seeing was impossible. I wondered if I was going insane. A part of me hoped I was losing my mind. Anything would be preferable to the reality of what I was seeing.

"I saw the unnatural, bestial, alien heads squirm and snarl and I stared at the carving of the thing at the top of the amulet. And I realized that it was *alive.*

"The coiling, writhing tentacles all vibrated rhythmically from the slowly undulating thrice-forked-tongue of the monstrous being. The grinding mandibles salivated menacingly from its colossal jaw. The saurian-like ears bristled, sensing things I could not imagine and would not dare to hear. The eyes set in the blasphemous face were closed. Blind. All but the central eye. That eighth eye burnt with a frozen eldritch flame. Blazing with all the black shades of midnight. Radiating an entire spectrum of anti-light. Darkness made manifest. I stared, open-mouthed, as the eye began to fold into itself.

"My blood froze in my veins. My limbs became heavy. Too heavy to move, as I stared uncomprehendingly into the awful eye. And in its place, I saw a *thing* begin to materialize. I can't describe it. I don't understand what I saw. I've done my best to mentally scrub my mind free of the vision, but I'll never truly be able to forget it. I felt myself vomiting as I watched. Mostly I remember it as an opening. It was fibrous. Like a canker. A tumor. A cancerous blight oozing into our world. It was forming itself in the frozen flame of the idol's eye.

"I suppose you could call it a mouth, but it might have been a vagina or an anus. Or all three.

"It was an orifice. A hole. A hole into our world.

"As I watched the *thing* that was appearing, it seemed to

be simultaneously consuming and producing itself, all through this single orifice. It was as though it was devouring itself, mating with itself, giving birth to itself, excreting itself out, and sucking itself back into a void, all at once. The cycles of creation and destruction had gone mad—there was no difference between them, not even a way of separating them into opposite parts.

"The thing hovered there, vomiting and swallowing and birthing and defecating itself in and out of existence. Again and yet again, in a twisted cycle that had no beginning and no end.

"And all the while it gibbered. Laughing with an inhuman, unearthly, insane sound. There was only one thing I could be sure about this unknown, unknowable entity.

"It was hungry.

"I could feel its desire to eat. To consume. It was all encompassing. The dark all-consuming lust to devour was all that motivated the *thing*.

"The tentacles writhed down from the talisman, spreading and twisting over the skeletal remains of the dead man, snaking toward me.

"Somehow I knew what was going to happen. They would engulf me. Draw me to the thing that that gloatingly gibbering in the frozen, burning eye. Then it would feast upon my soul.

"Without thinking, I took my semi-automatic and shot at

the talisman. My first shots went wide, echoing in the room but missing the carved stone entirely. Then one struck, chipping the amulet. An unearthly scream pierced my ears, my mind and my very soul. I shot again, and again, until the gun was empty. The last spray of bullets hit the *thing* directly. The stone shattered. Fragments of the metallic-crystal flew everywhere. One hit me in the eye, blinding me on that side.

"I'm not quite sure what happened next—I think I may have lost consciousness for a few moments. Groggily, I came to my senses, laying on the floor. The pain in my eye was terrible, but I ignored it. When I fell I'd knocked over the candle, and it had started a fire which was rapidly spreading. In front of me the desiccated corpse still stood, with the shattered stone screaming around its neck. I saw the flames reach the mummified cadaver and watched as the dead man began to burn. Perhaps it was only my imagination but, for a moment, I thought the skeletal face, with its permanent deaths-head grin, smiled a little more widely as the fire began to destroy the awful body. I felt a barbed, sucking tentacle brush against my leg, and that was enough to make me turn and flee. I found the door could now be opened and I burst through it, coughing and choking from the rapidly spreading blaze. I ran across the cabin, threw open the door, and headed into the night. Only then, once outside, did I dare to look back. The cabin was now fully ablaze. Yet above the noise of the fire I still heard that hideous, screeching, tormented wail coming from some other world, far beyond this one. It screamed in torment from a place that was not a place, in a time that was not a time. I didn't stop to think about what I was doing. If I had, maybe I'd have been more careful, but it didn't even occur to me to try to get clear. I fumbled inside my jacket and found the fragmentation grenade I always carried. There was never going to be another emergency like this. I pressed the ignition stud and tossed it into the blazing cabin. I heard more unearthly screams, but the sounds were suddenly obliterated as the grenade exploded, blowing the wooden building apart. I was caught in the blast. I never realized how powerful that grenade really was. I was lucky to have survived at all, but the blast cost me my leg. I tied off the stump to stop the bleeding.

"If it wasn't for the Silver Stallion I'd have died there, but somehow I made it back to the city. The tech-meds at the hospital fixed me up well enough. They gave me a new leg. And a new eye. But they couldn't remove the shard of crystal that had blinded me. It was embedded too close to my brain. So, they left it there.

"As I lay in my hospital bed, feeling the strangeness of my robotic implants, I remembered staring at the site of the cabin, little more than a crater. I'd seen only ashes and had been able to locate no trace of the remains of the dead man. Nor any surviving shards from the dark talisman. I hoped it had been completely destroyed in the explosion and the fire.

I prayed it had been.

"In relief that it was over, I closed my eye and mentally shut down the pictures from the implant in my empty socket. I settled back to rest. To sleep.

"And then I heard a noise.

"The sibilant, gibbering sound of insane laughter."

~ ~ ~

"I started running then. And I haven't stopped since. I keep travelling. Keep moving on. It's cost me all my savings. I don't stay in any one place for long. I can't. I hear it. The mad laughter. Because I know it's out there. Following me. Gibbering in the dark. I thought I might be safe if I hid in a city, among so many people. But it can find me anywhere. I must keep moving. I must. *It will be here soon.*"

~ ~ ~

At last, Grim Diesel fell silent. He would say nothing else, but he kept looking around, wildly, fearfully, starting at shadows.

I couldn't make up my mind if he was drunk or deranged.

Outside, the bombs were still falling.

I turned away to look in my handbag for a comb, and when I looked back Grim Diesel was gone. Out onto the streets, heedless of the explosions all around.

There were things he feared more than bombs. . .

I sat back, prepared for a long wait until it was safe to venture out of the shelter.

Exhausted, I closed my eyes.

And then I heard it.

In the darkness.

Echoing. Insidious. Eternal. Gibbering laughter.

WHAT'S BELOW THE SURFACE
by Hákon Gunnarsson

This tale deals more in pathos than in shock. What makes it all the more realistic for me is knowing the lake my family once vacationed at in my youth covered an entire town. Imagine boating a few feet above the rooves of decaying houses.—Ed.

EVERYTHING SEEMED SAFE, QUIET, and calm when he looked outside the window. No one was about. Charlie scanned the street again, then the houses, each window, slowly and thoroughly. When he finally was sure that no one could jump him outside, he turned to face the mirror. He always looked nice in these clothes. Black suit, black tie, white shirt. Once this had been his funeral outfit, but he'd attended the last one a while back. It hadn't actually been a proper funeral, with a priest, and all that. Just him burying Carol after she coughed for the last time. Fifteen years, was it? Something like that. Since then he'd been here all alone. Well, most of the time.

Of course, the trousers hung a little wide on him now, but that was to be expected, he wasn't what he used to be. Anyway, he adjusted the tie, and when he was happy with his appearance, he turned to leave, but grabbed the freshly picked flowers before he left. Like always, he went out through the cellar. Never the front door. He was too exposed there. It was too easy to spot him from a distance. Soon he was on the street, walking as fast as he could eastwards. From the distance he might have looked like any other old man taking a stroll. His long white hair and beard were a good indicator of his age. Up close one could hardly fail to notice that he kept scanning the houses for movement, and listening for any unfamiliar sounds.

Despite his age, he could take care of himself. After all, he had been doing so for sixty years now, or since he had been thirteen and his last family member died of the illness. At that time there were still other people living in the town. The only one that made much difference to him had been Carol. She could have been his Eve, but all their kids had died. Only one reached the age of five. It wasn't her fault. None of it was. Nor was it his. It was the way the world turned these days, months, years…

A sound stopped him in his track. It came from the next street. Cartwheels? People talking. No women. Men. At least two of them. He looked around, saw the burned car in a garage to the right, and walked there as quietly as he could. The back of the car wasn't the ideal hiding place, but it had to do. From his hiding place, he scanned the area for something that might give him away. Even though he couldn't see anything, he knew there was always the possibility that a good scavenger might detect something. Some of them had a frightening ability to sniff out food. It was the constant cat and mouse game, with him and others like him the mice. So, he made himself as small as possible. No hole was big enough for him to crawl into though.

He didn't dare look up, but the sounds grew louder. They were getting closer. This was a dead town, and he thought it obvious they didn't expect to find anyone. Otherwise, they wouldn't have talked as they walked. Or maybe they were so confident they didn't care one way or the other. There was a chill in the air. Slowly he put the flowers on the ground, and took a knife from the inside pocket of the jacket. It wasn't much protection, but he might at least injure one of them, if it came to that. He could feel the sharpness of the blade as he ran his fingertip across it. Then he heard them turn the corner, getting closer, and closer, and closer. First, he could identify one word, then more, soon he could almost make out what they were saying. Then:

"I'm telling you. It's dead. We've been here before."

"Someone might have moved back."

"Don't look like it. We should have gone north. The hunting grounds up there are more fertile."

Charlie pulled in as little breath as he dared. He kept his mouth open, and let the air flow in and out as soundlessly as possible. He could hear them directly outside the garage. His hands tightened upon the knife, but he didn't look up. Bloody scavengers. Over the years they had taken several of the people in the town, but they wouldn't take him without losing blood. He'd make them pay for their food.

"And we'd have to fight too many scavengers for our prey. You don't go hunting where there are predators. Use that tiny brain of yours some time. Sure, that is where the fertile hunting grounds are, but there is no need for a lot of prey, just enough to survive."

"But. . ."

"No buts, just keep your eyes open."

They stopped. Charlie could hear that. The cartwheels weren't moving. No squeaking. The footsteps slowed down, first one and then the other.

"Why did you stop?"

"Shh, did you hear something?"

Charlie closed his eyes. The drumming inside him quickened, grew louder almost to the point where he thought they might hear it.

"No."

"There is something about this town. Someone lives here."

"No. The place is dead."

"I'm serious. I felt it the last time, as well."

Charlie opened his eyes again. His back was starting to ache. Maybe it was time to take a stand, before he got so stiff that he wouldn't be able to fight at all. He wanted to get up to see if they had guns or not, but he stayed down.

"Here?"

"Close. I just realized some of the gardens had a fence that wasn't crumbling."

"To hide something?"

"Now you're using your gray matter."

"Okay, let's look at it."

"I can't remember where it was."

"Lets. . .What is it?"

"That garage."

Charlie heard the crunch of approaching footsteps. He tried to make out on what side of the car the man would come. From the sound of it, he would have to spin to defend himself. Not ideal. Not what he would have hoped for, but that's how the cards were stacked. If only he had a gun. He might have got them both before they could do anything. It sounded as if only one man was coming, the other must have stayed in the street. The footsteps stopped.

"Find anything?"

"Yeah, a wrench. Here among the trash. Could be useful."

"Perhaps."

The footsteps started again, this time heading out of the garage. Without looking up, Charlie loosened the grip on the knife. Both men were now walking, and the cartwheels began to squeak. As carefully as he could, Charlie peeked, saw the men on their way down the street. They were headed toward the house. It would probably fall to them, and worse, so would the garden with all its food. Lost. Forever. To those bloody...

Well, I'm lucky I wasn't at home, Charlie thought as he got up. He walked to the door, and saw that the scavengers were already at his house, looking over the fence. Yeah, it was lost. They'd find the other gardens when they'd start looking for him. All lost. While they were busy, he slipped out, but not without his flowers. Going through the gardens he tried to stay as much out of sight as he could. Even though he tried not to, he kept looking over his shoulder as he clocked down to the sea.

Soon he was by the tree where he hid his boat. The camouflage was in place. It was still there. Quickly, he uncovered it, turned it over and pushed it into the water. Once there he started to row his way through the maze of half-submerged houses. He almost took the road that once was there, but not quite. As he got further out, the houses were more submerged, damaged, and depressing. Back at his house, his home, were pictures from the time that the town was a thriving community. That was of course well before his time. In fact, the town had been dying ever since he could remember.

He looked around, and thought himself at the right spot. He stopped rowing. For a moment he let the boat drift, closed his eyes, and mumbled something. Then he opened his eyes again, and picked up the flowers. Without much force he threw them into the sea. They floated about a meter out from the boat. With a slight smile he watched them for a little while. No longer a bouquet, rather individual patches of color floating on the sea. Without haste, he started to undress. First the tie, then the jacket, shirt, trousers, and then the shoes. With great care he placed it all at the foot of the boat, then went overboard without making a splash.

For a minute he let himself float, letting his body acclimate to the cold, then dived below. The first attempt wasn't successful. He wasn't in the right place after all. He swam further out, and dived again. That was the right place. It wasn't deep, so he could stop for a while, to look at the tombstones one last time. He read the names, the dates. Images of people who once had been his life popped up in his head. Memories of life long gone. With his right hand he touched the stone nearest to him. Then let himself drift towards the sun again. The breath of air was nice, but as always, it was tinged with sadness. Why was he still up here? There wasn't much point with all his people gone.

He got onto the boat, a bit out of breath. Though he was in good shape, he was getting older, and the sea was cold. For a moment he thought about how long he had been doing this ritual, and he wasn't sure. It had been a while since the cemetery had gone under. His parents had been among the last to be buried there, and his late brother knew then that it would go under. Why the people were still using it at that point was beyond Charlie. Carol claimed a drier grave. One that wouldn't go under, a beautiful one under a tree on the outskirts of town. Not that it mattered in the end, but he'd made sure that her place was a nice one. Shame that he wouldn't be able to visit her today.

As he sat there in his wet underpants, and socks, he saw the scavengers coming down to the edge of the sea. For a moment they looked into each other's eyes. Without being able to hear their words, he knew. They looked at him, then around, but there was no other boat available. He knew that, and grinned a little. With a gun they might be able to reach him, but they would have to swim to get the meat of him. So he waved them. They didn't wave back. One of them expressed his anger quite comically, which made him grin a little wider. Then he started to row, slow, deliberate strokes, straight out to sea. He wouldn't be coming back. He'd go somewhere else, find a shore in time, and live for a while. And if he didn't, well, then he would at least not be dinner to a couple of scavengers.

A SHORT HISTORY OF THE FUTURE
by Han Adcock

Here's one about gamma rays. More notably, this story is a humorous look at a serious theme—or is that a serious look at a humorous theme?–Ed.

THEY SAY, "YOU'RE THE LAST GENERATION," and "You got to take responsibility for your actions," and on and on and ON. What they *really* mean is, "You got to sort out the shit when we're dead."

I hate death. It's always coming for us but never here. We're like ants running around in a shadow. Well, the kids en't, but older ones, the teenagers, get worried and stuff, sometimes, but the adults try to keep the scary stuff as far above our heads as they can.

I'm not a teenager yet. I'll be thirteen soon, but when I get to that age I swear I won't change. I'll still be the same, even if I get exposed to the shit. Anything else, any change wun't be me.

I said so to my best mate Xen. I said, "Whatever happens to us, I'm still gonna be me, and you're still gonna be you, till the day we die."

He din't get it. "Well, duh."

Today he en't here.

I came to school like normal. There's six of us left in my class. There's me, Xen, Pod, Randal, Whizz and 3251. Except that this morning, Xen's seat was empty.

"Hey."

It's Pod. He's the only feller in 8B I used to like before the shit started, and still do, apart from Xen. Randal and Whizz used to pick on us, and nobody likes 3251 because he's a bot. Pod can be a weirdo but he's a cool weirdo.

"Xen's not here."

"Yeah, I know." Pod pulls a daft face, which means he's really worried. "So now there's like five of us left, not counting Batty."

"Six. Xen's okay. He wun't. He wun't be stupid enough not to take his O2 or whatever."

"So how come he's not here?"

"Maybe he got a cold."

"Geez. Nobody gets colds anymore."

"He could still've."

Batty glares at us when he walks into the classroom. Not because we're late, but because he usually glares at everybody. It's his eyes. Ever since that accident with the acid, he's not been all that great with his new eyes. They were transplanted from a shut-down bot and everyone knows bot eyes are crap. Can't even blink proply, which is why we call him Batty. He bats them.

"No Xenon, then, I take it?" Batty clicks his eyeballs in our direction and spins them in all directions just for the thrill of it.

"No, Mr. Butts."

"Pity. He was a model student. Not a working model, but still." Batty gets out the register and crosses Xen's name off.

"Mr. Butts," I say. "Don't do that. He could be back tomorrer or the day after."

"Perhaps." He still crosses out Xen's name and his face dun't believe me.

"But he *could*," I say. "Xenon wun't...he wun't be miserable enough to..."

"Geronimo." Batty uses my whole name, which means he's getting mad. "Go and sit down and stop back-chatting me, please. Or I shall send you to the Head."

I stop and park myself next to Pod. Nobody likes being sent to the Head.

While Batty is up front drivelling on about science—nearly every lesson these days is science or maths if it isn't computers or P.E.—Pod talks.

"So, what do you reckon?"

"What do I reckon what?"

"Bout Xeno. I can tell you dun't think he's...Y'know...gone and done a Gilly."

Gilly was the last person to've gone. He lost a leg to the

Radiator Sickness, stopped bothering to take his O2 gas before bed and stopped bothering to check his portascanner. Then he died.

"He wun't have," I say. "There was nothing making Xen sad. He's okay. He'll be fine."

"He could've just. . .forgot."

"No." I NEED him to be okay. "He din't."

"He was the happiest kid I knew."

"IS. He *is* the happiest kid you *know*."

"Geronimo!" Batty yells from the interactive whiteboard. "Pipe down!"

"Sorry Mr. Butts."

"Well, I'm sure you've been paying attention." Batty is sarcastic. One eye rolls right back into his head and faces front again. "Maybe you'd like to tell us what day I just said it was."

"Um," I say. "Tuesday?"

Whizz collapses in a fit of silent, hiccuping giggles. Batty ignores her.

"No," he sighs. "I see you haven't been listening. Today, Geez, is the day when Dr. Abingdon discovered E2Q, the soul atom. If I catch you talking again, you'll be sitting with me at my desk."

Pod waits until Batty's back is turned, then whispers, "Do you think Xen was. . .taken?"

"Pod," I mumble. "We've been through this before. There

are no aliens. Nobody gets 'taken'. You've been watching too many old Spiel films." Pod loves Marty Spielberg.

"Han't."

"Have."

"I <u>an't</u>!"

"RIGHT," Batty barks. "Geronimo, you sit here. And I don't want to hear another peep out of anybody. Clear?"

As if to underline what he said, his left eye starts making that high-pitched ringing noise it does every so often. Someone mutters, "Peep," and we bite back our laughs as he scoops out the eye, still joined to the back of his socket with wires, gives it a shake and screws it back in the wrong way.

~ ~ ~

Three o'clock. Batty tells us to go away because we sicken him. Whizz and Randal start to pick on 3251.

They normly do it. We all walk home together because we live near each other, and nobody likes bots. They've always bullied 3251 since he got here, which is better than them bullying me and Pod. Being a bot, 3251 dun't mind, cause he dun't understand human feelings and he dun't have any feelings. He dun't need to eat. I don't know if he's even a he.

"Oi," Randal shouts at 32. "Tin-'ead!"

3251 turns around all stiff—joints prolly need oiling again—and says, "MY HEAD DOES NOT CONSIST OF TIN. I AM A PERSON, JUST LIKE YOU."

"Yeah, right." Randal snorts, wipes the snot off the end of his hooter. "Yer a GM piece of shit."

3251 says nothing, keeps walking. He walks quietly, like a ghost.

Bots dun't *look* like they're metal, and they en't, exactly. They look like a human from far away, but close up they're too symmetrical, too perfect. They never have acne, or freckles, or body hair. They never have earwax or bogies. I'd be able to tell one from a long distance but I guess if you'd never seen one before you wun't know.

"Where you off to then, tin-'ead?" Whizz says, and swings her bag against the back of 32's legs. "You goin home to your mother? Oh, I forgot. Sorry. Bots dun't have mothers. Stupid of me."

3251 nimbly jumps so the bag sweeps under his feet instead of bowling him over. He does it without looking, but I'm sort of glad about that. I en't sure what'd happen if he got hurt. Would he bleed? Or would he get mad and shoot kill-lasers from his eyes?

3251's forehead ratchets lower. "WE ARE ALL TO GO HOME."

"That was a rhetorical question, gearbox." Randal smirks. He's got this special annoying smirk where first one side of his mouth goes up, then his nose twists to one side.

We get to 32's street, and he goes off. I breathe a little bit easier, but Pod's face is white, or paler than it normally is.

"Why do you do that?" His voice is quiet.

"What?" Whizz blinks.

"Are you trying to hurt him?" Pod carries on, ignores my nudges for silence. "Cause it won't work."

That's the funny thing about Pod. He always wants to know why people do things, why people say what they say, what they're thinking. He thinks there's a reason for everything and dun't know when to shut up. His dad was a psychologist, before.

Randal's eyes narrow. He ruffles Pod's hair a tiny bit hard. "None of your biz, squirt."

"But...why?" Pod presses. "Why dun't nobody like bots? I mean, they're not really robots at all, they're, I dunno, androids?"

I whisper in his ear. "Leave it." His ears are so weird. One sticks out and the other's flat to the side of his head. "You'll make them hate us again."

"You whisprin?" Whizz says loudly. We shake our heads.

~ ~ ~

Xenon's house is near mine. It's one of the only houses still being lived in with the original people in it. Every other place except mine on Eville Avenue has been abandoned, left to fall down or get overgrown with weeds. Sometimes there are squatters, but they move on after a bit. They dun't bother you as long as you dun't bother them.

"You sure we should be doing this?" Pod says.

"I got to make sure he's ok," I say. "Want to check his family's not left the country or summat. Wait on the step if you're scared."

"I en't scared!"

Xen's dad answers the door, a short bald man wearing a breathing mask.

"Hullo. Is Xen in?"

He takes off his O2 mask. "What d'you think?" Xen's dad sounds annoyed even when he en't. "You just caught me doin me breathin."

"Is he OK?"

"Well, course he is. Why shun't he be?"

"Uh," Pod starts to plant his foot in his gob. "It's just that he din't turn up at school today, and we were wondering. . ."

I kick him.

"Ow! What did you do that f. . .? Oh. Sorry. Forget I said owt."

Xen's dad gives us a look, turns round and goes into the house, leaving the door wide open.

"You plonker."

"Don't you start," Pod says, and follows Xen's dad inside.

"Hey!" I say. "What you..?" But he can't hear. So I go in.

Xen's dad is upstairs, on the landing, shouting for Xen. There's no answer. His bedroom door's shut. Xen's dad opens it, walks past the drawings of teachers being herded and poked at by aliens, the Lost Band posters, and the papier-mâché head of our Head Xen uses as a stationary holder. He sticks the biros in the eye sockets. There's a huddled lump under the blankets, and my heart speeds up, worrying about the Radiator Sickness. But when Xen's dad flings off the covers, telling Xen not to be such a lazy-arse, his mates are here, Xen turns out to be a pile of cushions and junk.

Xen's dad's face goes lost and confused, like a stray sheep-animal.

"Where is he?" he asks us, mostly looking at Pod, but then it's kind of hard not to want to stare at Pod, he is strange-looking. "Is this a joke? Tell me this is a joke. What've you done with him? Where is he?"

I dun't want to get Xen in trouble. "Er. . .around."

Pod hares off sharpish, but before I can run out Xen's dad grabs the back of my neck. "You're stayin put til I've got to the cause of this problem."

"Fine," I say, shaking inside. There's been stories of what desperate adults do to kids now there's less of us around. If he touches me I'll kick him in the nads. "I en't done nothin to him. I han't seen him since yestday."

Xen's dad rings the school up. They tell him Xenon weren't there. He puts the phone down. Rubs his face til it goes red, then says he's sorry and that I can go away now.

Pod is hiding behind the brown, crusty hedge, waiting for me.

"D'you know what this could mean, Geez?" His eyes are

the size of plates.

"He wan't abducted by aliens, Pod." I'm tired. I want to go home. "He prolly just got fed up and run off to be alone. When he gets bored of that he'll be back."

Pod frowns. "I dunno. Xen's not run off before."

"That's prolly why he's gone and done it now, then."

"Well." Pod squints up at the moon starting to show in the dusky sky. "At least he dun't have the Radiating Sickness. You know, the ray thingy."

"Mm."

"Cause, y'know, everyone who's dead died of that."

"I know." My teeth are grinding.

"Why, though?"

"Why what?" We're almost at my front door.

"Why'd they die?"

"There's no cure for it. Once you have the, you know, the stuff—rays? Inside of you, they have to eat their way out. They burn you up. That's why no one's allowed near people who have it."

"I know that, Geez. My auntie had it, remember? I know it goes through skin and walls and stuff. What I mean is, why's nobody done anything about it? And where do the rays come from?"

"When the scientists were still figuring out how the portascanners worked, there was a test model they did with the built-in X-Ray app, right?"

"I know. They fixed it, I know, but if that's what started it, and it's all sorted now, how come people are still getting sick? How come the scientists dun't get their fingers out and find out where it's really coming from?"

"How should I know?" Pod flinches. "Pod, I'm sorry I'm off and stuff, but I dun't feel like talking about it. Save it for tomorrer, yeah?"

Pod always looks younger and smaller when he's hurt. "Yeah."

We are on my front doorstep.

"You'll be all right, walking the rest of the way?" I always ask him this. Pod dun't have a house any more. He lives with his ma in an old, burnt-out caravan, in a field round the back of some apartments too rotten to live in. The field used to be a car park, before we were born. Most of the flats are empty now, but still there's always the odd drunk or perve, and Pod's so skinny and short. Not very strong, but fast enough to get away.

"I'll be fine."

"Listen. Pod. I'm sorry. Things will get better. Xen will come back. The scientists will save us."

He pulls a face. "Er. . .yeah."

"See you."

At the end of the path, he turns round and asks me summat that makes my guts go cold.

"Geez. I wun't gonna ask if Xen had been taken by aliens.

What if he got picked up by someone else? What if he's got kidnapped?"

~ ~ ~

There's a picture in my attic only my family knows about. I go and sit up there and take it out of its manky old box to look at when I have stuff to think about, or when I forget what it looks like.

My great-great grandma painted it. She was a famous artist. Well, not *famous* like Damien Hirst or Claus Oldenberg, but she was known well locally. The picture is called "Eden in Reverse" and it's of a really, scarily tall plant with scabby-looking skin all over it. It forks outwards and upwards towards its top, like the blood vessels I see when I get lights shone in my eyes at the opticians. My great-great grandma went on a special pilgrimage, along with some other people—hundreds of them—to go see this ginormous plant. She said it was a tree, but on the back of the painting, in spidery pencil, it says "Pinus Negra" which I dun't understand.

It was all the way over in another country, I dunno which one, but it took her ages and ages to get back. I dunno why she wanted to go in the first place. Well, I do, sort of. I mean, how can something grow that big? Din't it get in the way of aircraft? But what was it for? What'd she do when she found it?

When I was little, I used to think it was summat to do

with getting married, cause when my great-great grandma set off to find the Last Tree, she was just a young girl, and when she came back she was with my great-great grandpa, with his kid, my great-grandma, in her belly. Now I'm old enough to know better. Trees en't used to make people pregnant. Maybe they went all that way just to touch it or pray to it or summat daft. Adults're always doing daft things. Maybe that's how the shit started.

Nowadays people dun't bother getting married or having kids. They can't see much point in it. There's not enough oxygen any more, and people keep dropping like flies. We've always had flies, I reckon, and they're dirty even though they're always washing their hands and faces, but the radiator sickness can't come from them. Pets, what about animals? People have dogs, cats, mice, rats and stuff, if they can look after them proply. You got to be careful, though. Some folks, like the squatters, or the weirdos, or people who still en't vegetarian, they, well, they'll catch your dog or your cat if it gets lost, and. . .well. . .At least that's what they tell us in school. Don't feed the squatters. I never saw a person eat meat before. I wonder if it makes your mouth bloody.

We got taught what it was like before, when the school still saw a point in teaching History, about how people in the olden days had sheep-animals, like walking bundles of old people's hair, and cow-things, with weird dangly bits underneath like rubber washing-up gloves. They died out, some kind of disease plus the O2 running out. Nobody thought of putting breathing masks on them. Nobody knows where the O2 gas is going to. My dad says it's leaking out into space. Sometimes, when I look up, I think I can see space through the hole in the sky, but I can't really.

These are some of the things I think about in the attic. I wonder what it'd feel like, standing next to a tree. Did the spindly bits at the top move? How did they? By themselves, like tentacles? Or not? Did they make a noise?

After a bit, I have to go down for tea, and feed Davie, who is my rat. Stuff dun't bother him. I get jealous of him, sometimes. His food prolly tastes better than what my mum makes us eat, which is mostly fungus. It dun't taste of anything.

Halfway through tea there's a banging on the door. Dad answers it, comes back in with a detective inspector, who has a head like the Old Millennium Dome.

"Now then, ah, Gerry?" he says.

"Geez," I say. "Everyone calls me Geez. Even better, call me G."

"Right. I need to ask a few questions about your friend Xenon. He's gone missing, last seen on Monday."

I en't surprised. "OK, but I dunno anything."

"When did you last see him?"

"Yestday, after school. We walk home together."

"Did he say anything odd? Did he seem any different?"

"He normly dun't say much. And he likes doing stuff that's diffrunt. Diffrunt's normal for him." Then summat clicks in my head. "Hey. Did you search his house yet?"

"Between you and me, yes."

"Did you find his portascanner?"

"No. . ."

"There you are then." I feel happier than I've felt all day.

"Sorry?"

"That proves it. He *has* run away. He wan't kidnapped. He'll be back."

"Well. . .we'll see. I can't promise anything. Did Xenon have difficulties? Was he bullied?"

"Both of us used to get beaten up, by Randal and Whizz, but that was last year, when nearly the whole class was ali— when nearly the whole class was still there. They dun't bother us now, they're too busy picking on the bot. Er, I mean, the exchange student."

The detective sucks his brown peggy teeth. "There's an awful load of that going on. What are Randal and Whizz's actual names?"

"I dunno their last names, I never asked. You'll have to ask Mr. Butts."

"Hmm, that's it. Remember, if anyone asks you about this, in school or on the street, you're to keep it confidential. Don't want to spread more panic."

He leaves. Dad looks at me. Mum stares at me from the

doorway. I shrug and shut myself in the attic.

~ ~ ~

It's Wednesday. My appointment with the school nurse is today. Every kid left has one, once a month. It dun't hurt. It's to check for what they call early signs.

I used to get really nervous, especially before my first one, when I was five, but it's a cinch. I was worrying about nothing.

When kids turn five, they either get given a portascanner by the scientists or through the school. We keep it for the rest of our lives. You dun't have to pay or anything to get your first one but if you end up losing it you have to, or your parents have to pay if you want another one. It's better if you do have one, cause then how else'd you know if summat was going wrong in your body?

"Right," Batty says, looking in both directions at once.

"You talking to me, Mr. Butts?"

Whizz laughs. Pod flashes me a quick grin, then goes back to staring out the window.

"Yes, I *am* talking to you, Gerry. I was going to say I know you have to see the nurse and that I expect you back within half an hour. Or else. And I do NOT appreciate you cracking jokes about my eyesight. It shows lack of sensitivity. You have detention at break."

I dun't care. Xen's coming back soon, and he's always in detention. He likes it. I have to keep thinking he's gonna be back, in case. But if I think it too much. . .shut up, brain.

"Sit," the nurse tells me, like she thinks I'm a puppy. I dun't think she ever had kids. She asks me if I brung my portascanner. I give it to her. She switches it on, taps her finger on the screen until it glows green, then gets me to stand up and take everything off except my pants. She X-Rays all of my body with it.

Then she turns the lights back on, and gives me a cam-pill to swaller. I swaller it. I'm not allowed to eat or drink anything except water until home time, then I have to come back so she can view the results on my 'scanner. That's OK. The pill you take's got a tiny little camera inside it, and as it gets digested it takes lots of pictures of the insides of your stomach and guts. That's why it takes all day to get the results, cause it has to take all them photos and send them up to a satellite, which sends them down to your 'scanner so you can see them.

"How'd it go?" Pod whispers once I get back to my seat next to him. We're halfway through maths.

"Fine."

"I really dun't trust it."

Pod's got a 'scanner but he's been refusing to use it since before I can remember. He's convinced the aliens—which dun't exist—might be able to find out stuff about him if he does use it.

"It's OK, Pod. Why d'you think aliens would be able to

'find out' about you?"

"They can find out stuff about anyone," he says, widening his eyes like a scared hop-rabbit. "It's the satellite. They've hacked into the satellite and are reading all this data about what we eat and drink and stuff. I just know it."

"HOW do you know, though?"

"I dream about it?"

I snort. "Dreams en't real. They dun't mean anything."

"But I have the same dream every night."

"Still dun't mean nothing, Pod."

"Does too."

"Dun't. Anyway, what's so bad about that, if they are finding stuff out about you? You're not important enough for them to come rushing to Earth once they find out you mostly eat ketchup sandwiches."

He pretends to hit me. "Twat. I meant—I *mean*—they can compile a load of information on us and then use it to...to...I dunno. I just dun't like it, that's all."

"I know that, but come on, mate. We're getting too old to believe in aliens. And dreams are only dreams. It dun't mean things like that exist. You prolly keep dreaming of aliens for some psycho-whatsitty reason."

"Dreams are messages from another world, where our true selves are."

"En't."

"Are."

"En't!"

"Are!"

"WILL YOU TWO PIPE DOWN?" Batty thunders from the front.

We shut up. But I can still feel Pod seething. I love winding him up. It's great fun. And he likes it too. He wun't bother talking to me if he din't.

~ ~ ~

The next day Pod comes up to me with a leaflet he's written and coloured in himself on his tablet.

"What's this?" I say.

"It's a thing I'm setting up. We need to let everybody know all about *them*."

"Them?"

"The aliens!"

"For God's sake!" I say, but let him give me the leaflet anyway. He goes around handing them to everyone in the playground. There's not a lot of us here, now. Prolly about seven kids to a class. At most, there's sixty kids left.

I look at mine. "IT'S US OR THEM" is on the front cover. It says we can't trust teachers, or strangers, or our parents. It says they're going behind our backs, not deliberately, but anyway they're sending information about us to the aliens, for an experiment. It says we should stop going for check-ups and bury our 'scanners. This is weird. I mean, Pod normly is weird, but this is verging on mad, now. He oughtter be careful. Randal and Whizz bullied us for ages cause of his space and aliens obsession. If they get wind of this. . .

I run after him.

"Pod! Pod?"

"What?"

"What's this all about? Don't you think you should talk to me about it first?"

"Why?"

"Well. . .cause. . .it sounds. . .it sounds mad, Poddo."

His face glows pink. "Dun't call me Poddo. Anyway, it wan't my idea to hand this stuff out, it were my dad's plan."

"Your *dad*?"

Pod's dad works as a cleaner in one of the scientists' fancy labs, now he's lost his job as a psychologist. Why does he want to spread weird lies? Portascanners help us be safe. They stop you dying of cancer and show early signs of the Radiating Sickness if you've got it. Dun't they?

"Right. Just *don't* show Whizz or Randal, OK? They'll pulverise you."

His mouth's set in a thin, grim line. "I have to. I've got to give one of these to every kid, but dun't let Batty or any grown-ups know, OK? My dad 'd prolly be arrested or summat."

"I dun't get it. Why's your dad asking you to..?"

"I'll explain later," he says. Whizz is shuffling over to us, looking confused and nosey. "Here," Pod says, giving her a leaflet. "Everybody's getting one. But not the teachers or your folks. 'Kay?"

Call me yellow-livered, but I dun't stick around to find out how Whizz takes it. I get lost sharpish.

~ ~ ~

After school my dad picks me up in the old van.

That's how I know summat's really wrong. Normly it's my mum, or I get the bus if she ever forgets or has to work late.

"What's happening?" I say when I get to the passenger window, which is rolled down.

"Get in." His face is blotchy, pink and white. He's been scrubbing at it with his hands, which is what he does when he's stressed. Red veins stand out in the corners of his eyes. I change my mind about asking what I need to know. I just do what he says, climb in and put my seat belt on. He drives.

He dun't look at me. He dun't say nothing till we get to our street.

"Look, um. . ." He coughs. Why can't he tell me? And why do I have to be told? My hands are slick with sweat, I feel sick.

"Look, Geronimo, it's your mum. She's not well."

"Why?"

"Well. . ."

There are Radiator Squad folks clustered around our door when we get there, going in and out, in bright orange suits and fish-bowl helmets.

The Radiating Sickness. She can't. She can't have.

"WHY?"

"Don't shout! Gero, you know she's not been feeling right for the past week—she woke up this morning and was losing her hair, I had to call an ambulance, and then the R.S. got involved—"

I dun't want to hear any more. I yank the van door open and scramble up the path, wanting to go in, wanting her to still be there. An orange-suit tries to get in my way. It's a small lady. I elbow past her.

The house dun't feel like ours. There are white lead-lined sheets over nearly all the furniture and walls, a flimsy white canvas tunnel thing running from the hallway up the stairs to my parents' room. Where my mum must've been last when they found her. More orange-suits are walking about slowly with radiation detectors, pointing the probes into corners and in the chairs and everywhere. It's a bad dream.

"What are you *doing*?" I say. It's a sensible question, but nobody answers me. Maybe they can't hear through their helmets. Maybe they dun't want to hear. It'd be just like them.

"Geez?" My dad's at the door. He wun't make himself come into his own house. Scared he'll catch it. How come he's not got it as well? Or me? "Geez, come on out of there. It's not safe. They've not checked all the rooms for gamma waves yet."

"Whoah!" One of the orange-suits turns around and

clocks me. I can hear his voice all right. "What you doin in here, duckie? You an't touched owt, have you?"

I'm shaking, furious. "I could ask you the same! Where is she? What've you done with her?"

"She was taken to the R.S. Ward, I should think. I'd just step outside till we're finished if I was you." He pokes his probe in my direction, moves it slowly from my head to my feet. There in't any noise, and he tells me I'm clean. I can go.

Kicked out of my own place, on top of everything else. I wish Xen was here. He'd prolly pull faces at the orange-suits or do stupid impressions of their walks, later, and make me feel better. Where is he? What's so important that he can't be here with me?

"She's in the Ward," I tell dad. I feel flat now, deflated. Behind the numbness there's a dull horror. "The old barracks."

"I know," he says. "We'll visit her. Come on."

"It wun't be a proper visit." I know what the R.S. Ward is like, from what Pod told me about his aunt dying there. They din't let the families into the same room as the patients, in case the Radiating Sickness spread. All Pod could do was look through a window at his auntie all sore and peeling in bed and talk at her through a tube.

"I dun't want to see her," I say, suddenly not wanting to at all. I dun't want to see her go like Pod's aunt Hellen. I want to keep her in my head like she was, like she's always been.

I thought my dad'd make me come with him, but he nods like a sad old man. "All right, boy. I need to see her anyway, but I'll drop you round to Xen's place. Maybe his dad can look after you."

"Not him," I say quickly. He's prolly still mad at me for calling on him and making him see Xen was gone. "Pod. Take me to Pod's."

"I don't know. . .it's a rough neighbourhood."

"Just drive me there. I'll give you directions, it'll be fine."

"No, no. It won't be safe enough. It'll have to be Mr. Paisley's."

Mr. Paisley is the name of Xen's dad. My heart and stomach lurch with nerves, but I dun't want to argue. I sit quiet in the van while he drives me up to Xen's.

The house is dark and still when we get there. A few orange-suits are milling about with their probes in the front garden, up and down the street now, poking in everyone's gardens. It's to check the R.S. han't spread, but it prolly wun't' ve spread to Paisley's cause he built the house himself using lead-infused bricks and cement before Xen got born. Lead's a pretty good shield. I can see why my dad thinks I'll be safest here.

We stand on the step and knock.

When Xen's dad opens the door there's no lights on behind him. He's wearing a ratty old dressing-gown, a cigarette half-burnt out in-between his lips. Fuggy expression, not shaved for a while. Red eyes.

"What?"

My dad flinches a bit, but not so you can see it. I feel him hunch up next to me.

"Have you heard the news?"

"News?"

"Izzie's ill."

"Oh. Isobel. The R.S. Yes. Sorry about that, my mind's been all over the place since. . .ah. . .will you come in?"

Dad shakes his head. It's starting to rain now, a fast, thin rain that drenches your hair and clothes in ten seconds. If you stand out in it too long, it can strip the top layer of your skin off like sunburn.

"I got to go to the Ward, got to be with her," my dad says. He is very deliberately not crying. This is how adult men chat to each other, I notice. They put up their own shields.

"You want me to take care of the lad?"

"Yeah."

Mr. Paisley nods. "He can't replace my own, but anyway, I'd be glad to."

Dad puts a hand on the top of my damp head. "Be good."

Then he's gone.

The R.S. Ward's in the next town over. He won't be back till tomorrer or the next day. It all depends on if he wants to stay with mum till she goes, or come back to me.

I think he's gonna stay with her.

"You'd better come in, then," Mr.Paisley sighs, flicking ash. "Getting soggy out there."

My feet drag over the threshold, reluctant. I know to take my shoes off. Xen's dad's a bit posher than my folks. In our house, you could keep your trainers on all day, but here it's different.

"You can sleep in Xen's room," he tells me. "My boy would've liked that. Hell, he might even have laid booby traps for you."

"Mm." I dun't know what to do, what to say. What is there to say?

"I'm doing macaroni cheese for tea, though really it's mushrooms pretending to be pasta and cheese," he says, like nothing's wrong and everything's normal. "Want some?"

"Uh, yeah. Please."

I foller him into the living room. The TV's on but not the sat-dish. Just a blue screen. Full ashtrays here and there. Photo albums thrown on the floor in a slapdash way, some open at pictures of Xen and his mum when he was at playgroup, some shut like tight brown mouths. Xen's dad must be the only bloke to print out his own photos and stick them in a book with glue. Normal people just save them onto a USB stick or summat.

"I was remembering a few things," Mr. Paisley says in the kitchen. "He was a nice kid. Then his mother left, and he went. . .well. I still miss him. I miss *her*."

"Mm," I say. "Is there Coke?"

He waves a hand at the fridge. "In there. Mind what you touch, though."

There's one can, not open, standing amongst bags of things that dun't smell very good and plastic boxes of stuff that looks like grey rice.

"Need to have a clear out."

"Where d'you reckon Xen is?" I can't stop myself asking.

"Dunno. Some hotel somewhere, if he's smart. Knowing him, it'll probably be a police station. That boy was always a mix of brains and lack of common sense. Me and his mum, we thought he was autistic when he started school. He stopped talking, wouldn't eat owt much, stared at stuff a lot. But it wasn't that. He was just mad. Stewing."

I nod. "He always hated school." Why are we talking about him in the past tense? "He said it was a prison camp for kids."

Mr. Paisley huffs a laugh.

I understood where Xen was coming from, though. I remember how he said it, eyes glittering under a lamp-post one Autumn when we waited to be picked up and took home.

"The world's not fair, G. People lock up their children just for the crime of being born, just cause their parents fucked. When I get to be Prime Minister, I'm going to change that. It'll be adults who get locked away in a stuffy concrete box. You just watch me. I'll put the teachers in the Year Six classrooms so they'll always have to do SATS and Eleven Plus exams. I'll put the police in Year One, and psychotherapists in Reception."

He had to see a psychotherapist once a week, and he had pills to stop the voices. Xen said the voices came from the reptile part of his brain and they told him to do stupid things, which is why he had to block them out.

Pod always said they were instructions from space. It's always aliens with Pod.

"He kept saying one day he'd run off to find his mother," Mr. Paisley says as I open my Coke. "Usually when we'd fallen out."

"Maybe that's what he's doing."

His smile's grateful. "Watch summat on telly if you want. Or grab summat to read. I dun't mind."

~ ~ ~

It feels weird reading Xen's pile of old Batman comics. They're his. I en't Xen. And every time I look up between forkfuls of mac and cheese I catch Mr. Paisley watching me in a funny sort of way. Like he's trying to see into my mind.

"They'll treat her right, you know," he says suddenly. "They'll give her stuff for the pain. She'll sleep most of the time."

What can I say to that? They can't give her time. They can't give her life. I'm looking at the same page, Batman strangling the Joker, but not really seeing it. The characters've gone blurry.

I swaller. "Where does it come from?"

"Eh?"

"The sh—the gamma rays. Where are they from? Why can't people stop them?"

"Space," Xen's dad says. "Dying stars or whatever, when they explode, a burst of gamma waves fires right at us. This wun't be a problem if our atmosphere was thicker, but there's a hole, see."

"A hole in the sky?"

"Summat like that." He blows smoke at the blank TV. It en't a good idea for him to smoke, but some people can't quit even now. "Too much carbon dioxide, not enough breathable air. Atmosphere thins. Boom. You got yourself a hole. Stuff from outside Earth leaks in."

"But why's it happening?"

He shrugs. "Shit happens."

Maybe these are the aliens Pod's always on about. Unintelligent, unstoppable, invisible, evil aliens. They take people everywhere, and they wun't stop taking till everything is gone.

I go to bed early.

Xen's room feels empty and strange without him in it. I remember last time we had a sleepover, and we threw ideas around about the future. He wanted us to write a book, all about the end of the world, he said. We were gonna call it A

History of the Future. Pod would be in it, fighting some ugly Martians. He could have editing credits. There'd be zombies, and giant custard monsters, and flying fish, and a prince waking a bot girl out of her mechanical sleep and kissing her to make her human.

I dun't think I'll be able to sleep. The air is too thick in here, and you can't open windows now, not when it's raining. I borrow Xen's mask and give myself some O2 for half an hour before turning off the light.

My tablet pings in my school-bag, and a white light glows. I shake the books off of it and pull it out.

It's a message from Xen.

No words.

Just a photo of a giant plant, with scabby black skin, and forked tendril-arms at the top. The photo's been taken at the base of it, looking up. It thins at the top from perspective, but the sun flickers green and gold through the leaves. They scrape the sky.

Next to it is a smaller one, a baby. So thin it could snap in the next strong wind.

By that tree is a woman. She has Xen's messy dark hair, and Xen's smile.

AFTER
by Jack Stone

Here are people who live underground. Why? It seems members of competing communities aren't very hospitable toward one another.—Ed.

THE WINTERS ARE BRUTAL. Frost pierces the thickest insulation. If you're not moving, the numbness takes over in an instant. Sometimes you pause just to get that quick fix of relief, a dangerous addiction that teases a quick, painless death.

The winds are unending and merciless, splitting lips and drying my frozen hands until they crack down the creases of my palms, temporarily reprieved only by the oozing blood from the wounds as it lubricates the cracks before it too freezes in place. Digging deep into the snow is the only way to survive for scavengers like myself.

The cities, if you can call them that, are all just connected tunnels below ground. We have learned to build like ants with tiered underground tunnel systems. The leaders, of course, live at the bottom where it is warmer in the winter and cooler in the summer.

The summer...Winters are brutal; the summers worse.

Everything above ground—and up to five feet below—is cooked, killing all but the strongest of wildlife and making the use of tools impossible after a few moments in the baking heat, turning them into hot irons that will melt your skin right off. At least in the winter I can feed my numbing addiction if I stand still long enough.

We live close to another group, no more than two miles away. While everyone in our camp is free to do as they please and performs a job of their choosing, the other group focuses more on slavery and forced labor. We do not agree with each other's methods of survival, but we are equally matched in our defenses and could never take over the others' city. Because of this, we trade and tolerate one another for survival.

When we find stragglers in the wild, we offer them food and shelter, whether male or female. The 'slavers,' as we call them, put men to work digging their tunnels; women are shared with their leaders. This, though vile, is what makes joining our city more appealing, and those we find have a greater appreciation for our help. When trading, we always meet between our two cities, never having actually been to the others' homes.

Tonight is an extremely cold one. I will stay home and sleep next to my wife.

~ ~ ~

Morning comes. One pair of socks pulled up to my knees.

Old Newspaper pages crinkled and wrapped around the sock. Another two pairs of socks, same for my legs. Tight pants covered in more pages and then my outer coveralls are slipped on. Three shirts with paper layers between each of them and my coveralls are zipped to the top. Gloves are not good enough for the cold; mittens must be worn to keep the fingers close to each other for warmth, but first the fingers must be wrapped together. This makes hunting difficult, at times, but prevents the loss of feeling—which is critical if I need to start a fire.

A final kiss from my wife and she slips my masks and hood into place, only my eyes exposed to the elements. The first moment I step out is always the same. A nice cooling sensation from sweltering in my clothes. The moment doesn't last, though, and I cling onto any of that warmth as the wind covers me in ice if I stand still too long.

I won't be back anytime soon. As my wife kissed me for the last time, she knew it may be for the last time. I have to go further than ever, as supplies are spreading thin this winter. More children have been born this year than ever before. We underestimated our needs.

Day one, nothing but the white out here (as I had feared). No animals, or even a rogue plant scratching its way up through the snow.

Day two, I can't see the flags that guide back to our home. I lay my own path markers and hope the white doesn't hide them from me on my way back. I stand on the edge of a vast valley that used to be my home. As with everything else in the winter, the white has erased any trace of civilization. I can't risk walking through it—I could fall through a thin spot near a house, and I would never be able to crawl back out. I must go around.

Day three, past the valley and further than I've ever been, I amazingly find a small patch of green fighting back against the white. The stark contrast of colors is almost shocking, appearing grey until I am upon it. The wind is almost calm in this little dip. A palm stands tall with small weeds and bushes huddled close to it. Amongst the burled mess is a treasure for sure: a yucca plant. I dig carefully to remove root and all and place it into my bag. From the roots out to its leaves it is an extremely useful plant. I gently remove a number of its leaves and place them into a pocket of their own.

Day four, I am awakened by the sound of salvation. A wild boar must have smelled the Yucca in my bag and has come to investigate. I lay flat with my knife at the ready, pretending to be dead. Some time goes by as the boar stalks around the area, deciding if it's worth the risk to come closer for the plant. He turns and moves straight for me, determined to get his meal. Just as he is over me, his breath on my face, I lunge up into his neck with my knife, and I wrap my arm around his head from underneath, holding him with all of my strength, burying my knife deep until his resistance fades and I am showered in his blood. I will have to build a shelter now. There is more meat here than I could carry in one trip, and I must protect the rest from other predators.

I use four small sheets of plexiglass scavenged during the summer months with cords wrapped around them to form an open-ended cube which I place on the ground and stuff full of snow, packing it tightly. Once a good cube of snow is packed into a brick, I remove the cord and slide the plexiglass pieces off of the cube leaving a perfect ice block in place. From there I stick three of the pieces into the snow to elongate the existing cube by stuffing more snow until I form an entire circle around ten feet in diameter. Once the bottom layer is complete, I stand in the center and dig up snow to place the next layer—which is where it becomes harder. Now, I have to make cubes and place them on the wall, slightly angled, using loose snow to fill in the gaps, welding the snow to itself. Layer after layer I place, raising the ceiling and lowering the floor at the same time until I can stand inside to place the final pieces. Once I am closed in, I dig underneath the first layer to create an entrance, using the extra snow to reinforce the bottom pile as I go. Once outside, I use more loose snow to fill in any gaps. It is getting dark—I drag the meat into the shelter and seal off the entrance for the night.

Day five, I slept better than I have so far on this trip.

Having the wind off you makes all the difference. I prepare the boar for transport. I remove the legs and cover the rest with snow to preserve it until I return for more. There is always a chance another scavenger could find my kill, but out here we take what we can and apologize for nothing.

Going home early will be a nice surprise for my wife. She hates knowing every time I leave could be the last. I am lucky to have her, and thinking of her worrying about me helps me focus so I can make my way back to her, to see that amazing smile one more time.

I used a lot of energy yesterday building the shelter, and it shows. I will have to make a fire using some of the yucca leaves and cook some of this boar to have the strength to make it home.

As night falls, the warm fire feels as good as the numbing cold. The smell of the boar somehow reminds me of before. Once every summer, my uncle would purchase and cook a whole pig, and the entire family would spend the day fishing, drinking, and playing games.

There is always a concern that fire will draw unwanted attention, so I stay on my guard while I have the best meal I've eaten in months.

I then hear the crunching of snow—footsteps, but not trying to conceal themselves. It was more of a struggling step. I look up to see a scavenger from our sister city with two prisoners in tow, chained together. A man and a woman.

Before he gets close to the fire he asks if he may join. I give him a nod and he motions to the pair to squat by the flames before seating himself. The man with him immediately pleads with me to help them, which I ignore, knowing it could incite a war between our two cities. The scavenger asks if I have any extra boar; I am reluctant to share any of my people's food with his kind.

"All out."

He snickers and pulls out a knife before reaching for the man prisoner's hand. He pulls his arm out, obviously ready to cut it off for food. I stop him mid-swing, offering some of my boar. He grins at my weakness and releases the hand he was willing to eat, pushing the prisoner to the ground.

It was getting late and my full belly made it hard to stay awake. I slipped my knife up to my chest as I rolled over to sleep and left them to their business. Just as I dozed off, I heard them arguing and the woman pleading. The scavenger was trying to rape her; her male counterpart was fighting the scavenger. I pretended not to hear until I heard her scream as the scavenger stabbed the male prisoner and killed him. I rolled over to see him preparing to gut him for his meat and, as he looked at me, I simply told him to take it away from the camp. He gave me that smirk again, acknowledging that I wasn't going to stop him.

He spent the next hour cutting the meat he wanted and was too tired to pay the woman any more attention for the night. Everything quieted until morning. The fire guttered in the night. When everyone wakes there is no talking, only hopelessness on the woman's face as she pleads to me with her eyes. She reminds me of my wife.

Day six, we head in the same direction, and so we travel together to get back to our cities. I have some of my boar and the scavenger eats pieces of his victim, with the woman refusing to eat her friend. At night, once he sleeps, I slip her some boar to keep her strength up. She quietly pleads every night for me to help her, but I have to do what is best for my people and ignore her.

Day seven, the wind is fierce and she can barely stand while being dragged. I keep imagining my wife treated that way, what I would do if it were her. The cold usually keeps any emotions at bay, as there is only room for survival, but I feel a fire building within me with every moment I see her struggle. He continues to pull her along like a trophy. I've seen many scavengers haul in prisoners before and never have I interfered. It is what we do.

We've been without a fire for a few days so the other scavenger reveals a few wood scraps. I toss in more yucca leaves to get it going, and we have a fire for a few hours. Once we are warm—and our bellies are full—he tries again to rape her.

She screams and he pulls a knife on her, threatening to cut off one of her hands if she resists. She quiets down and turns her head away from him, giving up any resistance. As he prepares to remove her pants, I make eye contact with her and note a single tear tracing down her face. She is broken, her hope completely gone. I close my eyes and see myself letting my own wife lose her hope by doing nothing.

In one quick action I draw my knife and bury it into his lower back, pulling the blade sideways to sever his spine, instantly paralyzing him. He falls limp; I roll him off of her and help her up. He tries to talk but is in shock. I cut her bonds and tell her to stay by the fire as I heft him across my shoulders. Over the hill I carry him before tossing him over a cliff like a lump of useless meat. Hopefully the wild animals will eat his body before summer. . .and hopefully he will still be alive while they do. Good riddance.

When I come back to the fire I give her an extra covering to keep warm and more of my boar. Over the next few days—on our way back—she regains her strength, and I see the same hope fill her eyes that also fills my wife's. This is a harsh new world we live in, and hope is rare, so we take what we can and apologize for nothing.

BEEN HERE BEFORE
by Jessica Mizell

This one belongs in a category all its own. Can you guess what popular pastime influenced the theme of this story?–Ed.

I AWAKEN.

I hear the ocean as I open my eyes. There is a terrible itch on my left arm. As I reach to scratch it I notice an unfamiliar metal object sewn into my wrist.

I am in my underwear, and—I am not sure, but—it feels like a dream. I rise to my feet and call out to anyone around, but my voice is drowned out by the rushing sea behind me.

Sticking to the beach I begin to hear noises in the surrounding areas between the trees. A little creature rushes up to me from the darkness and sniffs me before I can react.

It looks like a baby dinosaur. I quickly pick up a rock in defense but the little guy only stares at me. He seems harmless enough, so I continue down the beach and he follows close behind.

A few yards down the beach another one comes running up and follows along with its friend. One big, happy family. We dredge further on and a third one joins us, but this time they all three begin making noises—talking to each other, it seems. Before I can assess what is happening, all three of them jump onto me, biting my face and hands when I try to defend myself. They confuse me, and I fall to the ground. I have been betrayed and, although I fight, I slowly lose consciousness, and my body falls numb.

~ ~ ~

I awaken.

I hear the ocean as I open my eyes. My left arm itches and as I scratch it I notice a familiar metal object sewn into my wrist.

I stand up and see I am in my underwear. The ocean is so loud no one would hear me if I called out, so I begin walking down the beach.

I hear weird animal sounds coming from the nearby trees, so I arm myself with a rock. A little dinosaur runs out from the thicket toward me, and he looks hungry so I kick at him and throw my rock, scaring him away. I pick up another rock just in case as I continue on.

Around a cove another little one comes up while I am not looking. He seems to be friendly, so I let him follow along. A bit later, a second one joins us. I become suspicious of the little vixens.

After a tiring trek in the sand we come upon a weird-looking tree offering its shade. I lean against it to catch my breath, and my little companions seem leery, walking circles before me.

Suddenly, the entire tree lifts up, levitating over my head before crashing down in front of me, obliterating my two companions. The force of it knocks me on my bottom. A sound unlike any other rang through my body, shaking my bones and making the sand beneath me repel away.

I look up and see the underside of a creature larger than I thought could ever exist. I climb to my feet and creep away, hoping it won't notice me. When I felt I'd gone far enough, I turn to watch it eating leaves from the tree tops. I hid behind a giant boulder and watched in amazement.

At nighttime, cool air from the ocean began to chill me. Stomach empty, I can almost smell food cooking. As I top the next hill, I see a couple of small huts and a campfire.

I am so exhausted from my trip that I can't run down there, or I would have. I walk to the beach and up to the camp. There are three men there huddled around the fire, cooking meat on a spit. I say hello and, startled, they leap to their feet. It is some time before they realize I'm no threat.

They calm down and offer me a seat by the fire. One of them goes to find more firewood and I ask the other two about this place. Why there are dinosaurs here, and how we got there.

My head begins to hurt as I fall on my side. When I land, I see the man standing over me with the stick he had just struck me with. The other two run over and hold my arms down while I am dazed. The one who hit me lies atop me. I beg for a reason, but he punches me in the face. Blood covers my eye so that I cannot see. I begin to cry as he has his way with me. He punches me again and again until I can no longer feel him inside of me.

~ ~ ~

I awaken.

I am angry. The ocean is loud and that metal in my arm itches. I look around and pick up a few rocks before I start walking. There are animal noises coming from the trees, and a little dinosaur tries to run up to me before I kick him away.

I reach a cove a bit later and another of them comes running up to me. I hit him with a rock and toss him into the ocean to keep any more of them from gathering around the body.

A bit further and another one charges at me; I do the same to him. These little buggers are annoying.

I look around at everything and notice strange clouds that appear to be circling something. I see an enormous dinosaur down the beach eating from the tree tops. It must be an herbivore, but I definitely do not want to be anywhere near its feet. They were as big as trees themselves.

I waited until it moved off out of the area. It will soon be dark. As I top a hill I smell food cooking and see a couple of small huts with a campfire. Leery of this entire place, I sneak down behind one of the huts and note three men huddled around the flames with a skewer of meat cooking. I listen to them talk—they joke about how they recently raped a woman to death and tossed her body to the dinosaurs.

On the other side of the huts they have wooden spikes lining the beach, insuring the only way past them would be to swim around. I make my way back up the hill and slip into the water and slowly wade on my tiptoes until I arrive near their camp. I hold my breath and dive down to swim a bit past their blockade.

I watch their campfire fade in the distance. As I begin my swim back to shore I feel the water beneath me sucking me down. Before I can look, my entire body is surrounded by teeth as I am engulfed into something's mouth. When the enormous jaws close upon me, my body feels cold, and I see only darkness.

~ ~ ~

I awaken.

~ ~ ~

I awaken.

~ ~ ~

I awaken.

I am cold even though the sun pierces my eyelids as I lie on the beach. I can hear the ocean crashing on the shore as if daring me to join it. There are small rocks in the area, so I gather a few up in case I need them later.

After a quick look around, I walk down the beach and a tiny dinosaur runs at me from the nearby foliage. I throw a rock at it instinctively, knocking it cold. I was going to toss it into the ocean, but I instead gather nearby palm fronds and sit down to fashion a basket in which to carry it. How I know to strip and weave the back, I've no idea. It just feels natural.

As the morning rolls on it gets colder, and I gather some branches for a fire. While I sit close for warmth, I begin weaving clothing for myself. By the afternoon I've myself a shirt, some pants, a hat and make-shift sandals to help me walk in the sand.

There is a bad smell creeping over my camp area. With the little guy sleeping in his basket, I investigate. There is a nearby rock formation at the bottom of a cliff that seems to be the culprit. As I near it I begin to feel fear, anger, and shame wash over me, as if I already know what I will find.

Peeking beyond one of the giant rocks I see a pile of bodies—undoubtedly the cause of the smell. They are all in their underwear. They are female, and as I draw nearer I can see...they are all me. I am startled, scared. Immense shame washes over me, but I'm not confused. I don't know how or why I am standing here looking down at myself ten times over, but it feels like it's my fault that they have all leapt to their deaths.

I scavenge my own bodies. One has a weaved satchel; another a chest piece that looks like it is from a giant bug; another with a make-shift knife made from sharpened rock. When I have gently and thoroughly picked them over, I spend the rest of the day apologizing to them and digging their graves.

Before I bury the last one the little dinosaur wakes up and begins to yell. I know what it wants—but why do I even care? Cutting a piece from my own dead body was surprisingly easier than I expected. The little devil chomped it down almost too happily. He probably thinks it's a piece of me.

With daylight fading fast I cut branches from a tree, sharpen their edges and lay them out to dry for the night. There are different types of berries in the forest; while collecting them, I stay clear of the black ones. They give me a cautious feeling. After I fill my own belly with a few dozen berries, I restock the kindling and snuggle up to the fire to stay warm.

The next morning, I awaken to something touching me. When I roll over I see the dinosaur lying beside me for warmth. He chewed through his basket and could have easily killed me in my sleep. Instead, he wakes up and looks at me before yelling for his food. I think I will name him 'Complicated'—or Compy, for short.

I scavenge more berries for myself but don't come across anything Compy wants. We wander down the beach together and another little dinosaur runs toward us. Compy viciously attacks and kills it, then looks at me as if begging for approval, which I give, congratulating him on his kill. Quickly then, Compy eats what he needs from the body. . .making me glad he is on my side.

For now.

As we venture on we pass an area where a large dinosaur had been grazing. Great cuts of the treetops are missing, and some are toppled, as if stomped underfoot. We are careful as we walk through the mess, making sure we don't attract the attention of anything larger than us.

Soon I smell smoke—and ready one of my spears in case we are not welcomed. Over a hilltop, there are a couple of small huts with a campfire right on the beach. Past them—and running down the length of the beach—there are spiked formations setup, purposefully blocking entry to the camp.

Growing leery of the whole scene, Compy and I take to the forest. Not far in we find a small clearing. Must be where the owners of the camp cut their supplies. Within a few steps out into the light I feel a sharp sting and a familiar disorienting feeling, reminding me of the black berries. I look down to see an arrow stuck to my hip, and I begin to fade away.

I am drowsy.

We are at the camp. They are talking, can barely see. Campfire is bright. Compy tries to fight but is no match and runs away, fading again. Undressing me, going through my things. Compy comes back. . .he is hit with a spear. Compy lies still. One of them climbs over me. I fight, but I am weak—my arms feel numb. They laugh and have me throughout the night. I am awake through it all, but I cannot move.

When they tire of me they toss me with their scraps next to Compy. The only thing I can hear, can focus on, is Compy wheezing his final breath as I finally fall unconscious.

~ ~ ~

I awaken.

My insides hurt and I have a pulsing headache. I struggle to open my eyes. When I manage it, I see Compy had crawled up next to me, wanting me to protect him or—more likely— to protect me. I reach to him with what I fear will be my final touch, but our connection beckons the remaining life in him to show me that he, too, still fights.

It is dark and the men have gone to sleep with their doors tightly sealed. They have used us for their sick pleasures and thrown us away to die. I am furious with them, but I am mad at myself for letting it happen. Fighting back tears, I gently scoop Compy up and, with weak legs, I stumble out of the camp and deep into the woods.

The more I walk, the more my insides hurt. I note that I am naked and bleeding from between my legs. I become even more upset. . .and almost don't see the stream ahead of me as I patter into the water. I wash myself and clean Compy. Focusing on him takes my mind off of what had happened to me.

I pull some fronds and lay Comply amongst them,

checking his wound carefully. I get the bleeding to stop and then hunt in the stream to catch fish. We should be far enough away from the men that they won't notice a small fire.

While waiting for Compy to wake up I work on making new clothes, as well as some smaller sharp sticks to hide in my clothes—just in case I encounter those savages again.

Finally, Compy wakes up, but he can barely move. I thank my little hero and carefully feed him some of the fish before he falls asleep again. I fashion together a make-shift shelter and cuddle around Compy to keep an eye on him while I cry myself to sleep.

Boom

I am shaken awake. It is still dark, but dawn quickly approaches.

Boom

I am alert now. What could cause such a rumble? Is it another herbivore moving through the area?

Boom Boom

A quicker step confirms it is not one of the giant dinosaurs feeding near the beach. I peek out of our shelter to see a true monster part the trees down the stream from us as it lunges toward a giant turtle and bites it nearly in half with one bite.

A tyrannosaur.

Catching the spark of my dying fire, the giant carnivore barrels down the stream our way. I leave Compy safe (I hope) in the shelter, and I dart through the forest. The beast roars at my defiance and trains its focus upon me.

To the beach. To the beach.

The steps behind me getting ever louder nearly knock me off balance as their crashing shakes the ground. The tree tops shatter in the path it paves trying to get me.

To the beach. To the beach.

It draws close. A clearing allows it to gain on me unhindered; I feel its hot breath on my back as its jaws clamp shut just feet behind me. My body tingles with fear as I hit the trees on the other side of the clearing, nearly relieving myself as I jump over a log.

To the beach. To the camp.

When I come out onto the beach I run down to the men's camp and kick their fire while I yell and scream. They hurriedly come out of their huts just in time for the Rex to arrive. Too distracted by my ruckus they do not see it until it bites one of them at the waist. Another man ducks back into his hut. The gargantuan monster stomps on it, crushing it to splinters. The third screams as the Rex takes its time with him.

I am afraid, but I cannot help celebrating their deaths as if I were celebrating something more than vengeance. When I realize the Rex was almost finished with its current meal, my celebration cuts short and fear resumes control. I back away from the camp toward the spiked formations they have setup; I crawl carefully between them across the sand, making sure to stay out of sight.

When I come out the other side I peek to see it finishing off its rampage at the camp and letting out a roar that touches my soul. The beast does not dare storm the spikes between us, and eventually it wanders back into the forest.

Hours go bye while I use the spikes for cover. When I can no longer hear the distant booms of footsteps I make my way back to Compy. My headache is gone, and the sunlight feels good on my body. Arriving back at my shelter, it seems untouched. I look in to see Compy resting peacefully. Being in a dangerous area I scoop him up, gather my things, and hoist him onto my shoulder for ease of carrying.

We travel for days, seeing amazing waterfalls and encountering more dinosaurs that shouldn't exist. The further we go, the more I feel that I've missed something. Compy is doing better and has taken to riding on my shoulder fulltime.

We come to a cliff and see something unbelievable and amazing—yet I feel a sense of relief and a rush of emotion as I lay eyes on a magnificent stone city with its huge gates that overshadow nearby forests. I was leery of the men's camp, but this place instills in me the opposite feeling, like I've been here before.

As I approach, the giant gate opens, and I am greeted by guards who both welcome me back. They are mistaking me for someone else, surely. Everyone I see gives me a welcome nod and congratulates me on my return. Rather than correct them, I go along with it, thanking them.

Then I see him.

I grab a nearby spear from a weapon rack and confront the men who raped me, who stabbed Compy. He steps back and begs me not to harm him as I raise my spear to strike him. I am certain I watched the Rex eat him, but I would recognize his face anywhere after watching helplessly as he had his way with me. Others quickly join in and try to explain that he remembers nothing he'd done. That no one ever does.

Confused—but definitely outnumbered—I relent, and the frightened man scurries away. I am angry and emotional now, even in this happy place, as I am lead to the main building where I am supposed to meet the leader. She runs out upon hearing of my arrival and charges me, surprising me with a loving hug, washing away my angry mood. I do not know her, but I've felt this love before.

Once everything calms, I am given clean clothes made of smooth cloth and have my first warm shower (that I can remember). Later, we sit at a wonderful dinner, and the children play with Compy—who surprisingly hasn't tried to eat any of them. They are all surprised that I have effectively tamed him. . .or perhaps it is he who tamed me. Then I notice something while watching them play. None of the children have metal implants in their arms. . .but the adults *do*, just like me. The leader, Melissa, senses my confusion, but she also sees I have learned a lot in the time it took me to get here. As she explains what they know, I see flashes I have experienced these past weeks, and things begin to make sense as the mystery is unfolded. But she then reveals an even bigger one that they have been saving.

Ten years ago, she awoke here and began building this city on the cliffs from a small hut. She had no idea where she learned the skills to do this, but it came naturally. Slowly, more and more people appeared when she had awoken—and they joined in building. It wasn't until one of their hunters was eaten in front of them—only to come back a week later with no memories of anything—that they began to piece the mystery together.

They began compiling the names of everyone living in the community—this was to keep up with where they spawned after they were killed—and how long it took to come back. They made packages with each person's belongings to help them get a glimpse of who they used to be when they returned. All of the children had been born here naturally, and most adults believe if they die, the children will not return.

After dinner, Compy and I are shown to our room, where Melissa brings me a box. Inside are drawings and letters that she says were written by me. Some of the letters are years old. I sit up all night reading the life of a person whom everyone claims is me. I've been here from the beginning; I built the home in which I now sleep; I even had an intimate partner before they were killed. When they returned, they were (of course) never interested in my again.

The last few letters talk of me being a leader of an investigation team. We knew that we would return, and the city has one of those locations within its walls, but we did not know who had implanted us with devices that seem to be the reason we return. From our many discussions. the most we could conjecture is that we are being tested. While our memories are wiped clean, we retain any new skills learned between our deaths.

As I finish reading the letters and try to take this all in, I put Compy down on the bed and crawl up next to him. I am not sure what to think, but no matter what tomorrow brings, Compy and I will be ready for it.

~ ~ ~

I awaken.

~ ~ ~

I awaken.

~ ~ ~

I remember.

HANGING, JUST OUTSIDE THE WORLD

by Jim O'Donnell

Tell your family or roommate you'll be indisposed for the nonce, as this is a gloriously long tale that will command your attention until the last word.–Ed.

"See how the waters are rising in the north; they will become an overflowing torrent. They will overflow the land and everything in it, the towns and those who live in them. The people will cry out; all who dwell on the land will wail."
  Jeremiah 47:2

SOMEWHERE WITHIN THE FITS of reason that assailed her, Sunny caught a glimpse of the boy. There, between the sleeping and the dreaming, she knew she always would.

"I saw him again."

"Oh?" The nurse pulled a thin blanket over Sunny's shoulders. Sunny lay in a deep chair, curled into a ball. Her hips ached and her back was tight. The nurse opened the curtains. The sun streaked in, lighting the bed in front of her. Instantly, she felt the heat and pushed the blanket onto the floor. The bed was still empty. She'd hoped that, maybe, the bed wouldn't be empty. She hoped that, maybe, it had all just been one long nightmare. She took a deep breath.

"Yes," she said.

"Wait. Which boy?" The nurse was cautious.

"The one there on the docks."

"Huh? Oh...Ok." The nurse pulled at his blue scrubs, adjusted his surgical glass, and sat down on the empty bed. He ran his fingers through his dark hair and sighed. "Do you want to tell me about him?"

"He's gone. They're all gone," she said. "It hurts."

"Nothing hurts forever."

"A mother shouldn't have to bury her own son."

The nurse nodded. He didn't know what to say to her.

"You remember the ferry that used to go out there?" she asked. "Do you remember? You could still see the island from shore that spring."

"Not anymore."

"No."

"It wasn't so far away then."

"No...Of course, it was actually there, then. And then it wasn't." Redoubt had reinforced the old ferry in the winter because of the waves. They'd grown so big out there almost anything would roll. They took out all the windows and welded in steel plates. The third deck was like a fortress. They reinforced the hull and put in padded chairs and seat belts. It wasn't supposed to be fun. Just transportation. "Do you remember?"

He didn't. He was too young. The ferry hadn't run for years.

"I had to get out there to the island to get back. But I was afraid to go home."

~ ~ ~

Sunny gasped when she crawled up into the devil-eye of the sun. It was very hot. The stench of sweat and breath and bodies had overwhelmed the cabin. But the island air wasn't an improvement. It was still and humid and stunk like seagrass, brine, and oil. Sunny felt the apprehension she held for this place well up inside of her. She pulled her shirt over her head. Then, like all the others, she popped open her white umbrella. On the dock, the captain waited. She was stiff and sweating. She was nervous and impatient.

"I don't understand why you come back here, Sunny," the Captain growled. "This place is a prison. Everyone is leaving and you come back." She shook her head.

Men and women in blue Redoubt Ferries uniforms stacked boxes, trunks, and suitcases. Then, one of them scanned each tab and printed a bar-tape receipt in black thermo-print for its owner. Others formed a line and passed the luggage into the ferry. The old LNG Wärtsilä engines grunted against the waves to keep the boat steady. It was all very orderly. Sunny walked down the dock and into a silent crowd. The families, relieved for the moment of their possessions, crowded around under their umbrellas. Sunny recognized faces but couldn't place them with names. They were all drenched in sweat and swatted at the mosquitos and bugs that rose up in clouds from the edge of the marsh. Some broke off into small groups and mingled to the side. One family set about trying to build a smoky fire against the bugs. The others simply watched.

The boy was standing just there. It was the first time she'd ever seen him. He was blond, like all the rest, but his skin was a deep bronze color. He was grimy and hungry-looking. He watched the ferry with intent hazel eyes.

The Captain walked over to Sunny. "Look. You've got to talk them off of here. This island is a death trap."

"That's not why I'm here."

"What is it you want, Sunny?"

"I want my mom's things, and that's it. Then I'm out of here."

"They're all going to die. You know that, right?"

"I know."

"You want that on your conscious?" the Captain asked.

"I hate them. Why would I care?"

"Family. You have to talk them off."

But Sunny just looked at the ground. "Fuck it," said the Captain. "But you listen to me. If they don't go on the Guard boat...the last boat out is us. And for the return trip we'll have just your seat left," she said. "If you bring out any of them after the Guard leaves you'll have to give up your seat. Think twice about that, considering your condition." Sunny nodded.

The Guard had set a perimeter just beyond the boathouses and Gillie's Fish Shack. They funneled the islanders in along the white-picket fences of Sheridan Lane and down to the docks. Most of them were unarmed. Sunny could see the strain on their faces. Someone had taken shots at them earlier in the day. For some of the islanders the Guard weren't to be trusted. The soldiers on the perimeter had rifles. They scanned the tree line and the cliff faces with ancient binoculars, a single laser-sight, and rifle scopes.

Tom met Sunny at the end of the pier. He was thin and brown from the now endless summer. His eyes were a baked brown. He didn't try to hug her. She couldn't believe they had once been close. "I told you not to come back," was all he said.

"It's good to see you too, cousin."

"I didn't mean it like that. It's just not smart. It's not safe."

"It's my home, Tom," she told him.

"No. It's not."

"This isn't exactly the reception I'd expected."

"Ya," he said. "No bags?"

"No. I'm here two nights. That's it." She made a sound like a jet taking off. "I'm not sticking around for your storm."

Tom led her along Sheridan to the deck at Gillie's. The

bar sat on this side of the mouth of a treeless and swampy spillway that cut back up into the island to where the bridge used to be. The spillway was lined with white, red, and pale blue crab shanties. Sunny and Tom sat under Gillie's fabric shade.

"Let's drink a beer," she said, wanting something to calm her nerves.

Tom shrugged. "They're hot."

"Everything is hot."

"You want the local?"

"Tastes like ocean."

Tom stuck his head in through a hole in the wall of the structure. "She wants the better!" he shouted.

"Of course," came a reply.

Gillie waddled out. He brought two glasses and two bottles. He looked at Sunny. She was looking off at the turbines in the bay. They were white in the sun. None of them turned in the still, and half of them were in ruins. "They look like monsters," she said.

"I've never seen a monster," Tom said.

"I have."

"Long time, girl," Gillie said, breaking in. His bald head was shiny in the sun. "They're warm, of course."

"Nothing at all cold?"

Gillie shook his head. "My panels have been down for months. I can't afford new ones."

"I'll need a shot before I can down that swill," she said to him, trying to smile.

"You've gotten weak there in the city, Sunny. We've got one last bottle of whiskey on the island," Gillie said. "We'd hoped you'd bring some more."

"For the funeral?"

"Come on," Tom said.

"Well? Who will be left to drink it?" she said, looking to the growing crowd over at the docks. "They're not sticking around."

"I'll drink it. I'm not going anywhere." Gillie poured out three shots of whiskey and capped the bottle.

"What? Gillie. . ."

He took his shot and passed into the cement structure.

"When are you going?" Sunny asked Tom, although she knew the answer. "One Guard evac, one ferry ride. That's all that's left." Tom downed his whiskey, sipped at his beer, and looked out over the water, saying nothing. "You have got to be kidding," she said.

"So? What are you doing here?" he asked.

She sighed and shook her head. "I'm going to get Uncle Frank and get my things from mom's place. . ."

"What's so important out at your mom's?"

"My future."

"Just the past, more like."

"I've got to take care of me. Nobody else will."

Down along Sheridan someone shouted. It was a man. The Guard wouldn't let him in. They'd stopped him at the checkpoint just beyond Gillie's deck. Several of the Guard rushed the perimeter and held him back. He pushed at the men and yelled. "Those are my kids too!"

A woman and three children stood along the gravel road and down past the white picket fences. She turned. You could see she'd been crying. She set down her bags and checked her device. She shook her head and placed it into her pants pocket. "Then, come on!" she shouted back. He didn't respond and dropped his shoulders. The Guards stood off of him. A Lieutenant walked over and said: "If you're leaving, you're welcome in. But we can't have you in here making a problem. We've got enough to deal with."

"I know," said the man. And then he just stood there.

"Jesus Christ," Sunny hissed to Tom. She stood and walked to the railing. "You didn't build the jetty high enough did you? It's just gone now. There's sea junk in the streets, Tom. The whole place smells like a sewer and look at me…I've sweated off ten pounds just since I got here. And you got a guy there who doesn't want his family to leave? What is wrong with you people?"

"You never tried to understand us," he said.

"But would that have helped? I mean, what's the point of trying to understand people who reject reality?"

"You abandoned us."

"You abandoned the world." She waved her hand at the water. "So now the rest of the world is at fault for not coddling your willful ignorance? For Christ sake. Somebody should've fixed this place."

They were both silent, and then: "It's all on His timetable," Tom said.

"God won't save you, Tom."

"I've got faith."

"I've got no faith that you'd ever make a smart choice," she said.

Tom sat silent, fingering the empty glass. He wiped the sweat from his face.

"How many are there?" she asked him.

"A couple dozen."

"Jeanie? The boys? Are they doing this? That's why the Guard won't round everyone up, isn't it? They don't want a damn shootout with a pack of kids."

"But they. . .we. . .wouldn't go anyway."

"Jeanie won't let them go, you mean. You're all a God damned cult," she said, shaking her head. "Who is that?" She pointed at the boy she'd seen near the dock.

"Nobody."

"Oh. You mean I'm seeing ghosts now?"

"Don't worry about him."

"I've never seen him before."

"Don't worry about it."

"Frank will come. I'm going to get him. He's too smart for this."

"No. No he won't, and you leave him alone, Sunny. Do you hear me?"

"I'm going out there, Tom."

"You get what you need and be back here to get on that boat when it comes back. You don't belong here. I'm warning you."

"And I am warning you."

"We know how you are. Do you think anyone's forgiven you?"

"Thanks for nothing, cousin," she told him. "I remember when we were friends." She left the terrace.

"Sunny," he said. "Island Road. . .you can't drive on it anymore. Chantel took the truck down there just last month. There were waves crashing in on it. . .she tried to cross, and. . ."

"Ya. I know."

"I don't know if you'll have time."

"It's all on His timetable," she said, waving her arm at the sky.

"Just go out and come back. Nothing else. They'll be watching you."

"Good."

~ ~ ~

From the open window the broad sweeping sea reached

to the sky. Thin floral curtains fluttered in a light breeze that had just begun. It wasn't cool, but at least it was moving. The holoscreen hovering above Frank's drafting table flickered a series of numbers and graphs and comparison model runs. Along the bookshelves sprawled her uncle's collection of shells and flotsam and old photographs. One of them was of her and Tom, children, fishing from the dock. The others were all of various cousins or island sunsets. There were no pictures of Frank's wife. In one photo, however, Frank stood on a corner in the city. He held an eye-catching younger woman in his arms. He was very good-looking, Sunny thought. Sunny couldn't recall her name, but Frank had left his wife for her. Later, when Triana fell silent and funding dried up, he also left the young woman. He left her alone in the city with a child so he could return to the island. The woman wanted to come. He said no. He had work to do. He wasn't a bad man, Sunny thought. Just a man.

The curtain snapped and Sunny looked up. She watched as the tri-drone dropped out of the sky and approached the house. A swarm of smaller drones buzzed in behind it then split off and made for the mainland. The tri-drone slowed just before the window. It judged its surroundings then slid into its cradle. It powered down and linked itself to the main system. Radar reflexivity values, barometric pressure readings, and other numbers she couldn't evaluate appeared on the holoscreen beaming over the drafting table. A second holoscreen came to life, and the video of the flight looped there.

Then the room darkened and the video moved off the holoscreen into the center of the room. Sunny found herself in the middle of the approaching storm. The clouds swirled around her, some puffy white, others a battleship grey, and a growing number nearly black. If she stared long enough at one area, each point appeared, grew, then shrank back to a single dot, and was gone. The winds powered up, and the rotation was nauseating. She braced her feet. The eye centered on her and above, the roof of the house disappeared. She could see the cold tops of thunderstorms climb into a blue sky. She looked down. The floor gave way to a violent dark ocean tipped in frothing streaks of white. She gasped.

"In this tool," said Frank, "you can see the vertical structure of all the radar echoes. You can see the difference in structure between convective and stratiform echoes."

"It's fantastic," she said.

"It's a simple looping four-dimensional rotation. This is what NASA hired me to build."

Again, the eye of the storm centered on her, and she watched the cloud walls swirl like a meaty stew. "It's beautiful," she said.

"It's also the end of us." The storm flew back to the holoscreen and the lights came back on. "This is the only time it will ever get used. We're going dark."

"Frank," she said. "It's time to go."

He shook his head.

"Uncle Frank. . ."

"There are some tides you just can't swim against, Sunny. No. Not me. And did you see? Jeanie and the boys. They're not letting people leave anyway." Frank walked into the room and past her. He was limping. He looked old to her, but he smiled, his eyes dry. He'd trimmed off his moustache and most of his hair.

"Well, why are there dozens down at the docks?"

"It's just family members they're keeping. That's me."

"But. . .*just* family? That's half the damn island! It doesn't even seem human," she said. "You'll all be dead."

"Well. . .Human and human. I'm not sure there's much humanity in any of this." He took in the breeze from the window, flapping his shirt.

"That's the point of it all, isn't it? We've gone ahead and destroyed humanity."

"No," he said, "that's not right. Humanity won't die off, even if our civilization does. Humanity is more like a garden, Sunny. There are beets and corn and squash and snow peas. There are zinnias and tomatoes and spinach and chard and raspberries and marigolds. When the carrots are pulled, the tomatoes ripen. When the corn dies, the squash produce. Aphids come; ladybugs come next. A grasshopper and then a blue bird. Life and death all at once. All the time.

"In the garden you describe, Sunny, there are tomatoes. Only the tomatoes. When a blight or a wilt comes along all your tomatoes die, and that's all you had. Everything is dead. That's not a real garden. You talk of the death of one plant and equate it with the death of the garden. Technology won't save us. We will be a fundamentally different people before too long. But we are a civilization-creating species. We've signed the death warrant for our civilization, but humanity will continue on."

"So, why are you letting them keep you?"

"They can't keep me. I'm staying."

"And all this?" She waved her arm around the room. "For this?"

"Of course. I'll send all the data along to NASA as long as I can. These machines are the last one's they'll make." He pointed to the drone on its perch. "They're not getting anything from GOES 16 anymore. It was an extraordinary machine. It lasted decades. But it's gone dormant now. We'll go dark with what we don't know and choose not to know." He fell silent. "So. Anyway. Tell me. How's the city? I've heard the refugees. . ."

She relented. "You wouldn't recognize it," she said. "The water came up too fast. And the people—they've been pouring in. They're coming from everywhere now. All up and down the coast. The governors, the mayor, and the Feds struck a deal to house the new ones in the suburbs. The first ones? They've built cities within the city. Out on the edge they started printing tents and kitchens. The idea was that they'd be there just for a few months before they could be resettled out west. Of course, there's no water out there. Just space. All the water is here," she said. "Now they'll never move. Most of them, at least. The camps just get bigger. I heard some people from Florida started printing permanent structures. Even their own drinking water and sewage system. They aren't going anywhere. They're going to build their own city. It's a mess. It's hard to imagine no one ever planned for this."

"But what's that like for you? I mean, personally? How does reality impact my favorite niece?"

"The museum is fine. But I'm just the same, Uncle Frank. Marooned. But that's nothing new."

Frank nodded and sat. "What's so important out at your mom's place?"

"The road forward, I think."

"Explain."

She sighed and walked in small circles until Frank cleared his throat. "I've got a little boy growing inside of me," she said.

"Oh?"

"Ya."

"Enhanced?"

"No. Not enhanced. And no, I don't know who the father

is, so don't ask." She sighed and dropped her shoulders. "And I'm not going to have a job anytime soon."

"Ahhh, so that's it. A baby. No job. So, you come home. And just in time for the party, too!" He laughed.

"The city decided to sell the collections to help pay for the seawall. I'm about to be a mom with no money. Rent and food...the price keeps going up. I'm in a bad way."

"And your mom's?"

"The journals."

"You know where they are?"

"I hid them. Right after she died. I couldn't take them then, so I hid them. I didn't want Jeanie or Chantel to get their hands on her stuff. I figured they'd be worth something someday, anyway. I hid them all out at the house. I figure I can either edit and publish them or just make an offer to the University. No doubt they'd pay to get ahold of all that. I guess. I don't know. I hope."

"Ahhhh. I'd wondered where it had all gone," he said.

"She didn't want any of our idiotic family to get their hands on them anyway."

"My sister was pigheaded," said Frank. "That doesn't mean wrong, just stubborn as could be."

"Some things are genetic, I guess."

"Will you stay?"

"Yes. Please. Just the two nights."

"The front room is always yours." He smiled at her. "Are

you hungry?"

She nodded. He led her, pulling his right leg behind him, down the stairs to the kitchen. He didn't offer an explanation for the leg, so Sunny decided not to ask.

The kitchen was dark. It remained neat and tidy like she remembered. From the cold box in the floor, Frank pulled out a slab of smoked fish, a loaf of bread, and a mass of carrots. He made two sandwiches and packed them in a small bag with the carrots. He filled a bottle with water from the filter. "Come," he said.

They pushed through the humidity into a small and buggy grove of oaks out along the shore where they opened the umbrellas. "See that crab boat?" Frank said. She nodded. It wasn't far. A football field, maybe two. A tern crashed into the waves, hunting. Sunny herself dove deep, conjuring the past from the waters. "The school," she said.

There were thirty children at the school. It had been square and blocky, made of cement against the storms. Just next to the school there had been a playground that flooded at high tide. And a store. Tom had been one grade younger than Sunny. She remembered waiting for him outside after school, then running off together to the store for ice-cream. They would sit on the swings, running their toes across the rim of the water while slurping at the melting chocolate. They were happy there watching the freighters round the cape going up to the city.

Tom was Jeanie's son, so he had always been a part of her group. He was raised into it. But he seemed tangential to it all somehow, and you could see the strain on his face when, one windy Sunday afternoon, he'd told Sunny and her mom about the baptisms and the cuttings and the marriages. He'd told them not to tell. The next day, he'd paid for Sunny's ice-cream from his allowance. "I have faith in you," he told her that day. But that was all under water now.

"It's coming up too fast," she said.

Frank nodded.

"It's not easy to be here," she said.

Again, Frank nodded.

"It is everything I want to leave behind."

He nodded yet again, and then led her to a small rise. Two tombstones stood in the marsh just feet from the waves. "The Georges came and dug up their people before the cemetery drowned. They reburied them in the back yard. Eskridge did the same. Like they think the dead care."

"Maybe they do," Sunny said. "Jeanie and the rest are obsessed with our dead."

"But they're human, too, Sunny. I'd like for you to try to get them off of here."

"No."

"Try."

Again, a breeze lit across the water. "Oh. Thank God," Sunny said and lifted her arms. This time it was cool.

They ate the sandwiches and carrots and continued along the shore. When they came to Island Road, Sunny gasped. She could see her mother's house out on the rocky point. It had been there for more than two-hundred years. It stood alone. The little neighborhood was gone. Island Road was covered in sea, and the crabbing boat they'd seen earlier crossed over it, heading home. The crabber waved.

"I'm going to need a boat," said Sunny.

"Try the one in the cemetery forest."

"Will it float?"

"Let's see." They walked from the shore.

"The water," said Frank, "it's turned on us." Frank had been alive long enough to remember when the island was a peninsula. "Now we're hanging, just outside the world."

"Come off with me Frank."

"No. I've had enough. This is home."

"You have a future you know."

"Sure," he laughed. "But it's the past I want!"

~ ~ ~

The figure moved, wraith-like, through the oaks and into the bramble about the cliff. Sunny called to it but there was no response. She wiped the sweat, left the overturned skiff, and followed.

The path wound through the cemetery grasses and up past a spring that had turned salty. The oaks were thick. Small splashes of light reached the forest floor moving like fairies if the breeze pushed against the branches above. Fairies. Or souls. She followed out along the cliff's edge, calling ahead, but found nothing. When she dove back into the oaks she saw it again. Two this time. Or perhaps three. They moved parallel to her. She called out to them. They disappeared. She stopped. She recalled Tom's warning and it occurred to her she was being hunted. She tensed. Then she could feel their eyes peering at her through the forest. Several pairs. . .dozens? Hundreds? She tried not to panic.

Sunny despised the eyes of the island. When her mother brought her back from the city after the Guard raided the island she'd felt them. The eyes of the whole family. Of the whole island. She had betrayed them all. Without the protection of her mother and Frank she might have just disappeared. Disappeared like the girl who had run away from her marriage and told the sheriff she was too young to be married—and to an old man, at that. The sheriff had simply taken her back, and then the girl was gone. Sunny never saw her again. For a long time, Sunny wondered if she had even done the right thing.

The figures moved again and Sunny called out to them, trying to be brave. "Come out," she said. "You need to leave. There is a storm coming. A big one. A killer. You won't survive." But there was no answer and no movement. Still, she could feel eyes on her. Then a rock thumped to the ground next to her.

"Go home, Sunny!" a small voice called out. "You don't belong here!"

Sunny ran.

The ground was uneven and she stumbled straight off. She came up and raced past the old headstones and up along the fold in the land where the spring ran. At the top, she could see them weaving among the trees. Her heart dropped. Jeanie's boys. The one's she had collected around her after she'd left prison. The children of her cult, the cult the Guard had broken apart.

Sunny raced on toward the old boat, aiming for the clearing below Frank's house. The boys moved in closer, paralleling her on either side. She weaved among the trees, gasping for air. They caught her at the boat. Twelve shirtless, barefoot, grimy boys with grim faces. They were armed with rocks, lengths of pipe, and timber clubs. She stopped cold. "I'm pregnant," she told them.

"You're not one of us," said the tallest boy.

"I'm sorry," she said. But she didn't mean it. She was frightened.

"Leave."

"Come away with me," she said. "I can help you if you come. I can't help you here."

The boy looked at her and considered, shook his head.

"Hey!" someone shouted.

The boy took a step towards Sunny and raised his club.

"Back off!" Tom came from the clearing. "Go on back, boys," he told them. They disappeared into the trees, like ghosts.

Sunny watched them go. Then her fear turned to rage. "What the fuck was that about?" she screamed at Tom.

"I had nothing to do with this. But I warned you," he shouted back.

"They listen to you! You're part of this? Your mother is a fucking child molester and you're OK with that?"

"Why do you persecute us for our beliefs?"

"I've never given a damn about your beliefs! It's about your impact on others! Dammit!" she yelled, kicking at the boat until her foot hurt. The rage inside drained to sorrow, and she tired. She paced and rubbed her belly. "Just dammit," she said. She fought back tears. "I've got this life to grow," she said and pointed at her belly. Then she rubbed it again, gently.

"I didn't know."

"Of course not."

"Did you come here for forgiveness?"

"What do I need forgiveness for?"

"You're not Jesus."

"I didn't lie, Tom."

"Honesty isn't the point."

"Loyalty above truth, then?"

"Something like that."

The oaks swayed in the wind, creaking and groaning. Tom pointed up. "Our dead sing from the trees. We've always buried our family here, Sunny. You know that." He pointed at the ground. "Our blood, our bones, our genes...they're all a part of this earth. And the trees have grown here, taking up our material as part of them. Even they're family. How can we not have loyalty to that? It's our land. Our home. You want us to leave that?"

Sunny nodded. She watched the smears of sun play across the grasses. If she understood anything, she understood this part of it all. "We were friends once. Cousins. We played together. I loved you."

"Yes," he said.

"Tom. What I did had nothing to do with our family's history, or to our roots. I told because your mom...that side of the family...was hurting people. Marrying little girls to old men."

"But this is what God told us. It's a way of life. And if we live right with God we save our land. Our roots."

"No," she said. Then: "God never told you that." She paced again. "Do you have a little wife now? Is this happening again?"

"You know nothing about loyalty, Sunny. You've always been out for yourself. I'm protecting a whole way of life."

"You're all going to die. And you deserve it."

Tom laughed out loud. "You know nothing of faith."

"No," she agreed. "I've never had any faith." Sunny walked away towards the clearing.

"I'll keep them away from you, Sunny. But you have to hurry up and leave."

Somewhere in the distance they heard the pop, pop, pop of gunfire. And Tom was gone.

~ ~ ~

The bottom level of the house was full of water. The mangrove had moved in and backed up all along the rear where the dock and garden had been. Sunny hesitated and closed her eyes. She left her shoes and umbrella by the swing set, hiked up her dress, and waded inside. The water was warm, like a bath. She could see through to her feet, the sidewalk and the crabs creeping along what had been a well-maintained yard. Cattails and a dark-green bramble grew just on either side of the front door. A cloud of mosquitos lifted when she came into the gloom. She covered her face with her dress and closed her eyes. She could smell the mold and rot.

"Hello?"

"Upstairs, sweet Sunny!"

She crawled up onto a platform of two by fours lashed together and set on piles above the water. They led to stairs—she climbed to the third story. A thick tarp served as a door and she pushed her way through. The room was dark and cave-like. Hot and stale. The ceiling was low, and the room was filled with a thin smoke and the stench of unwashed bodies.

Jeanie sat in the gloom in a wide wooden rocking chair that creaked when she moved. A reedy beam of light fell on her from a crack in the curtains. Her hair was gray now, her skin ghost-white. She smiled with oversized yellow teeth. She was almost too large for the rocker. The blond boy from the docks stood next to Jeanie. His eyes caught Sunny's and held them.

"Hello, my love. It's been far too long. Actually, I'm surprised you'd even come here. Bravery isn't your strong suit."

"Hello, Aunt Jeanie. It looks like there's been some changes."

"The world is always changing, my love. We can't do anything about that, can we?" She laughed.

"Hi, there," Sunny said to the boy, but he remained silent. "Who is he?" Sunny asked.

"That is Chantal's boy," said Jeanie. "There is something wrong with him. He doesn't talk much. He can't choose for himself. Now. Tell me about you. I love it that you've grown your hair back out. You look like a woman again. Scrawny, but still like a woman. I hope you got rid of those awful tattoos too."

"I saw him down at the dock. Where does he live? Does he have a name?"

"What's the point of a name?"

Sunny sighed. "I'm fine." They stared at one another, waiting. "Where is everyone, Jeanie? Where are the boys? Do you know the house is flooded?"

Jeanie stared at Sunny, then began rocking again, pushing with her rough, bare toes. Her eyes adjusted to the dim light. Sunny took a step back and assessed the room. A huge cross, one of the old plastic ones, hung from the ceiling. There was a line of chairs stacked against the wall. A hundred-year-old transistor radio crowned a stack of boxes. A large, empty table dominated the room. Smoking coils of mosquito repellent hung by fishing line from the ceiling. It was all very bare bones and, despite the curtains, the windows were open in false hopes of catching a sea breeze.

"Frank says you're not letting anyone leave."

"Why should they?" Jeanie's voice dropped.

"Do you know what's coming?"

"Nothing is coming, Sweet Sunny. That's what." Sunny started to speak, but Jeanie waved her off. "Your problem, Sunny, just like your mom's, is that you believe everything they tell you. They want this island cleared, Sunny. And they think it will serve somehow to scare us off with stories of a big, bad Cat 6. They think that we'll just up and run away and let them get it. No dear. Enough of that."

"Frank, too, says its coming. I've seen it on his holoscreen."

"Hollywood."

"Jeanie. . ."

"He works for them, Sweet Sunny. Don't worry. Frank has had his warning."

"Warning? Warned about what? What do you mean?" She put a hand on her belly and paced in a circle, thinking. "Is that why he's limping? Did you hurt him? Is that your warning?" Her mouth went dry.

Jeanie resumed rocking and folded her hands into her lap. Sunny paced more. "Does he stay?" Sunny asked, pointing to the boy. "I can get him on the Guard evac ship."

"No," she said. "There is something wrong with him. He wants to learn how to swim. Seriously? He said one thing in 2116: Can you teach me how to swim? Can you believe it?" Jeanie laughed in her grunting way and slapped her knee. "Can you honestly believe it?"

"You're keeping him here to die, then?" Again, Jeanie didn't respond. "That's just not human," said Sunny. "He doesn't have the ability to speak for himself and what he wants. So, you decide?"

Jean simply looked at her. "You have nothing to say, sweet Sunny. Nothing after what you did to us."

"Where are the boys?" Sunny asked again. But there was no response. The house groaned and settled. "This is happening before your eyes, Aunt Jeanie. How can you deny this?"

"We don't deny it," she said. "This is God doing what God does. For all we know, God wants the Earth to get warmer."

"Whatever, Jeanie. It's God's will. Fine. But it's time to go. This island is going to be under twenty feet of water in a few days."

Jeanie smiled. "Your sea walls, those drones flying around seeding the ocean with iron? Folly. All of it. Money can't buy back what you had then. You can't fight God. You can't violate God's will. If God wants the change you can do nothing to stop it."

"Then why do you live in this house? You were born naked. Isn't it against God's will to cover yourself up if you were born naked? To live in this house made of God's trees that humans cut down?"

Sunny heard shouting outside. There was splashing and a cry for help. She darted to the window. A pack of bare-chested boys splashed through the water. They were the boys from the forest, and her heart sank. None of them were more than twenty years old. They carried the body of a man drenched in blood. A gaping hole marred his chest. A cloth covered his face. Behind them, two other blood-soaked boys limped through the water, crying. "They shot us, mama!" someone shouted.

Sunny pushed aside the tarp and ran downstairs. They boys clambered onto the planks and passed the body along between them up the stairs. They looked at her and stopped.

"Come on," she said, pulling one boy by his hand. Sunny tried to help with the body, but they pushed past her. She waited for the other two and helped them onto the stairs. They were covered in blood; they sobbed and winced in pain. In the dark, Sunny couldn't see the extent of their injuries.

"The Guard shot us!" yelled one of the boys. He was trembling. "We did what you said and they shot us!" They placed the body on the table.

"Who is that?" yelled Sunny. No one responded. The boys paced about looking at the floor and breathing hard. The two wounded boys slumped down into tears. Jeanie still sat in her chair and asked for a prayer.

Instead, Sunny shouted again. "Who is that?" She pointed at the body, shaking. "It's God's will to destroy all the people?"

"It may be," said Jeanie. "Those that experience God's wrath. . ."

Sunny rushed the table and pulled the cloth from the dead man's face. Her breath caught. It was Tom. The room went silent, and Jeanie asked for a prayer. Sunny stepped away.

"And you? Why is God about to kill you?" Sunny shouted at them all, interrupting the prayer. "You're religious. Why do you deserve to die?"

"We won't."

"Tom did!" Sunny covered her cousin's face. "That's your

son!" The boys stood around in silence. Sunny cried. "What is going on here?" She rubbed her belly, feeling ill. She paced again. "Get some clean water," she ordered the tallest boy. To another, she said "Get clean rags or towels. Something. We've got to help those two." She didn't know who was who. Were they all family? She couldn't remember all on the island. "Why did the Guard shoot? I've never heard of that before."

"They want our island."

"Crap," she said. No one had moved.

"I guess we don't need to bother ourselves any more by taking responsibility for our actions. Right? We make a poor choice, there are negative consequences. . .but, oh! Wait! God actually wanted those negative consequences! So it's no one's fault. No responsibility. Is that how it works?" Again, no one responded. "What's your name?" she asked the tallest boy.

"Michael."

"Get some Goddamned water, Michael!" she shouted. This time he moved. The tables had turned, she noted. He was frightened. "Is there a medical kit around here?"

"I know where I can get one," another of the boys said. He was filthy, and you could see the sorrow and fear on his face.

"No," said Jeanie. "Sunny, it's time you leave."

"Jeanie—"

"What is it you want, Sunny?"

"Let the boys come with me."

"No."

"Let that boy come with me, then." She pointed at Chantal's son.

"No."

"You have to come with me. You have to let others go. You have to let me take them."

"No, Sunny. You're not taking anyone. This is a test of faith."

"It is a Goddamned test alright. God is testing our intelligence. And we've failed. You're right. Judgement is at hand, and hell will cook us into extinction." Sunny kicked at the wall and threw aside the tarp, walking into the mass of mosquitos. She covered her face again. She followed the trail of blood down the stairs and into the dark, dank of the bottom level. She jumped into the water.

Outside, she heard Jeanie's voice call after her. "It's Judgment Day, Sunny."

~ ~ ~

Sunny told Frank Tom was dead. His shoulders dropped. "I'm not surprised," he said. "Let's get the boat before they see us."

They walked from the kitchen to the clearing and into the oaks. A Black skimmer passed over the dove at the water beyond the cliff. "I thought they were going to kill me," Sunny said.

"It's a mess, Sunny. We're just a damn mess." Sunny

could see the weight of it all riding on his back, his shoulders, his head. Sunny's heart sank as she realized that Frank had lost his hope. She needed his hope. He was the only one who ever had hope.

Using two logs as levers they turned the skiff over. A spider crawled away. Sunny realized the boat was hung up on a trailer sunk deep in the soil, and overgrown. "Dammit," she said, lifting her shirt over her head to wipe at the sweat and bugs. "Goddammit."

"No kidding," said Frank. He was breathing hard in the heat. They looked at the boat.

"What's the point of being dead?" she asked him.

"No point, really."

"Then why die for an idea? For a religion? What does that help? Go and shoot at some fucking Guard—for what? To get shot?"

"Doesn't seem so smart, does it?"

"You're no different."

Frank considered. "I don't know why I'm not afraid. Maybe you have to care to be afraid."

"You don't care?"

"I don't care."

"And Gillie? He doesn't care."

"I don't think there is much hope to spread around, Sunny." Frank took one of the logs and pushed at the skiff until the boat shifted off the trailer and into the grass. He winced.

"Leg?"

"I'm just old."

"Jeanie."

"It was a warning."

"And you listened."

"Well enough." Together they got the boat up on a line of logs and rolled it into the clearing. Then they sat, breathing hard and swiping at the bugs. Frank pulled the boat along by the dock line while Sunny raced back and forth carrying the small logs from back to front to keep it moving. It was an ancient way. At the waterline, she felt the first kick of her pregnancy. She was surprised and sat in the boat, laughing. Frank pulled his leg behind him and asked, "First time?"

"Yes. Yes." She laughed again.

"An end, a beginning." They sat the in boat, resting.

"Why didn't you say anything, Frank? Why didn't you and mom just say? And why didn't you back me up?"

"I don't know."

"You do know right from wrong, don't you?"

"Maybe."

"Ya."

"Jeanie won't come off. She won't let those kids come off. Its ok. That's not why I came here anyway. Let the water cleanse the world."

"No. It will just make more of them," Frank said. "It

seems that when the world comes undone folks try to understand it through their Gods. And then they think: *if we only can go back to the old ways*. . .whatever that is in their minds. When it all falls apart, new religions are born. I guess the challenge is: Who controls the vision of the future?"

"And Chantal's boy?"

"Ya. The kid who likes the plastic birds."

"Maybe I can get him."

"You, your boy, and Chantal's messed-up kid. That will be the end of us. Amazing, eh? He hangs out at The Tiles. You can find him there." A river otter poked its head above the small waves, assessed the two, and moved toward the inlet. "It's their world again now," Frank said.

"Help me."

"No. You can do it. You've got to do it. Go. Come back. Make it fast. It's also your world now."

~ ~ ~

In the morning, out on The Tiles, the place where the rocks broke off into neat plates, Chantal's boy found her. The rocks were covered in bird shit. Sunny sat, poking at a pile of plastics with a stick while watching a trawler move across the bay from where Norfolk had been. It was an older vessel. They were all old now, or most of them anyway. It had been retrofitted as an iceberg catcher, probably for West-coast work, and you could see the giant harpoon placements on deck. But they were empty, and the trawler pulled nothing.

The boy came and sat next to her. He pointed at the shadows of the clouds passing over. Then he put his hand on her shoulder. She looked at him and acknowledged that he would be dead in a few days. "I'm sitting with a damned ghost," she sighed. He pointed at the trawler. "I heard that out there...down there," she pointed, "the ocean steams. That's where it comes from."

Sunny talked at the boy about the city, about her mother, her child. She told him how her father died working on the New York seawall when she was a teenager. She told him how her brother joined the army and got sent off to Mexico, that he was still there. She told him about her job and her apartment in the city. She told him how the storm was coming, and that he was going to die. "It's one crap-ass world," she said. The pile of plastics she poked with the stick had once been inside a gull. The feathers were all gone. Only the skeleton and plastics the bird had consumed remained. "It's one giant pile of shit," and she poked some more.

"We're a civilization-creating species, so we'll just create a new one. Sure. Though it's not likely to be a better one."

"Money can't buy back what you had then," the boy said. And that was all. She asked him his name; he said nothing. Eventually, he stood and walked away, drifting off down The Tiles, occasionally touching the water with his foot.

The day faded. The shadows of the kittiwakes and terns cut the horizon. The breeze grew. Sunny walked back among the houses towards Frank's place. The roofs glowed with golds and oranges against the matte of the greying sky.

~ ~ ~

Sunny crossed along the roadway chest-high in the rising water, pulling the skiff from the forest behind her. The breeze grew into a wind. The sky was mostly gray. The water lapped at her chest, but her footing was secure. For the first time since childhood, she was cold. Her body shuddered, and remembered. The storm surge was pushing the water higher. The driveway had eroded into chunks of asphalt; Sunny tied the skiff to the handle of the garage door. The old oak with the swing was drowned. Inside, the house creaked in the wind. It groaned with the gusts. Most of the windows were broken out, and some of the furniture was missing. Tiny piles of sand had accumulated in the strangest spots. A family of gulls nested in the reading alcove where she had kept her books and basked in the streaks of sunlight. Upstairs, in her favorite room, Sunny found the toolbox and fingered through some of her dresses still hanging in the closet; she decided to take none of them. She took the toolbox and walked past the bathroom into the master bedroom. It appeared untouched and the windows were still intact—but everything was blanketed in salt and sand and dust. She kneeled, opened the toolbox, and removed a crowbar. She pried up five floorboards, looking in to see the box. She opened it.

The notebooks that had made her mother famous lay

tied in neat bundles. They were wrapped in plastic and appeared to be in good condition. Sunny sighed. She cracked one of the plastic bags, untied a bundle, and took out a solitary blue-covered notebook. She ran her fingers over the equations and chards and doodles that were her mother's lifework. Sunny smiled. A powerful gust, the strongest so far, hit the house, and it groaned. Now, she told herself, it's time to get off the island.

She heard water slapping somewhere downstairs. She dropped the notebook into the box, sealed the plastic, and pulled the package from the box. Then she lifted the whole thing from the hole in the floor and placed the notebooks back inside. She closed it tight, running her fingers along the edges to check for a water-tight seal. She felt the house sway and nearly lost her footing. She ran back to her favorite room, grabbed a pile of her old dresses from the closet, and looked out the window. The blue sky was gone, replaced by gray. To the south, she could make out the storm's black wall. The ocean beyond the headland was choppy. Roiling. "Shit." It was moving faster than anyone imagined.

Sunny raced back to the master bedroom and took up the box. It was heavier than she thought it should be. She draped the dresses over the box and lugged it downstairs, past the gull nest, and outside. The boys were there, waiting. Her stomach tied itself into knots. Then she set the box gently into the boat, making sure the dresses kept it hidden.

"You came back for dresses?" said Michael.

"They're mine."

"Dresses?"

"I want my things."

"You don't belong here."

"Neither do you. Not anymore. You're scared. I can help you." But the look of fear she'd seen in Michael's eyes was gone. "I can help you," she shouted at the other boys.

They rushed her. Some of them grabbed her arms and held her. Michael punched her repeatedly in the head. Her fear again turned to fury, and she kicked at them. But they knocked her to the ground. She curled into a ball and wrapped her arms around her head as they kicked at her. At some point, a curtain came over her eyes. They left her.

Sunny woke when the water swallowed her feet and licked at her ankles. She pulled herself up and sat with her knees wrapped into her chest. She felt her belly. "Please kick, baby," she said. And then she cried. It was a deep, long and sobbing cry. The little skiff bumped her legs. Out beyond the point the water was dark and tipped in frothing caps of white. You could see the black storm to the south. The Guard evac ship crawled into view, fighting the sea. Then it disappeared behind a curtain of rain. "No," she breathed. "No. No. No." The wind grew. It threw her hair all up in her face. She checked her device, but it was drowned. When she wiped at her face her hand came away bloody. Her arms and legs ached from the beating. She struggled to stand.

"Goddammit!" she yelled, standing. "Dammit. Dammit. Dammit." She climbed back to the porch, opened the door, and walked into the house. Her body relented out of the wind, but the house moved in great groans and creaks. In the garage, she found two old oars and hustled outside. She tossed them into the skiff and climbed in. She untied the line from the garage door and floated free, down Island Road.

The wind took her as soon as she crossed the rocks. Her hair flew again in her face. She dragged the box between her feet. She pulled hard on the oars. She barely moved. She pulled again. And again. Her arms ached. She kept pulling, slowly propelling the skiff towards the opposite shore. She could see pieces of the road under the waves. Her nose bled into her dress. She could feel that her ribs were bruised, maybe even broken. A cold wave slapped the side of the boat and turned it sideways. It drenched her, and she cried out. The salt burned a crack in her cheek. She began to cry again as she pulled the skiff back on course. Sunny pulled hard on the oars several more times, grunting with effort. When she turned to see the shore ahead, another wave hit—and the boat tipped. Sunny crashed into the water.

The sea lashed her in circles. It flooded her body. A wave pushed her down and she smashed into the pavement. Her shoulder popped loose as she tumbled along the road and into a boulder. Panicked, she kicked to the surface, but the sea roiled her, and she hit her head on the pavement. Desperate, she turned and pushed off again. When she hit the surface, she sucked in a lungful of air. Then she screamed. The skiff was gone, and the waves began taking her out to sea.

Sunny heard her name, and a rope slapped across her face. It stung. She grasped at it, wincing every time she tried to move her right arm. Her legs crashed against the rocks before she regained her footing. Frank scrambled into the water and took her up.

"It's gone!" she yelled. "All of it is gone!"

"Goddammit, girl!" Frank drug her through the boulders and marsh and onto the shore. He laid her down in a pile of gravel. "You've got to get off of here!" he shouted. "The ferry is. . .what the hell happened to you? Who—? Goddammit." And then she was gone.

~ ~ ~

Sunny woke on the dock. The wind whistled like a train. As she sat up, several Guard members rushed past. Gillie's was all burned out. The shanties were all on fire, and the wind carried the flames to the sky. The sky was black and the blades on the turbines spun far too fast. More Guard came past her, and then a man hustling along with a group of crying children. "It's OK," he told them. Painfully, Sunny pushed up and steadied herself in the blow.

Down at the little beach, Chantal's boy stood with his toes in the water. He held a cup and collected small bits of shell and stone and flotsam. When the wind whipped his hair into his face he pushed it aside and stepped deeper into the water. He smiled, reached down, and came up with a smooth piece of glass. He held it up to her, beaming. He stepped in deeper. Sunny felt a kick in her belly. Then another. She burst into tears. "Thank God," she said.

The captain came at her, angry. "Goddammit it all!" she yelled. Sunny could see that she was scared, and the sweat on her dark skin shook like tears. "I'm not one of these idiots," she yelled, sweeping her arm at the island. "I have no interest in drowning here. The future won't be dry, that's for damn sure. It's time to go."

"What about the boy?"

"Grab him," said the captain.

She looked at the boy again and caught his eyes. He held her gaze, but said nothing. There was a kick inside of her. 'Go', it seemed to say. Alone and empty-handed, Sunny turned and limped into the ferry.

~ ~ ~

"Everyone was silent," Sunny said to the nurse. She told how they were thrown around the ferry like dolls. She told about the silence, then the screams. Then silence again. You could hear bones snap at times. Then more screams. Then it was quiet again. Not everyone had seats. The ferry was overcrowded, and it nearly rolled several times. The storm moved faster than anyone imagined it would; it pushed the ferry just ahead. What she remembered most clearly was the white-knuckled silence. "When we got to the docks they carried them off on stretchers," she said. "Just as they carried me. In some ways, it seems like yesterday. In other ways, it seems like centuries ago."

"It was a long time ago," said the nurse.

Sunny nodded, closed her eyes.

When she woke, she stretched, lifted the blanket, and walked to the window. The nurse had placed her son's things in a small box and left them on the bed. His keys. His glasses. His books. His rings. His clothes. Even his medications. The ones that had failed them both. Sunny looked out on the slackwater of the city. The tide was out, and the fresh continental waters flowed up against a line of seawater. It was almost sunset and you could see the printed platform walks snaking along 14th Street, tight up against the buildings. Their shadows lay long on the silvery water. Small mercantile boats and Guard craft crawled up and down the canals past canoes and rafts (and an occasional sailboat). The lamp posts, poking just above the water, were covered in white crust from the birds. A man and a boy fished from an island of cattails in a corner below the International Trade Center. On the Mall, the stilted shantytown sprawled in a haze of smoke from the dinner fires. The white marble of the monument lay where it had collapsed a decade before, poking above the water like the spine of a dead leviathan.

Traders gathered around the fish farms in a tight pack of skiffs and canoes. The sun lit a line pointing to where the sea met the sky and hung there just a bit too long.

THE BEGINNING, AGAIN
by Justin Bloch

Boy, this one has a bit of everything in it! See if this doesn't set your inner eye on its ear.—Ed.

EVERY DAY THERE WAS more blood on the comforter, and every day Darius Pham thought about washing it, but he never did. What was the point? He would have to drag it all the way down to the river, bring it all the way back still soaking wet, and then wait for it to dry in the sun on the line in back. It would take all day, and he'd be exposed for far too much of it. Then he'd put it back on the bed, and guess what? More blood when he woke up the next morning.

He sat on the bed, used his candle to light the wick of the kerosene lamp on the nightstand, then blew the candle out. The lamplight washed across the bedroom, illuminating it in soft, dim yellow. He fitted the hurricane glass down over the lamp's base and lowered the wick until the flame stopped flickering. The pleasant smell of the extinguished candle suffused the bedroom. He slid his legs under the stained comforter, lay down, and stared up at the ceiling and the sooty stain directly above the nightstand.

He read for a little while, an old Judy Blume he'd been

through half a dozen times already. It wasn't his preferred reading material, but at least it was better than the Twilight books. The library, if it was even still there, wasn't an option after what had happened last time.

The cat came in and meowed at him. He glanced at her, finished the paragraph he was working on, then marked his place and set the book aside. She leapt onto the bed, and he waited for her to get comfortably curled up before blowing out the lamp. He spent a few moments as his eyes adjusted staring in the direction of the bedroom's window, searching for any chink of light. But the darkness was complete. The cat was purring happily and he closed his eyes and fell asleep. And that was the end of the 383rd day in the house.

~ ~ ~

When he woke up the next morning there was more blood on the comforter. He sighed and went to find the cat.

She was in the center of the fuzzy square of illumination from the skylight in the otherwise dark living room. She was licking her back paw, and he went over to her, sat cross-legged on the floor and set the lamp down. He gently took her paw in his hands and lifted it to where he could see it in the light.

The pads were a raw, red mess, with bits of fur and dirt stuck in the wound. Between her toes was just as bad, licked bald and bloody.

"Oh, Santhy," he muttered.

She pulled her paw out of his grasp and went back to licking it. That was the problem, the licking. This had happened before, she got a cut or an infection and then wouldn't leave it alone. And now that he looked at it, he could tell the paw and leg were both swollen too. Back before the Shivers, a quick trip to the vet would have solved the problem. It wasn't that simple anymore.

"I'll take care of it." His chest hitched at that, but there was no other choice. He'd known for the last two weeks that things were probably heading this direction. He didn't know how bad the infection could get, but if Santhy...No. He wouldn't think about that because it wasn't going to happen. He would do what he needed to. "Fucking hell."

He stood up and looked around the room, checking the windows. Not a pinprick of light snuck in past the window coverings, and he headed for the kitchen. He had a breakfast of stale cereal while he pored over his provisions. He had the box and can quantities memorized, but counting them while he ate his breakfast was a ritual at this point, like a Hare Krishna's mantra, and the act calmed him. Early on, when he'd been stocking the larder, he made rationing rotas, trying to figure out how long the food would last, but he'd given up on that pretty quick. There were too many variables, too much chaos; it stressed him out. Plus, once the Shivers got going, every person had been a hoarder, and every house became a treasure trove. He'd raided with abandon, increased their supplies until whole rooms of the house were crammed full of food. His parents' bedroom was stacked floor to ceiling with cases of bottled water; he'd never been able to sleep in there after finding them side by side in bed. He'd known that it was a good possibility, but it didn't make it any easier to dig the graves in the back corner of the yard, by the fence.

Once he finished eating, he toweled himself off with a few baby wipes and walked back through the house. The cat followed him, limping. Into the bedroom to get dressed and she jumped up on the bed, leaving a fresh smear of blood. He sat beside her and stroked down her back.

"I'm sorry, Santhy," he said. "I shouldn't have let it get this bad."

She ignored him.

He stood back up after a moment and dressed. All earth tones, light enough to move quickly but heavy enough to keep him warm. He checked that the window covering was still flush to the wall, then repeated the process at every other window in the house, doubling back in a few places until he realized he was just stalling and forced himself to stop.

In the living room, arranged carefully near the barricade, were his guns. He looked longingly at the long guns, but a rifle would only hamper him on the bike. He tucked a semi-automatic pistol into his belt and packed ammunition and a revolver into his backpack. He was a better shot with the pistol, but it had jammed on him once when he needed it, and he wouldn't trust anyone's life to it again.

He added a roadside flare, then dropped the bag on the floor and crouched to undo the locks on the barricade. The door through it was two and a half feet wide and eighteen inches high, made of carefully nailed and glued two by fours. He swung it open and wriggled through into the pitch-black entryway, a narrow box about four feet square. He stood and carefully slid the sheet of aluminum covering the window in the center of his front door aside, just a half inch.

He peered out across the screened-in porch and into the street beyond, where nothing moved. He glanced up at the drugstore mirrors he had attached to the porch's ceiling, great, heavy, convex things that gave him a view of the entire floor space. There was nothing there but a tangle of lawn furniture, some of it scorched and melted. Satisfied, he slid the aluminum further to the side to give himself a wider view. Nothing changed, though. The street was deserted, quiet.

He covered the window again, hunkered down, and crawled back through the door in the barricade. He stood, shrugged into his backpack, and headed to the rear of the house, feeling jangly now, his heart thumping in his chest. His respirator hung on a peg on the wall, and he snugged it over his nose and mouth and cinched the straps tight. He went through the barricade at the backdoor in the same way and checked through the window. The yard looked like a jungle at first glance, the grass run to riot, with a mess of common pokeweed tangled out along the back fence in spite of the change of season. But he had cultivated the yard wild on purpose, and despite the appearance, there was nowhere in the snarl to hide. The only evidence of his presence was the humped rectangles in the corner, the grass still patchy, but he kept his gaze away from those. There was no porch here, but the twins to the mirrors out front hung suspended in the big oak outside and gave him a clear view of both the back of the house and both sides. Just as in front, nothing moved, and he undid the locks, deadbolt, chains, and security bar. The hinges were well-oiled and opened without a sound, even though he hadn't been outside in four months' time, since that final trip to the library.

He was breathing too quickly, almost hyperventilating, light-headed as hell. He shrank back further into the shadows of the alcove, counting off minutes on his pocket watch, trying to focus on the second-hand spinning around the timepiece's face instead of everything waiting to kill him in the world beyond the house, his breath whistling in and out of the respirator filters. The cold started to sink into his body, and once five minutes had gone by, he had to admit to himself that there was no one out there and that, if he was going to try to help Santhy, he was only postponing the inevitable by cowering here. He shoved himself out of the house, taking the wooden steps down to the yard smoothly but certain his feet would tangle together any moment, leading with the gun shaking chaotically in his hands. He swept the weapon over the yard, checked one side of the house, then the other. That done, he retreated to the back door, closed and locked it, and descended the steps once more. The steps were open beneath, but he'd blocked both sides with cheap pieces of plywood and a pair of padlocks. He undid one now and swung the plywood to the side. His bike was stashed beneath on a raised platform to keep it out of the mud when it rained, and he pulled it out, keeping his head and eyes moving, always moving.

He wheeled the bike to the side of the house, peered around the edge. Another mirror set up at the end of the neighbor's fence gave him a view of the street. It was clear, and he pushed the bike through the shin-high grass to the front. Still nothing, but he forced himself to stay sharp, stay alive. The thin sunlight felt good on his skin.

The street in front of his house was deserted. Or, at least, it looked like it was. There could have been someone in any of the houses, even the burned-out hulks, but he couldn't do anything about that. He had to hope that if there were people, they were just like him, holed up and isolated inside, barely even ever looking out, terrified of getting sick. The front of his house was charred, part of the porch collapsed in cinders, graffiti splashed against the rest and no glass in any of the windows except the one in the door, which was nearly unreachable across the disaster area that was the porch. But he'd tagged the house himself, and smashed the windows, and set the blaze that had done almost as much damage as he'd wanted before he put it out, all this before things had really fallen apart and the utilities quit. The house needed to look abandoned if he didn't want to wake up in the middle of the night to harriers ready to kill him for his stash of food. He thought he'd done a pretty good job, but it didn't make him any less uneasy when he left. Because anyone could have done the same thing to any of the other houses on his street, and could be waiting and watching from within right now.

He rolled the bike out into the street, hopped on, and started pedaling. It was downhill out of the neighborhood, and he pushed himself, leaning over the handlebars and pumping his legs as hard as he could to gain speed. The gun was still clutched in one hand; he'd given himself plenty of practice taking off and keeping control while still holding onto the weapon. He'd cleared the street of abandoned cars long ago, venturing out late in the night to shift them into neutral and coast them out of the road. He'd had nightmares for weeks afterwards: some of the cars still had corpses in them. Things had fallen off.

He took the corner swiftly, flying now, the tires rolling smoothly over the asphalt, paying just enough attention to avoid any debris while searching for any movement past the sidewalks. Beyond his street there were still vehicles littering the road and he slowed some so that he could weave without danger. He didn't dare let himself drop to anything resembling a leisurely pace. He would spend less time outside on the bike than he would on foot, but there was no hiding when you were zipping down the road on two wheels. He preferred the risk of the bike, though, when it came down to it. Anything to get him back to his house more quickly.

Fifteen minutes later he was out of the suburbs and onto Route 42, two lanes on either side with a wide, now-overgrown median strip separating them. The blacktop here was clear again, although the shoulders looked like the remains of an epic demolition derby. Cars and trucks were twisted together, smashed, overturned, crumpled: the remnants of the military's last-ditch efforts to keep major thoroughfares open.

He kept alert as he rolled. There were myriad places along the shoulders where someone could be hidden, but he knew the side streets and backroads were worse. Clogged with cars, hilly, too many blind curves. He could run into anything. Here, if something popped up, he could be in the high grass or hidden among the wrecks within moments.

But nothing jumped out at him, nothing attacked. The most movement he saw was a flock of geese heading south, and they paid him no mind. He coasted down the road, right down the dotted center line, a sheen of sweat on his face now, and for a little while his fear receded.

He pulled off the highway into a parking lot of a square, boring brick building: Santhy's veterinarian's office. There were two dogs snuffling at something at the back of the lot, surprising him enough that he almost toppled over on the bike. Like the geese, they seemed to ignore him, and he cruised up to the building's entrance and propped the bike against the wall, facing the highway. He kept an eye on the dogs. He had no idea whether they'd been born before or after the Shivers had come, but he had no interest in being mauled. He supposed there was a decent chance the dogs would all turn back into wolves now.

The glass entrance door had been smashed in, which wasn't surprising. He checked that the safety was still off on the gun, then peeked one eye past the edge and peered into the building. Everything was shadows and stillness within. He waited a minute, but didn't hear anything. And more, the building felt empty. He'd learned that feeling, after all this time on his own. People vibrated, and you could sense it, especially when you were so infrequently with them.

The vet's office was empty, he was almost sure of it, but he stepped through the door with the gun held straight out in front of him, his pulse racing. His shoes crunched on the shattered glass of the door, and he checked the waiting area and behind the reception desk, then dipped into his backpack for a flashlight.

He used the narrow circle of light to pick his way through the examination rooms. Cabinets had been toppled over, and in one of the rooms it looked like some animal had constructed a den, but he was able to find a path through to the staff-only area where once, long ago, they'd kept the medications. It had clearly been ransacked.

"Goddammit," he muttered, and set to work organizing the shambles of what was left, dividing everything into neat piles on the laminate floor, the flashlight barrel clenched between his teeth. It took him half an hour, during which his breathing came more and more quickly, but finally he had sorted through the last of the vials, bottles, and blister packs. And there was nothing he could use. Nothing Santhy needed.

He closed his eyes and tilted his head back, his jaw working. He rose stiffly to his feet and looped his hand through one strap of his backpack, began to raise it and halted with it halfway up. He hadn't had much confidence in being able to find the antibiotics Santhy needed for the swelling, but he thought there was a chance for the steroid. Why would someone loot an animal steroid? Her foot was really bad, he had to get her something. He had to. He dropped back to the floor, scattering empty bottles, thinking he must have missed something, *knowing* he must have. He didn't know where another vet was, and there was no way he was going into an area he wasn't familiar with. There had to be a steroid here. He scrambled on his hands and knees from pile to pile, batting trash and empty pill boxes across the tile, making growling noises deep in his throat. Santhy flashed before his eyes as he searched, and the comforter with all that blood, and sitting beneath the big oak in the backyard, staring at his parents' graves while he worked up the nerve to dig another.

He shoved one entire pile to the side and slammed his fists against the floor where it had been. Impact shock vibrated up his arms, and his teeth clicked together painfully. He rocked back on his butt, braced himself against a counter, and kicked out again and again at the cabinet in front of him, first denting the metal doors, then breaking them off of their hinges with a thunderous din. One of them fell onto him, cutting his forehead, and he threw it off and lurched to his feet. He gripped the top shelf of the cabinet and yanked it away from the wall, crashing the entire thing to the floor. A box that had been out of sight on top bounced across the laminate and came to rest in the parabola of light from the flashlight, and he stood staring at it, breathing raggedly, shuddering.

The box was labeled "Depo Medrol." That was the steroid they had given Santhy last time. He licked his lips and went to the box. He picked it up, turned it over in his hands. The top was folded closed, and he separated the cardboard flaps and pulled them open.

The box was empty.

He dropped it and raised his hands to his face. For long moments there was nothing, just silence and the stillness of the world. He remembered Santhy as a kitten, when he first got her. He'd been working at a photo developing place, and a lady came in with pictures of newborn kittens, and he asked what she was doing with them. He hadn't been able to get used to the quiet of his apartment after the boisterous clamor of his parents' house, the frenzied noise of his little sister Mai, and he thought that maybe a pet would help. Two days later he was at the lady's house, looking at a tussling, tumbling litter of kittens, and he'd picked out the one he wanted almost immediately. The kitten had sealed it when she took a running start and jumped right into the sliding glass door. He'd known instantly that her name was Chrysanthemum.

Darius began to weep, and he didn't stop for a long time.

~ ~ ~

He turned onto his street and stood up on the pedals to push up the hill to his house. His eyes were red rimmed and bloodshot, and he was sniffling like a kid with a cold, but the ride back had given him some time to pull himself together. Although it was kind of ridiculous, thinking Santhy would even notice he was upset. She was just a cat.

Thinking that made tears well up in his eyes again, and he bit his lip and broke his cardinal rule by turning his face down to the surface of the road. He grunted with every rotation his feet made on the pedals, focused on defeating the hill. Fuck this street, fuck this hill, fuck this fucking world. He was so intent on his anger that he went most of the way past his house and had to hook back around.

He walked the bike around to the rear of the house and stowed it once more beneath the stairs. He let himself in and stepped into the darkness, then replaced all of the security measures and slid through the barricade. The respirator went back on the peg, leaving bright red weals across his cheeks where the edges pressed. He felt weary to the bone, but routine was what kept him alive, and he relocked the door on the barricade and shouldered the heavy backpack. He lit a lamp, waited for the flame to settle down, and then headed to the front of the house to replace the guns.

Through the kitchen, past his bedroom, into the living room. Santhy was there again, curled up under the skylight. A man was standing over her.

Darius shot him.

The rounds struck the man center mass. Or, at least, Darius would have sworn they did. It had seemed for a moment as if light was pouring from three holes in the man's bare chest, but an instant later the skin was unblemished and whole once more. They were in close quarters here in the living room, but Darius's hand was shaking badly and he felt like he'd been shot full of adrenaline, so he guessed it was possible he'd missed. But Jesus, if he got out of this alive, he needed to target practice more. "What do you want?" he barked.

"Darius Pham, last living man on Earth," the man announced. His voice seemed to come from far in the distance, from the peak of a mountain or the depths of a canyon. His face was strange as well, almost as if it was blurry, like a charcoal portrait that had been smudged. "I have been sent to lead you from this place."

"I'm not going anywhere." He could see the barricade at the front door, and it wasn't disturbed. And he remembered unlocking the back door to get in. Right? He had unlocked it, right? Yeah, no, he definitely had. He crouched long enough to set the kerosene lamp on the floor, then straightened and used his free hand to steady his weapon. He didn't intend to miss again. "How did you get in here?"

"Walls pose no barrier to the hosts," the intruder said. "Please—"

"What did you say?" Darius growled, and backed away. He hooked the collar of his shirt up over his nose. A goddamned host in his house. He hadn't survived this long just to contract the Shivers in his own fucking house. "Santhy, get over here."

The cat looked at him from behind the rack of rifles where she had fled at the gunshots, but didn't move. The intruder remained rooted to his spot as well.

"Please, lower your weapon," he began again. "I have not

come to harm you. There is no one left on this world that would harm you."

"Shut the fuck up, man," Darius snarled, still retreating, thinking now about how to get through the barricade. He hadn't designed it with escape from this side in mind, and crawling through was going to leave him exposed.

"You are safe, Darius Pham."

"Santhy, please. Come here, girl. *Please.*" He halted at the doorway out of the living room. If the cat wouldn't come, he was going to have to leave her. He hovered where he was, unable to force himself to take the next step. But he couldn't die like the rest, he'd made it so far, he couldn't let himself die just because of a cat. He took another step back.

The room exploded in brilliant, prismatic light. Darius buried his eyes behind his elbow, trying to shut it out, but the intensity lasted only an instant.

DARIUS PHAM, the intruder intoned, and now his voice seemed to come from all around, to shake the foundations of the house, to quake the bones of Darius's body, OPEN YOUR EYES.

He did as he was commanded. The intruder stood unmoved, just as before. Two scintillating wings extended from his back, stretching across the living room. They seemed to have no substance, but to be made of light itself, the light of a more perfect sun. Looking at them felt obscene, sacrilegious; they weren't meant for his eyes.

"I am a member of the hosts," the intruder said, his voice returned to its previous, distant timbre. "What you would call an 'angel.' I have been sent to lead you, the last living man on Earth, from this place."

Were delusions one of the symptoms of the Shivers? Darius racked his brain, trying to remember. Out of all the horrific things the Shivers did to your body, was hallucinating one of them? He was pretty sure it was an early sign. Was it...wait. Wait. "What did you call me?" he said. "Did you say I'm the last man on Earth?"

"Yes."

The gun, still pointed at the stranger's chest, faltered. Everyone else, everyone else on Earth. Gone. Dead. In all the world, there was only his voice now, just a single human voice. How could that be? How could he really be the last one left?

"Please lower your weapon."

Darius did as the intruder—the angel?—asked. He felt like lowering himself, for that matter. It was like standing in the surf when the ocean was rough, as the sand was sucked from beneath your feet and the water dragged you toward the depths. "Are you..." His voice cracked, and he started over. "Are you sure?"

"That you are the last? Yes. It was believed that we would collect you much sooner than this, but the disease traveled more slowly through the Amazon than anticipated, and the Man of the Hole only succumbed a few hours ago."

It was hard to think. He knew there were things he should ask, things he should do. He was alone. What would he do now? An angel was here. His ears filled with a sound like the roar within a conch shell. An angel, a fucking *angel*. The room was darkening at the corners, despite the light given off by the angel's wings. He didn't deserve to be the last, there was no reason for it. He realized he was panting, tried to control his breathing and couldn't. It couldn't be true. He couldn't be the last.

"Darius Pham, calm yourself."

He looked at the angel, the fucking angel standing in his living room. "Fuck you," he said, put the gun under his chin, closed his eyes, and squeezed the trigger.

Nothing happened.

He opened his eyes. The angel was standing a foot away from him, his hand on the barrel of the gun.

"I'm sorry," the angel said. "I can't allow you to do that."

"I'm freaking out, man."

"I know. This will help." The angel touched one fingertip to the center of Darius's forehead, and the last living man on Earth passed out.

~ ~ ~

He woke up staring at the ceiling of the living room. He was lying on the floor right where he'd been standing, half through the doorway. Everything came back to him, but as if through a sieve, and he pushed aside the bits he didn't feel like he could deal with right away. There would be time, he knew, all the time in the world.

He sat up. His forehead felt hot, and he ran his fingers across it. In the center, where he'd been touched, there was an oval of warm, ridged skin, just above the level of his eyebrows. He dropped his hand; this was also something else for later. Right now, he had to figure out what to do about the angel that had given it to him.

He turned, and the angel was once more standing beneath the skylight. His wings were gone.

"Darius Pham, last living man on Earth, I have been sent to lead you from this place."

He got to his knees, facing the angel. "Lead me where?"

"To a better place."

"Then why did you stop me from shooting myself?"

The angel blinked at him and cocked his head a fraction to the right. After a moment, he said, "I see. You think I mean the human conception of Heaven. No. I have been sent to lead you to a better place than this, on Earth."

"Why me?"

"I don't understand."

"I'm nobody. I'm literally nobody. So why did you pick me to survive?"

"We had no hand in either the coming of the plague or your resistance to it. We believed the disease would destroy all human life. When it became clear you were immune, and when it was obvious that you were the only man on Earth to be so, we made plans to lead you from your life of exile. We were not permitted to do so until you were the last, however."

"This is crazy, man."

The angel said nothing.

"Where are you supposed to take me?"

"I do not know."

"Then how are you going to take me there?"

"I can feel it, drawing me."

"Jesus Christ." He got to his feet. "Do you know where my cat went?"

The angel pointed toward the back of the house. Darius retrieved the lamp from the floor and headed toward his bedroom, ensconced in the yellow glow. Santhy was at the foot of his bed.

"Hey," he said, sitting down beside her. He scratched her behind one ear, and she pressed her face against his knuckles, the corner of her mouth pulling at his skin. "I couldn't get the medicine for you. I'm sorry. I tried, but it didn't work out."

The cat flopped onto her side so that he could pet her belly, and he scooted a few inches away so that she wouldn't get blood on his clothes. Which he realized was impossible, because her paw was no longer weeping and inflamed. The skin had healed, now pink and fresh, still furless but undeniably whole.

He tried to examine the cat's paw more closely, but Santhy was having none of it. She leapt off the bed and left the room, and he followed her back into the living room. She rubbed against the angel's legs, then settled down at his feet.

"Did you do that?" Darius asked. "Heal her?"

"I did not believe that you would leave without the cat, and she would not be able to follow with her injury. I healed her while you were unconscious."

"Well. Thank you."

"Are you ready to leave?"

"What?"

"I have been sent to lead you from this place. Are you ready to leave?"

Darius stared at him for a moment. He had to remind himself that this was an angel, and clearly not one well-versed in human interaction. Still, it had been a stressful day, and he had trouble keeping the snap out of his voice. "No, I'm not ready to leave. I have to get food, I have to pack."

"Everything you could need will be provided to you. You will want for nothing on the journey."

Darius left the room without reply. Into his bedroom, onto his bed, staring up at the ceiling. He wondered again about delusions, but he knew it didn't matter. If he had the Shivers there was nothing he could do about it, and he wouldn't care about the truth of reality when he was dead.

But he was safe here; the house was a fortress he had built for them. Out beyond the barricades there could be anyone waiting. Although the angel said there wasn't anyone left, just him. Jesus, really, was he really the last one? He felt the clouds start to rise up in his mind and he pushed them away with an effort. He gathered up some clothes, a few mementos, and stowed them carefully in a backpack.

Back in the living room, the angel still stood beneath the skylight. "What's your name?" Darius asked.

"The hosts do not have names as you understand them. I am one of many."

"What can I call you, then? There's gotta be something."

Again, that almost imperceptible head tilt. "I have no name as you would understand it. You may call me Many."

He grunted. "I guess that's better than nothing."

The angel made no reply.

"I'm going to get some food together, and then I'll be ready. Apparently, I'm going with you." He laughed, a wild sound bordering on a cackle. He was surprised to discover that his fear was muted at the prospect of leaving this time. Not gone, not completely, but quiet, a background murmur. He felt almost crazed instead, manic.

"You won't need food. Or anything else. You will want for nothing on the journey."

"You don't even know where we're going. You don't

know whether I'll need food or not." He crouched and picked up the handgun and added it to the backpack.

"You will not need that," the angel said.

"Yeah, but I'd feel better if I had it." He looked around the living room. Was this really it? Was he really leaving the house he'd grown up in? Leaving with an angel? He moved before he could overthink it, through the house to the back, undo the locks, under the barricade, undo more locks, through the backdoor, down the steps, into the yard, and if there were harriers or anyone else out here, he was fucking dead.

Santhy crept along at his feet, sniffing the air, the grass, her belly close to the ground. Many was somehow waiting outside already.

"Follow me," the angel said, and headed toward the front of the house.

Darius remained where he was. He stood in the air, the cold nipping at his skin, his eyes closed, and then he forced himself to turn toward the fence and the three raised plots. He made his way over to them and stood at the foot of the smallest. Many appeared at his shoulder a minute or two later, looking at the ground.

"My sister's down there," Darius said eventually.

The angel said nothing.

"She was still here when I left my apartment. I kind of expected her to be...you know, when I came, but she was still healthy. Like me. She used to help me around here, building the barricades, putting the coverings over the windows. She actually yelled at me when I set fire to the front of the house. She didn't know I was going to do it, and she freaked out, jumping around the front yard, yelling. She made me put it out before I was ready." He grinned at the memory, the smile spilling tears from the corners of his eyes. God, she'd been pissed. "She was only thirteen. Just like, a kid. She was always a firecracker, you know, just…just a crazy little kid. But there was nothing to do here, holed up in the house, no electricity, just the…the two of us. Cataloguing food isn't any teenager's idea of a good time. So, you know, it was lucky that she loved to read so much. But she'd already read all of her books a hundred times, even those damn Twilight books, and she wanted something new. She wouldn't stop begging me to take her to the library.

"So, I did. I mean, why wouldn't I? I'd been out of the house plenty of times, raiding other houses for food, supplies, I'd gone to Lowes to get stuff for the barricades. Things were shitty out there, but I stayed away from people, I wore my respirator, I hadn't gotten sick. So, I took her to the library."

He halted, suddenly. He glanced at the angel in his peripheral vision, but Many was still staring at the ground in front of them. For all he knew, the angel wasn't even paying attention, wasn't hearing a word he said. "We loaded up our backpacks with books and headed out. Out, and straight into a bunch of harriers. Big fuckers, loaded down with weapons, one of them even had a fucking sword, and they wanted Mai. So, we had a gunfight," he said, still not really able to believe it, even now, four months later. The death of the entire human race seemed somehow more plausible than the fact that he'd been in a gunfight. "My fucking gun jammed, and we were pinned down behind this wall. I had a flare in my backpack, and I lit it and put it back into the backpack, and the books we'd taken caught fire. I tossed the whole thing into the bushes near them, and the bushes lit up, and we got away, but Mai...she, um, she...

"We made it home, and then. Then." He motioned at the grave in front of them. There was nothing else of the story to tell. The dirt said it all.

~ ~ ~

Eventually Darius turned away, rubbing at his eyes as he walked toward the front yard with Many beside him. Santhy traipsed along between them, apparently already used to the outside world. They came around the corner of the house, and Darius flinched at how casually the angel moved into the open. This was crazy, this was the stupidest goddamn thing he'd ever done. "Are you sure?" he asked. "I really don't need any food?"

"I have not been sent to lead you into danger. You will want for nothing on the journey."

"Why do you talk like that?"

"I do not understand."

"You repeat yourself all the time. You've told me three or four times you've been sent to lead me away. It's like you're...I don't know, like you're programmed or something. You don't talk like a human does."

"I am not human."

"Yeah, that's obvious."

"The hosts have not come to your plane since before the first human touched the Earth. Speaking with you, thinking like you, is foreign to me. Your language is alien."

"And what's your language like?"

"It is..." He trailed off for a moment. "Your language is linear, expressing each thought piece by piece, each word building on and dependent on the previous. In our language, all thoughts and ideas are conveyed at once."

"What's that like?"

"The closest analogue on this plane would be a symphony. Come, it is time we began."

Darius glanced at the houses across from his and up and down the block. He supposed they were empty, if the angel was telling the truth. It was a little bit of a letdown, if he was being honest with himself. He had always feared meeting someone else when he left the house, but he had also romanticized the idea of being just across the street from another living human. But it was beginning to seem more and more unlikely that the angel was some kind of delusion. If he had been, Darius would be showing other symptoms of the Shivers by now. It was not a disease that fucked around.

"Which way?" he asked.

"You will need to hold the cat."

Darius frowned, confused, but located Santhy sniffing at the porch and gathered her up in his arms.

"Take my hand," the angel said, offering it.

Darius did as asked. The angel's hand seemed as insubstantial as seafoam.

"We will travel in this direction," Many said, and pointed across the street. Darius supposed that was one of the advantages of traveling by foot, not being limited by terrain or obstacles. "Are you ready?"

"Sure. Why are we holding hands, exactly?"

"Step forward," the angel said, taking a step of his own and pulling Darius along with him.

The world flashed past them, as if someone had spun the globe while holding them motionless just above the surface. It lasted only a moment before Darius, shocked and terrified, yanked his hand free of the angel's and went tumbling violently across the ground, end over end, Santhy yowling in protest. He came to rest against a tree trunk, his knees bleeding through his torn pants, his palms scraped, ribs groaning in protest at every breath. He swiped at his face and discovered he had reopened the gash on his forehead from the vet's office. The angel was nowhere in sight, until suddenly he was.

"What the fuck was that?" Darius exclaimed.

"We have far to travel, and I wish to reach our destination today."

"That doesn't answer my goddamned question!"

"Many thousands of miles separate us from our destination. It would take you too long to complete such a journey in a human fashion."

Darius shot to his feet, fists clenched. "You couldn't have warned me you were going to do some kind of weird angel shit?" he shouted. "You can't just do that kind of thing."

Many said nothing, only looked at him. Darius spun away in disgust, rubbing at his chest where he'd struck the tree. They were in a small park, with a scattering of trees, a small jungle gym, and a dry fountain. He looked at the fountain in consternation for a moment, then turned back to the angel. "Where are we?" he snapped. "I don't recognize this place."

"I do not know the names of the places on this plane."

"How far did we come?"

"Far."

"That's helpful."

"Do you wish to continue?"

"Doesn't seem like I really have a choice."

"I have been sent to lead you from this place. This is the fastest method, but there are others. Using them, however, we will not reach our destination today, and I am not certain we will find shelter when we stop for the night."

"You didn't think you should warn me, at least?"

"It didn't occur to me that I should warn you. I told you that I was not leading you into danger."

Darius groaned and went to track down Santhy. She was much less pliant this time, wriggling in his grip and pawing at him, but she stopped short of extending her claws. He made his way over to the angel, who looked at him before proffering his hand.

"When you take my hand and we step forward, we will travel at a great speed across the face of the Earth and toward our destination. The effect may be disconcerting and jarring."

"Jesus Christ," Darius mumbled. He linked hands with the angel and they took a step.

The scenery became a blur of colors and indistinct shapes rushing past. His foot came down and everything paused for a moment, only long enough for him to have an impression of tall buildings and cement, and then his other foot had lifted from the ground and they were traveling again. Each instant between steps showed him something different, a suburb, a highway, a desert. Once he was in the middle of a body of water, whether a lake or river or ocean he had no idea, but he was unable to glimpse any land before the world was roaring by again.

He didn't have any concept of how long they walked, but

at last they came to a stop. Darius dropped to his knees, releasing Santhy, breathing hard, his pulse pounding at his temples. He felt like he'd just run a marathon, and he closed his eyes and laid his forehead against his hands on the ground. He remained like that for several minutes, getting his wind back, his muscles burning, before finally rolling onto his back. A thick canopy of tree branches arced above him, laced together tightly across the azure sky.

The air here was cool, and crisp, and clean. Now that he was beginning to breathe normally, he could smell pine and loam, and he looked for the angel. He found Many standing off to his left, watching him. Santhy was beside him.

Darius pushed himself to a sitting position, pulled his knees to his chest and brushed the dirt and pine needles away. Some had stuck to the cuts from his fall in the park, and he was rewarded with a bright sting of pain.

"So, this is it?" he asked. "A forest?"

"No. We are close. Follow me."

He climbed to his feet, still somewhat shaky, and set off between the trees. Darius was worried about keeping up, but the angel kept to a pace he could maintain. They hiked through the woods, past a small brook, across a meadow, once startling a family of deer. The ground sloped gently upwards, the trees closing in and spreading out rhythmically, and before long Darius's legs were aching again, but the angel showed no signs of stopping, and he pressed on. They came to a paved road, devoid of any painted lines, and turned along it, tracing its curves. It ended a mile or so later at a large Victorian house, painted yellow with white trim, awash in sunlight and beautiful. Many had halted, and Darius forced himself to stop as well, although all he wanted to do was climb the steps of the porch and let himself into the house. This had to be it. This had to be where they were going.

"We have arrived at our destination," the angel said, as if reading his mind.

He wanted to cry out in joy, but before his lips had parted, movement caught his eye. Coming around from the far side of the house was another angel. Many turned toward him and spoke, now in his native tongue, and Darius understood what the angel had meant when he described their language as a symphony, although this made Dvořák sound like a child plinking at a toy piano. The other angel joined in after a space of seconds, and the entire forest seemed to reverberate as the two voices blended together into something nearly beyond comprehension. Tears sprung to Darius's eyes, but before they could fall the angels lapsed into silence. The forest was absolutely quiet.

"Darius Pham, last living man on Earth," the angel said, and there was movement on the porch. Another figure, stepping out of the house, a woman with a great, flowing mass of thick black hair and eyes wide with shock. "This is Anjali Singh, the last living woman on Earth."

They looked at one another across the garden, the last man and last woman, and then Darius broke for her, racing across the space, stumbling, one knee into the dirt and back up, flailing, running. And she was coming for him as well, flying down the porch steps, hair streaming out behind her. They crashed together with enough force to knock the wind out of Darius, the impact spinning them amidst the remains of the autumn black-eyed-Susans.

"Oh my god, oh my god, oh my god…" the woman was saying over and over, practically choking him with her embrace. Her voice was throaty and ragged, interrupted by her sobs, but it was beautiful, Darius thought it was beautiful, it was another human voice and Darius thought he'd never hear something so beautiful again.

"The Gandharva said I was alone," she cried. Darius had forgotten her name already. Words had abandoned him, he knew he should say something but could think of nothing, could focus only on her hands gripping the skin of his back, her tears slicking the lobe of his ear. He wanted to pull away, to look at her face, to look into her eyes, but he was terrified that if he let her go, she would fade into mist.

"I thought," she stuttered, "Oh my god, I thought the world had ended."

"It did," he managed, his voice just as thick and muffled as hers and already breaking down again, "and…and now…"

WHAT REMAINS
by Kamron Taylor

Even in a collection of "strange" tales, this one is pretty strange. The dietary habits herein are eye-opening, but sensical. Don't try this at home, kids.–Ed.

THE SUN SHONE BRIGHT in the eastern sky. The cloudless expanse stretching beyond sight. The desolate terrain, windswept and devoid of movement, seemed to go on forever. Walking though the morning air, Xander Coulter cast a long shadow as he trekked ever westward towards his destination. The man, if what was left alive in that frame could still be called a "man", leaned heavy on a makeshift walking stick two meters tall as he trudged on through the sand. His head was wrapped in a scarf to keep the beating sun off his face and the billowing sands from his nostrils. The threadbare clothing he wore resembled what once was a military uniform. On his back was a pack that represented every item he owned in the world. Slung across his chest, and hanging to his side, was his only friend in the world, a pulse-rifle. The only thing he knew without doubt that would stand with him when the shit hit the fan. The only thing he'd had in months as a companion. It had been a long time since he'd heard a voice other than his own.

Even now, as he slogged along his way, the only sound he heard was the rhythmic whirring of the servo motors connected to various parts of his anatomy. The series of gears and motors that made the mechanical abomination of his left leg and arm, and the left side of his face, kept up the constant sound, forever present in his ears.

"No chance of sneaking up on something to eat anymore" he mused aloud, just to hear something other than his own droning. It had been days since he'd had a proper meal, his last opportunity thwarted by those damn "enhancements" to his body that he had "volunteered" to have implanted. Moments before daybreak, he'd been slowly advancing on a wild dog, trying to stay downwind, and had just pulled the rifle up and gotten a bead on the creature, when the sound of his left eye, auto adjusting into focus, had perked the canine's ears. Before he could squeeze off the shot, the pooch shot off into the dunes, and out of his range.

"Guess it's the usual for supper" he'd grunted. The "usual"…the thought made him cringe. That meant another day of taking out of his pack the amino emulsifier he'd had since his deployment to the Dead Lands and doing what he'd done more times than he'd care to remember. The amino emulsifier was a solar powered wonder of technology. It had the ability to take any component of organic origin and extract the amino acids from them and turn them into a paste. The paste would sustain an individual, providing the bare minimum of calories, and keep one from starving to death. Taste was determined by said organic component. When he dried meats, he found it made a pâté of sorts that, if one closed one's eyes, it almost tasted like a chewed-up hotdog. Not the most appetizing flavor, but better than the potential flavors one would have to endure when times got lean, and currently, times were as lean as they'd ever been. He reluctantly pulled the "cat box" out of his pack. It was nondescript. Just a plain aluminum box that sealed with a clamp across the top. Standard issue. The contents of said container; the owners most resent bowel movement. The amino emulsifier wasn't picky. It didn't matter the organic compound put into it—it would do its job.

"Looks like shit" he chuckled to himself as the device produced a dark brown, pungent goo. "Tastes like shit too" he said as he choked down the necessary sustenance. Holding down a final wretch, he put away the contraption, gathered his gear, and continued on his way. He knew it was going to be a long, hot, and exhausting trek. By his calculations, he was fifty kilometers from the nearest settlement, as the crow flies. He couldn't fly...he'd not been lucky enough to get that upgrade, so, on foot, it would not be an easy task.

He raised his left "arm" and checked the atomic chronometer imbedded into its wrist.

"0630" he muttered, "I'll never make it before sundown

at this pace". He shrugged his shoulders, stiffened his back, took a deep breath, and quickened his pace. He had to make up some ground before the sun rose higher in the sky—or he'd be stuck in the heat of the day. No one could walk nonstop in the Dead Lands. Between the heat and the terrain, it wore you down. The temperature would swing from below zero at night, to over a hundred degrees in the heat of the day. The sand would shift from soft, flowing dunes, near impossible to walk in, to slick glass flats, the reminders of the nuclear blasts that had hit the area years ago, and the jagged spikes of glass, like stalagmites sticking up, could spear a man instantly if he lost his footing.

As high noon approached, Xander looked for a spot to assemble his small shelter and escape the rising temperatures. As he crested a dune, he saw a small outcropping of rock, and what looked like a small puddle of. . .

"Water!" he cried. He zoomed in with his telephoto settings on his cybernetic eye to get a better look. Sure enough, below the pile of boulders, a small, clear pool of water.

Xander half ran, half tumbled down the dune as he made his way to the little oasis. As he got closer, clearer thinking replaced the joy of seeing fresh water, he realized this would be a perfect spot for ambush. He slowed his pace, readied his pulse rifle, put his ocular implant into infrared mode, and scanned the area. Methodically he panned, from north to south, up and around all the boulders, the training he'd received all those years ago, kicking back in as he was on high alert. After a scan showed no heat signatures or signs of life, he switched his left ear to scan for radio signals, in the off chance there was a remote triggered device nearby, just waiting for an unsuspecting traveler to get near. No signals. Finally, he conducted a third sweep of the area, in the full visible spectrum that his eye would allow. Convinced he was alone and therefore safe, he lowered his weapon and approached the pool. He produced from his pack a water tester, lowered it into the lagoon, pulling up a sample to analyze. Placing the vial into his left arm, the micro-sized mass spectrometer checked the levels of the water. The Geiger counter in his wrist mounted display showed no signs of radiation in the area. No signs. Nothing. Ambient radiation was everywhere, but here, nothing.

"Damnit, this bloody thing is going out" he thought. Just then, the scan on the water sample finished. "Non-saline, contaminant free water" the read out stated. "Impossible" Xander said. He fished out his canteen and pulled the cup from around the bottle, and scooped water into the vessel. "What the Hell," he mused, "this place ain't killed me yet, what's a drink of water going to hurt?" He pulled the tin cup to his lips and dipped his tongue into it, barely tasting the water. It was true. . .clean water! Gleefully, he gulped the rest. He reached down and filled it again and drank that down as fast as he put it to his lips.

"This is amazing," he thought. He'd had no clean water from the ground in...he'd forgotten how long it'd been. All the water he'd been surviving on was produced by the sweat and humidity collection system made into his implant along his left side, and it didn't taste near as good as the fresh water he was now drinking.

He checked his GPS locator. He was now thirty kilometers from "Glass Town", the shanty village toward which he headed. "Surely they know about this place," he thought. "How could they not?" Was he poaching someone's private well? Folks would kill for a hell of a lot less, but poaching water—the most precious of resources out here— "They'd not only kill me, they'd probably eat me." He shuddered.

Another thought occurred to him. Maybe the village didn't know it was here. It was conceivable. It sat thirty clicks east of the settlement, not an easy journey to make a "water run," and walking east is never easy, with the sun in one's face and eyes. It is possible that he is the only person that knows this water hole exists. Amazing.

Coming back to reality, Xander thought it time to make his sun shade and get out of the direct noon rays. He placed the little tent-like structure up against the largest boulders— to maximize shade potential and the cooler temperatures of the sand below its mass, and settled in. As he lay there, pondering how the little pond came to be where it is and how in the world it was so clean and not contaminated ... he drifted off to sleep.

He awoke disoriented, confused, his head pounding. He strained to see through the darkness. Pitch black. Nothingness. He slowly realized he was not lying on the sand where he last was. He was on a hard surface. He felt the smoothness of it.

"Concrete?" he mused. "How did I get here?" He snapped to his senses, felt around his chest for the strap of his rifle. . .it wasn't there. He went to adjust his artificial eye into the infrared spectrum to get his bearings and glimpse of his surroundings, only it wasn't working. He reached across with his right hand to bring up the holographic display from his left arm control panel and gasped in horror—his mechanical left arm was gone! He felt his shoulder; there was a bandaged stump where his arm had once been. He felt for the motorized leg that should have been attached to his hip and felt only the stump of leg that was left. He slowly touched the left side of his face, feeling cloth bandages instead of the smooth titanium alloy that had once been his left profile.

Dazed and panicking, he screamed into the abyss. "What the hell is happening to me? Who did this to me? Where am I?" Silence answered him. He worked his way onto his one knee and hand, and stood upon one organic foot. Swaying a moment, he soon found his balance. He loped forward, hoping to find the edges of his containment. After a few paces, he felt the smooth, cool surface of a wall. He ran his fingers across it, feeling for mortar lines or cracks. Nothing. Incredibly smooth. He decided to work his way down the wall to see if he could make out the size or shape of the room. Slowly, deliberately, using the wall for balance, he hobbled down and to the left.

"A corner," he said, noting an intersection between two walls. "I'm in a cell of some kind." Repeating the process to find the corner, he continued down the wall. On the third wall he found what felt like a panel or door or window. He steadied himself and banged against it. It felt hollow and not as smooth as the walls. "Could be a way out."

He repeatedly beat at the casement, hoping it would give way, or that someone on the other side would hear him. Nothing. No reply, no movement from the aperture. Defeated, he sank to the floor. "Guess I wait," he said, half chuckling. What else could he do? Half the man he once was sat in a dark room on a cold floor.

Time had lost any reference point; he didn't know how long he'd been there. Without his chronometer, it didn't really matter. Hunger flared in his stomach, the cold of the barren floor chilled him. The incessant darkness encompassed him.

"All I've survived—and this is how ends," he mused. "This is what's left. This is what remains."

DUST & FINGERS
by Luke Kondor

If there's one constant in post-apocalyptic fiction, it's this: Trust no one. I know I wouldn't.—Ed.

THOSE ANCIENT WINDING ROADS of old Great Bright-Land lay flat against the burnt shades of orange and brown. The dusty hills that once were so green and fresh with life now simply fizzed like gas-leaks in the heat-that-never-ends. Where life once flourished, now lived only rock and sand and the devils who drank the spoiled air and turned sour in their skin.

Or so they say on the coast where the waters feed them. Or so they say in the south where the bunker-folk emerged only years after the bad-times. Or so they say in Neal and Cork's township—the watered lands of London-Stone.

And as they'd driven so long in that diesel-machine, with the wheels singing a tune and the engine playing a beat, as their bodies dried in that heat-that-never-ends, the two of them spoke little and pined for water and food. They'd gotten through their boiled water by the time they'd reached the eastern coast in search of more bunker-folk to come with them to join their cause, to rebuild a society, to turn London-

Stone into something like what it once was. But all they found in the east was sand and radiation. Their radi-meters ticking louder and louder and warning them to turn around for if they continued their skin would bubble right off the bone.

So, they didn't drink. So, they didn't eat. And now, with many more miles travelled and the old diesel-machine whose singing voice now rasped and coughed, they ached so badly for water; they ached so badly for food. And they hoped to hell their engine would keep going until they made it to the northlands. There were people there. It had been confirmed by the last junkers who drove up. Normal folk looking to survive just like them.

So, they drove...

So, they drove...

In the middle-lands they passed stone walls that once separated property and farmland and noticed a sign that read Snake Pass. It took them up and up until their ears popped and they saw sprawling yellow hills that had been rolled into dunes by the angry winds. The winds that had left them to burn and crisp up in that heat...that goddammit heat-that-never-ends.

So, the engine churned and Neal's stomach knotted. He held back the urge to scream and might well have done so until he saw what lay up ahead. A speck at first but growing larger with each passing minute. A little black bundle of rags with a face hiding beneath.

This was the first person they'd seen since they'd left a week before. The way Cork tells it, there was a time when the Great Bright-Land was full of faces. Too many, he said, "That's why they went coo-coo, made them bombs that killed and scarred, and left the world to the rest of us."

That was Cork, though. He always talked about the old days. Long before his time, too, but he was one for reading and was always talking about how one could learn from history and make not the same mistakes again. But Cork was growing as old as the land itself, his skin wrapping itself up in layers of history, wrinkling like the rags that dressed the hitcher up ahead.

The hitcher was stood where the hills went down and up again. Next to a bundle of rocks that once made the banks of a stream. Cork squinted and those deep-set wrinkles somehow deepened as a bead of sweat danced down his cheek.

"What do we reckon then?" said Neal.

Cork's mouth lifted. He chewed at his clammy fingernails and made a whining noise. The cogs were turning in his head. The pistons were firing. On any normal day, Cork would have driven right on past.

"Don't trust the hill-folk," he'd have said. "The radiation's turned em, made em bad. They ain't human at all, Neal. No point treating em like one neither."

But this wasn't any normal day. The heat-that-never-ends was oppressive. It would kill them soon if they didn't drink something. And the cogs clicked in Cork's head and he nodded, turning on his radi-meter resting on the diesel-machine's dashboard. They slowed as they passed and it was a man indeed. He didn't look much more than a disembodied head with a body made of cloth and leather but down by his feet was a promising looking canvas sack.

What presents lay within?

What wonders did the ragged man hold?

They slowed to a stop and pulled up on the side of the road. The radi-meter remained calm. The ticking of its beat at a steady zero.

Before they climbed out they looked at each other and grabbed their weapons. Neal had his wooden club, stained with fish gut, and Cork took out the boom-gun. The old man had held onto that weapon for half his life and fired it twice. It had three more uses and that would be the end of it. It would expire. No way of getting more rounds for it in this world.

They walked over, trying to take in the oddly beautiful vista of desert, feeling their skin burning in the sun, and stopped a good twenty feet from the man.

"Easy now," Cork said, holding out his boom-gun. "Watchu sayin?"

The ragged man turned to face them. His face was all dry skin and warts. He eyed them left, right, to their weapons, and then back to their faces before smiling. He had a wide grin of yellowed decaying teeth but not without an odd beatific charm to it. With a quick dance of movement, he whipped open the rags and bowed to them.

"Well now. . .Am I looking at two fine gentleman men of the coast?"

His face peered up at them again. That smile still wide.

Cork looked to Neal and swallowed dryly.

"Yup," Neal said, resting the bat across his shoulders. "We're making our way to the northlands. What about you?"

The man stood up, but not before reaching to his feet and grabbing a hat and placing it on his head. An odd-looking hat with a wide circular rim that reached out to his shoulders. The man's clothes were old and torn and unlike anything Neal had seen before. Like he'd stepped out of one of Cork's history books. His hair was matted into thick knots resting on his shoulders and his face had more edges and grooves than a rock and looked harder to break.

But those eyes of his, placed in those deep jagged sockets were brilliantly blue. They sparkled saliently amongst the browns and yellows. It was a watery blue that reminded him of the seas of the coast.

"I'm Neal," he said. "This here is my mentor and travel-companion. He goes by the name of Cork and that weapon he's holding is a real old-school boom-gun. It'll take your leg right off if it disagrees with you."

"That's right," Cork said, sucking his gums. "You best tell us your name?"

"Please to meet your acquaintance, gents. They call me Jean-Paul. I'm from a small bunker down near Nottingham. Been out here walking amongst the sand for so long now I'd almost given up hope."

"Well, Jean-Paul of the hills," Cork said. "Our diesel-machine is in working order. We could potentially take you back to your bunker if you might have something of worth to trade."

Jean-Paul eyed the horizon to his right, his smile faded.

"I have much to trade, but I have not what you look for."

Cork eyed Neal again.

"You a mutie?" Neal said suddenly, struggling to hold back the contentment in his voice.

With that, Jean-Paul looked to him, the smile returned.

"I have water and food. But not here. Back in our bunker we have meats and drink and biodiesel for your motor. Even have tea. You men ever have tea before?"

Cork lowered the gun a little.

"I read about it."

"Well you take me back to the bunker, and we'll see about getting you watered and fed, eh?"

Neal thought the answer obvious. The man had what they needed. What else was there to talk about? He took a step forward but Cork lifted the gun again.

"Now hang on, tell us what's in that sack of yours first. We don't want to be travelling to your bunker if you're carrying water there."

Jean-Paul nodded and kicked the sack towards them.

"In this bag is my personal effects and nothing more."

A beat. A slight breeze blew past. The dust rattled.

Cork waved Neal on and he sauntered to the sack, holding his eyes on those majestic blues as he pulled it away. It was a large canvas, heavy, tied up with leather string. He undid it to find more rags inside, along with an empty plastic bottle, an odd assortment of mirrors and looking glasses, and books. Five of them. Each of them were falling apart and the art on the covers had faded to near nothing. He held them up to Cork who nodded. The old man was a fool for a new book, but he didn't seem interested in these. His attention was fading. The heat was getting to him, turning his skin an odd shade of pinkish yellow. A fine film of sweat glistening on his forehead.

"You still breathing, Cork?"

The old man nodded, hacked up a lungful of dusty phlegm, and told Neal to "Keep looking."

Inside were more empty plastic bottles and finally, a cardboard box. The art on the box had been lost completely but upon opening it he saw a small stack of cardboard sheets inside, each with illustrations on them that were so wonderful to look at, so vivid and rich in colour, they almost had Neal welling up with tears there and then. Pictures of green hills and grass and humans so beautiful and perfect looking with pale skin and animals of which he'd never seen before and a skeleton. . .a skeleton in a hood with a dagger on a stick.

"What the hell are these, mister?" he said.

Jean-Paul took a step forward and dropped to his knee. Cork held the gun straight but allowed it. The man looked Neal in the eye, the smell of rotten earth in his breath. A raspy-whisper escaped his lips.

"Neal, oh Neal, they be the source of all my magick."

"Magick?"

"These cards know more than the sun above us. These cards have insight into the threads that connect us, when we'll live, when we'll die, who we'll mate with, and who we'll kill. These cards will teach you much about yourself."

With his curiosity piqued, Neal looked at them once more before handing them over to Jean-Paul.

"You want me to give you a reading, boy?" Jean-Paul said.

"Come on, Neal. No time for this. This damn heat. . .It's turning my head. I need water, boy. I need some goddam water!"

The old man hollered but Neal couldn't quite help himself. The charm of the ragged man was palpable and alluring. Just being this close to the magick-man had his heartbeat thumping, had his skin turning to sugar-paper.

But no. . .

There would be time for this later.

"Okay," Neal said. "We go now and you can show us la-"

"But a minute. My bunker is a short drive away. This will only take a minute and will change your life, Neal. I promise you. It will change your life."

Neal looked over his shoulder at Cork. The man wiped his brow and took a deep breath. A slight drunken sway had taken him.

"We better move," Neal went to say but stopped as Jean-Paul had already begun. He'd flipped over the top card and Neal couldn't help but look upon it, curious as to what the cards knew about him that he didn't know himself.

The picture was a man in a long cloak with a staff.

"The hermit," Jean-Paul said. "You will wander, Neal. You will wander alone for a while."

Neal couldn't help but look at this picture through the filter of his life so far. He had never been alone. Cork had always been in his life. Cork had been his family.

Another card flipped.

A beautiful blonde baby with dove wings, holding some sort of golden instrument to his mouth.

"Judgement. You will have an awakening of sorts. You will know new truths you'd never known before."

This meant little to Neal but he couldn't deny the odd

tickle in the base of his spine, the thumping of his heart, the quickening of his breath.

He turned to look at Cork but the man was now looking straight up, paying no mind the dalliances of the reading. He was staring at the sun, at the heat-that-never-ends, whispering sweet-nothings to the sky.

"And now your final card, Neal," continued the ragged man.

"It's so hot," Cork said to no one, his voice a notch higher, full of melancholy. "I miss you, Jood. I want to be with my Jood again. She was so sweet. . .so sweet."

The final card flipped and Neal paid no attention to his mentor. His senile ravings were a distraction to the magick happening before his eyes. Magick that he may never get to witness again. The heat-that-never-ends bore into him from above and yet he still felt the chill of the cards. They were peering into him, discovering parts of him he wasn't aware of.

The last card was a skeleton. The one with the dagger and the stick. But this time Jean-Paul said nothing. He simply looked up at Neal and sighed.

"What does this one mean?" Neal said.

And with that the ragged man whispered its name, a name which seemed to bring with it a breeze that pushed the dust of the hills onwards, pattering against the hot road.

"Death," he said. "Neal. It means death."

A sudden bang slammed their eardrums. Neal turned to see Cork on the floor, eyes closed, smoke billowing up from the end of his boom-gun. The old bastard had fainted and lost one of the few rounds that he had left.

"Cork!" screamed Neal as he went to stand, but before he could climb to his feet a hand grabbed hold of his shoulder. He turned to see the clammy lines of Jean-Paul's clenched fist before it slammed into his mouth, splitting lip and tongue against teeth. "Ack!"

He spat blood, spit, and the tip of his tongue into the air as his head lolled back. If he were quick enough he would've grabbed his bat from the floor but Jean-Paul was unnaturally fast. Another fist slammed into his face. Before he knew it, the ragged man was on top of him like a spider on its prey, slamming fists into his mouth, nose, head, again... again...again...

Neal's vision went dark. The world seemed to spin. Minutes passed in moments. By the time he opened them again and felt the throbbing pain of his face he saw the silhouette of Jean-Paul standing above Cork, who was awake long enough to cry out before Jean-Paul brought down Neal's own bat against his mentor's head.

The old man's face fell inwards, more so with each crack, until the brains that made up his friend spilt out and hissed against the heat of the road. The smell of cooking meats quickly finding Neal's broken nose.

But his vision went dark again. The ragged man had dislodged something in Neal's head and it was still trying to correct itself; he was still trying to reboot.

"You're in for great enlightenment," Jean-Paul said as he picked up Cork's boom-gun. He walked over to Neal and aimed the gun at something out of his view. "Don't disrespect the cards, Neal, oh Neal, for they tell us all."

Another gunshot. This one louder. This one more painful. Neal writhed in pain, seething blood and bile onto the road.

"You're right, Neal. This boom-gun'll take your leg right off."

A cackle of laughter escaped the ragged man's lips as he picked up his sack and wandered to the roadside. He walked to a rock, lifted it, revealing a deep hole in the ground. He reached in and pulled out a bottle of water covered in more rags to shade it. The man opened the lid and drank greedily from it, spilling some out from the sides.

"Sure is hot out here," Jean-Paul said. "Thirsty work, indeed."

Neal rolled to his front and crawled towards his dead friend. He sobbed at the disgusting sight that looked so alien to him now. Crying what little moisture he had left and burying his face into the man's bloodied shoulder.

"No..." he cried. "Cork...no...no...no..."

Jean-Paul walked over to him and rolled him over with

his boot. He flashed his six-fingered hands, dabbing his finger at Neal's bloodied face, licking it as he looked out at the horizon once more.

"Brother, brother," he began, not talking to Neal at all, but to some unseen abstract on the horizon. "We ride on and on, the tickling of the tongue as we taste the road we're on. I call it the golden eternity, Neal, and I say it is perfect."

With that, he picked up the rest of his belongings and climbed inside the diesel-machine.

That familiar song of engine and wheel-on-road. It was to be Neal's final lullaby. That radi-meter ticking away like crazy at the new driver inside. Neal managed to sit himself up, just to watch as it disappeared in the hills of Snake Pass, melting away in that warbling heat-haze; its song faded into nothing until Neal was alone again.

He grabbed that fish gut stained bat and hoisted himself up. His foot was non-existent now. A frayed tangle of blood and bone and trouser-thread in its place. And then he began, leaving Cork's body to rot and cook in the heat-that-never-ends, feeling that walking would be better than nothing, well aware that he'd be dead before the hour was up anyway, but still he hobbled on, still he saw those soul-touching blue eyes of the ragged man, and still he heard those final verses that he spoke, and he mouthed them himself until there was no air left in him to speak with.

"Brother brother," he said, again and again, laughing,

delirious and bubbling in the radiation-heavy wasteland. "Brother, brother. I call it the golden eternity. I say it is perfect."

VERITY
by Megan Manzano

Here's a tale that is best described as being gonzo–in the best possible way, of course. It features a cast of young people I think you'll enjoy getting to know.–Ed.

ACE.

Fucking Ace.

Aleks hadn't seen him in over a year and he had every reason to think he was dead—just as Ace had every reason to think the same of him. Aleks couldn't have gone back home. It would have been the first place they searched for him. He hadn't wanted to get anyone else involved nor did he know what could be said of the situation.

What Aleks did know was the government went crazy after his trial. Boy on the run. A boy willing to expose everything, if he hadn't been half-traumatized by the fact someone had made him believe he lived an entire year outside of his head. A doctor assumed to be under the command of the President, had fabricated his memories. Where he had actually been: strapped to a bed with wires looped around his body, monitors buzzing as they took every detail of him in.

His pulse.

His brain activity.

His identity.

"He was the best one so far." The voice was static against Aleks' ears. "Get me another copy of those scans. Gregory will be beyond pleased."

"Yes sir."

Aleks had thought he was dreaming until he acknowledged the pressure on his wrists and ankles. He noticed a continuous beeping, chords entangled with his limbs. This slight awareness repeated for several weeks until the day he didn't submerge into nothingness as expected.

He swallowed.

He wiggled his fingers and toes.

His eyes opened.

The beeping spiked.

Footsteps rushed towards the source of the noise.

Aleks exhaled, an attempt to detach himself from the memories. They weren't important right now. What was important was talking to Ace. He knew the man would want every last detail of his disappearance.

He was the only one Aleks knew out of the group of refugees. Unless, of course, the government had fucked with Ace's brain too. His stomach dropped at the thought.

The refugees were either escapees or rebels, constantly on the move to avoid capture. There was a no tolerance policy for those with sober minds. If someone roamed about without smiling like a rocket of happy juice had been shot up their ass, it was considered suspicious. Anything suspicious was considered dangerous and, well—the rest was obvious. Aleks couldn't stand sneaking into the city for supplies for this reason. The complacent smiles burned his skin. The steady, uniform steps made him want to shudder. And the voice of the government over loudspeakers, drawing every ounce of undivided, malleable attention made him want to scream until there was no energy left inside.

He never did, of course. Grin and bear it. Don't be seen. Get in. Get out.

Those who followed a similar path as Aleks, their only chance was the woods. This particular group had set up camp in the abandoned house Aleks had hid in the past few weeks. It was a two-story building atop an uphill driveway, sporting blacked-out windows, crumbling brick, and chipped paint. It creaked with every step, making Aleks distrustful of the stairs connecting the floors. Nina, the leader of the refugees, said they'd try their luck—or rather—she would. Aleks noticed whatever she said often was the case.

He didn't feel the need to abide by such rules, not at the moment. He had wanted to speak to Ace since their reunion that afternoon, but ground had to be covered before nightfall. Nina also seemed keen on their separation, assigning them differing tasks throughout the day.

There was no time for chit chat, she argued.

Luckily, Aleks overheard Nina telling Ace to take the night watch prior to curfew.

Aleks slipped from his corner of the house. He moved carefully through the evening shadows and the refugees that lay scattered about the floor. He attempted to be as light on his feet as possible until he reached the door below flight of steps. His teeth clenched the entire way down.

Once outside, he scanned the perimeter for Ace. It took quinting and stifling through closely bound trees until he caught sight of him. He was off to the right, curled into himself atop of a branch. Aleks bit back a smirk. There was one thing about Ace that hadn't changed.

He approached the tree after deducting no one else was there with Ace. "Finally got over your fear?" he called out.

There was rustling from overhead and in the gaps between the branches. Aleks caught sight of blue eyes, the same color as his, though much softer, as if they were water as opposed to crystal.

"Christ, Aleks!" The gun in Ace's hands lowered. "Way to give me a heart attack."

Aleks chuckled. Relief swelled in his chest. God, when had he last laughed?

He found his footing and climbed to a branch opposite Ace's own. While he rested comfortably, as comfortably as one could get on a piece of wood, Ace's spine was straight, practically leaving a mark on the trunk of the tree behind him.

"I'll take that as a no to my question," Aleks quipped.

"Yeah. . ." Ace nodded, his fingers sweeping through his blonde hair which was shaggier, dirtier than Aleks remembered him having it. Trimmed, but just enough where he could either be a businessman or a skater boy, was where Ace had worn the length of his hair in the past.

Now, that seemed like a distant memory, a lazy Friday afternoon when they had finished classes and both of them were in a playful tiff about what look would best score a date. Ace had called himself the best of both worlds. Aleks had called him a cocky asshole. And Kelsey—

Kelsey.

What had happened to her? Their third roommate.

There was so much to say and Aleks wasn't even certain where to begin. His fingers laced together.

"We have a lot to talk about, don't we?" Ace asked, as if reading Aleks' mind.

"Yeah, we do. I—I didn't expect to see you again. I didn't know what I was expecting."

"You were gone a whole year, Aleks. Me and K—" Ace paused, confirming what Aleks had suspected.

His gaze fell briefly to his lap. "Do I want to know?"

"You tell me."

He should have the knowledge of his friend's death, add

it to the list of reasons why he loathed the government. Innocent people dying for profit. And what did they do in response? They called it a success.

"Yes." There was conviction in his voice.

Ace waited a moment and when Aleks didn't protest, he began. "I'm not sure what happened with you. I've heard your name spoken among the refugees. You were different. And I believe—or the most logical explanation to me is—since we were intertwined with you, they came after us."

"Who's they?"

"The government. The police. Someone who wanted us dead. They raided our flat, held Kelsey and I hostage. They kept asking where you were and we told them you were dead because that's what we thought. They didn't believe us. A guy pulled a gun on Kelsey, and I started thrashing. I managed to create a distraction so we could run. But. . ."

"Kelsey—they got her." Aleks was shaking, his nails digging into his palms.

"Yeah. They shot her. She went down. I—I wanted to go back. You have to believe that. There was just. . .so many of them and only one of me, and Aleks. . .I see her face all the time. They got her right here." Ace tapped his finger between his eyes, and it was then Aleks saw he too was shaking.

"It wasn't your fault." Aleks said. "It wasn't."

"Bullshit."

"It's not. You did what you could. It wasn't your fault."

His lips, however, curled into a frown.

It was *his.* If he hadn't run, if he hadn't fought, they would have never had a reason to come after his friends.

Everything had happened in a rush. Aleks remained still as a doctor ran in to assess the sudden change in his vitals. The bonds were undone from his wrists and ankles, and he sprung to life.

Fists were thrown. The doctor stumbled backwards, tripping over the legs of a monitor stand.

Aleks yanked the wires from his arms. He felt something warm and sticky trickle downward to his fingers. He removed the electrodes attached to his head.

The doctor regained his balance. Aleks lunged at him, attempting to pin the other beneath him. The man anticipated this and kicked.

It was Aleks' turn to stumble. Someone grabbed him before he fell and shoved him against the wall. Hands closed around his throat. He felt the man's thumbs press into his windpipe, as if they desired to pop his voice box from place. His body bucked. His lungs burned for air they could not receive.

An alarm roared. Red lights flashed along the edges of Aleks' vision.

He wouldn't die here. He. Would. Not. Die. Here.

He saw a pen in the pocket of the doctor's jacket.

"You say that like you know for certain," Ace finally

replied, seeking out Aleks' gaze.

Aleks blinked in succession. The trees came back into focus. "I do. They came after you and K...Kelsey because I escaped. Because I killed someone who was important to them."

"What—what happened to you, Aleks?"

Aleks felt a knot in his throat. He had been with Ace and Kelsey one day, gone the next, squeezed from existence itself.

"I had gone to that job interview, the assistant producer position. It started off alright, but the interviewer pushed me to answer questions the way he wanted. When he refused, he got mad and then I got mad and he said I was no longer qualified. And then I...I remember calling you and K...Kelsey to go for a drink—"

"We never got a call."

"I know that now, but everything after that interview was real, Ace. I lived an entire year in my head while I was..."

Comatose.

Gone.

Erased.

He had never left that building.

But Aleks could say none of that. "They, this doctor, tapped into my brain and constructed memories I...I thought were real. A year later, I woke up to find they were a lie. A few seconds after that I'm fighting for my life."

Ace was still, his face drained of color.

"What? Ace. Say something, please."

"What Emilie said was true."

"Emilie. . .The agent who went rogue?"

"That one," Ace confirmed. "When I joined Nina's group, Emilie explained the government was putting chips in people's brains, had been doing it for years until it leaked and everything devolved into chaos. But yeah, they were pulling people from all over the country to test this idea—particularly trauma victims, or people with shady histories. She said something about susceptibility. I don't know the logistics, but it worked by attaching chips to the part of the brain associated with memory. A particular kind of manipulation and—"

"—they can create whatever they want." Aleks felt his stomach lurch. It was slowly expanded outward.

There would be no protest without a reminder of wrong. There would be no protest without a sense of who one was. There would be nothing other than compliance.

~ ~ ~

They had tried their idea on Aleks. They tested to see if he was compatible to be a nation—approved dummy. They took interest in a past he had left behind in his small hometown: the crunching of metal as his friend's car was hit by a drunk driver, the overwhelming cloud of smoke that seared his lungs, screams that began and ended with him, the obituaries in the paper. There was constant guilt eating at his insides, commanding them to twist and turn when it seemed fit. To leave it all behind, Aleks physically removed himself from the environment. With university only a few months away, that was what he had done.

But moving away hadn't healed the wounds. They were scars bright, throbbing, and eager to be opened again.

Fuck them. Fuck every last one of them. The thought of killing one of their own didn't seem as despicable to Aleks as it had five minutes ago.

It seemed right.

"All of it. . .sounded mad, but when I look around and see people as mindless zombies, how keen the police are on making sure everything is as it should be, I can't think of an alternative."

"And to think we thought stuff like this was good television. We're in the middle of a series." Aleks joked. He didn't want to break apart.

Ace returned the gesture. "Pretty sure we can't sit around debating who shows up first on the opening credits or the fact that you can't act—at all."

"Thanks, I'll remember that." Aleks rolled his eyes. "We have all night, don't we? Teach me a few things."

"Technically, I have all night. You're supposed to be asleep." Ace shot Aleks a look a disappointed parent gave a child.

"Right, okay. I'll sleep after seeing my best friend for the first time in ages."

Ace's face softened and he released a breath. "I really did miss you, Aleks. When you didn't come back...Kelsey thought it hadn't gone well and you needed space. Something told me otherwise."

"I wish that was the actual case. Did you...when you realized I wasn't...did you call the—"

"Of course, we did. Of course!" Ace's hand slammed into the branch below him. He immediately recoiled, pressed his back against the trunk. When he spoke again, it was in a whisper. "Of course. They took your information, a photograph, and then nothing. They closed the investigation long before there was even a case to be made. Ruled you off as a dead end."

Aleks' hands curled into fists. His attention landed on the gun that was slung from Ace's shoulder. A pull of the trigger and he could kill another and another and another.

"Don't."

Aleks said nothing, focusing on the pressure exhibited from his closed palms, a wave of energy centering itself there.

"I mean it." Ace's voice was stronger this time, breaking Aleks from his trance. "I understand wanting to. God, Aleks. Just thinking about what they did to you makes me mad. Completely and utterly mad. But if we pull that trigger, we're just like them. We become them."

Normally the jokester. Normally the one who would

wear boxers when either Kelsey or Aleks had guests over. Now, a light in the dark, marred and altered from what he had seen.

It clicked in Aleks' head that Ace had killed, and not always with mercy in mind. Aleks' felt a chord wrap around his lungs that Ace didn't deserve it. He didn't deserve to know what death was like, how revenge was an anchor that grew hotter in the pit of a person until it couldn't be ignored.

He had been the meek heart with an intelligence that baffled Aleks. While he scraped by, a speck in life, Ace could code. Ace had entered and won scholarships based on research that furthered the knowledge of bacteria.

Aleks always thought he'd be great. Aleks thought he'd be someone who left a mark on the world. He would remember Ace and make sure what he could do was never forgotten.

"You and I were always different. But. . .you're right. Look. . .I. . .If there was one person I wanted to see more than anyone, it was you." Aleks' nose wrinkled. When had be become that sappy?

"Did they take the douchey part out of your brain?" Ace teased. He was quick to follow up. "Pretty sure the nicest thing you ever said to me before now was thanks for washing the dishes."

"Fuck off," Aleks retorted, though he was smiling. If anyone else had joked about what happened to him, there would be no guarantee of the same response.

"The...feeling is mutual," Ace continued when the territory between them was deemed safe. "When Bones and Char dragged you out of the house, I thought I was being tricked, that it was some horrible joke. But you were there. You were real."

"I am real, Ace."

"And you're not going anywhere?"

"No. Not without a fight. We're in it together."

"Together," Ace affirmed, extending his hand. "I'd hug you, but I'd like not to fall to my death."

"Together." Aleks took Ace's hand, held on for seconds longer than he should have. He felt alive. He felt he could be whole again. "Don't worry, I'll spare you the anxiety attack."

Aleks finally let go of Ace's hand and brought the same hand upward to stroke his chin. "It's not that high, you know."

"Shut up, Aleks." A grunt. "Nina gave me the worst job possible."

Aleks bit back words that were inching along the tip of his tongue. He knew Ace respected Nina and he understood his time with her had warranted loyalty. It hadn't happened for Aleks himself and he doubted it would. There was something negative she reflected when she had seen him dragged out of the house. Just when it seemed Ace was going to pursue the matter, a cracking sound. Both boys's heads turned to catch what might have caused it. Darkness, endless darkness. Aleks remained still in the tree, desperate to find a possible threat before it caused any damage.

Aleks had been in encounters with the police force before. They were relentless in pursuit with shoot to kill orders to quell resistance. It was the reason for the scar that lingered on his upper right arm.

"Al-"

He placed a finger to his lips, shifted so his legs dangled off one side of the branch. He scooted toward the backside of the tree and used it as leverage to stand.

Don't look down.

He extended his right leg, his foot coming into contact with the branch Ace was sitting on. He applied as much pressure as he could. The branch didn't buckle and he took that as his cue to cross over.

"How good are you with guns?" Aleks asked as he heard the crunching of leaves. Closer this time.

"Good enough," Ace replied, raising the weapon, squinting to find the source of the noise.

"Give it to me."

"What?"

"Give it to me." Aleks held out both of his hands. He would not allow any more blood to taint Ace's life, not if he could help it. Aleks could handle taking lives. He had resigned himself to it. Ace, however, never would.

Ace hesitated at Aleks' demand at first, and then gave in

with a sudden haste as if the same resolution had clicked within his mind.

Aleks slid the gun over his head, motioned for Ace to stay as close as possible. He searched for movement, a flash of someone lurking where they weren't supposed to be. His finger was already on the trigger.

One.

Two.

Three.

Snap!

"There, coming through the bushes," Ace observed.

"How many?"

"Four, from what I can see. We need to draw their attention from the house."

Except the police were moving quickly across the yard, showing no interest in the house. Aleks shifted the gun. He would take no chances. A single stir from behind the walls and the police would swarm.

Aleks steadied his hand, aimed at the person closest to the end of the pack, and fired. He tipped backwards from the recoil but Ace's hands were quick to catch him.

A body dropped to the ground with a thud and a voice rang out, "Man down. I repeat, man down!"

"Direction of the shot? Anyone?" Heads turned. Silence echoed in response to the demand.

"Keep your eyes fucking open then!"

"They're not leaving," Ace said. Aleks fired another shot. It gave away their position—the soldiers advanced towards them, dressed in padded uniforms of navy and black. They were part of the night, shadows with guns pointed in Aleks' and Ace's direction.

"You—we need to get down now," Aleks instructed. Ace didn't need to be told twice, but as he swiveled to drop to the next branch, he froze.

"Ace, you can do this," Aleks insisted from above. "You have to."

He inhaled sharply and made his way down, Aleks keeping up with him.

The instant their feet hit the ground, bullets fired.

"Targets spotted!"

"Run!" Aleks cried.

"What did you think I was going to do?" Ace spat, his feet gaining speed, gravel and dirt being upturned.

Aleks kept up behind him, the beating of his heart echoing in his skull, pulsating through his ears. He ignored the throbbing in his legs. One wrong step and he'd tumble. He already felt as if the air was tugging him downward, pulling him by the edges of his clothes.

A bullet whizzed past Aleks' hip. Another by his shoulder. Ace was almost at the bottom of the hill. He jumped, as desperate as Aleks to reach leveled ground. Aleks followed suit and the two pivoted to the right, hiding themselves in the blanket of surrounding trees.

"They went towards the barn!"

Instead of hearing pursuit, there was emptiness. The forest was quiet. Aleks tugged on Ace's wrist and jerked him to a stop. His chest rose and fell rapidly. His mouth felt like sandpaper. Ace bent down, hands pressing against his knees, before rising to full height.

"Where did they go?"

Aleks searched frantically. "I. . .don't know. We need to keep moving."

". . .Aleks?"

"Wh-?" Every ounce of air rushed out of him. Ace's head was tilted downward to his hip, fingers pressing against skin and being met with dampness.

"Stop right there!" Aleks' feet dug angrily into the dirt below. Three men emerged. The man who spoke, presumably the leader, wore a malicious grin. "You're not the only one who can shoot from a distance."

Aleks couldn't focus. Blood. Ace was bleeding.

Ace caught sight of the other. "I'm okay," he mouthed. "Stay."

Aleks' mind whirred a thousand miles per minute. His panic held weight as it came crashing against his skull.

"You have one of two options."

The voice fizzled at the edges, as did the trees.

"You can either surrender and come quietly with us—"

Aleks' head felt suddenly as if it were splitting in half. He had gone rigid. His eyelids fell shut and he squeezed them tight.

"ALEKS!"

"Where do you think you're going?" There was a crunch of a boot against the ground followed by a loud whimper.

Aleks dropped to his knees. His hands cupped the sides of his head. The gun hanging from his shoulder swung to and fro. The police stared at Aleks as if they were trying to decipher whether they should bother to place an ounce of concern into his distressed state.

The pain traveled throughout Aleks' body, his muscles stiffening, stunted by agony he couldn't explain.

Ace lay crouched on the floor, his wound bleeding profusely after having been dug into with the butt of the man's weapon. He forced himself to look at Aleks, writhing, screaming. The sounds were raw, scraped from the back of his throat.

"Aleks! What did you do? What did you do to him?"

The guards remained stoic, dismissing Ace without a glance.

Aleks begged for the world around him to stop spinning. It dissolved further. When he forced his eyes open, the police were ink blots on a page. Ace advanced toward him on his elbows only to be kicked hard in the side.

Aleks was slammed against a rock. He had to be. There

was no other explanation. A slam and another and another and another. He swore he tasted metal on his tongue.

The world around him broke into glass fragments and Aleks was encompassed in swirling darkness. His body felt trapped in a wind tunnel, yanked upward by a heavy hand until he was released and gravity rushed up to meet him.

~ ~ ~

"Make sure those cuffs are tight. I don't need a repeat of last year," Doctor Webber instructed, his fingers brushing subconsciously against the dime-sized scar on his neck. He studied the monitor before him, square framed spectacles settled on the brim of his nose, nodding at the slow ascent of Aleks' blood pressure and pulse. The boy would be waking soon.

"Sir." The woman who adjusted the restraints on Aleks' arms and legs turned to face the doctor. "Raven told me to pass on the word that we were able to pinpoint the source of Aleks' disembarkment from the experiment."

Doctor Webber straightened in his seat. "Where is Raven to tell me this news herself, Colleen?"

"You know the answer to that. Slipping away now would look immensely suspicious, don't you think? Doctor Webber scoffed and straightened his spine, a shadow cast over the cream-colored tiles due to his height. He towered at six-feet-two.

"Do I have permission to take care of the matter at

hand?" Collen asked with a tone of apathy.

"Permission granted." Doctor Webber matched Colleen's enthusiasm, despite the importance of the matter they were discussing. With this decision, Aleks would have a slim chance of breaking from the experiment. Human volition was not as powerful as it used to be. Neither were emotions.

"Excellent." Colleen brushed her hands together and made for the exit. There was a stride in her step, a twitching of the corners of her mouth.

"Colleen."

His tone made her stop. "Yes, Doctor Webber?"

"I want the source eradicated. Do you understand?"

"Completely."

As the woman disappeared into the hall, Doctor Webber stood above Aleks. He watched the rise and fall of his chest, relished in the stillness of a defeated subject. "Let's see how strong you are—alone."

BLACK WATER
by N.J. Reynolds

The best part of waking up. (Also, the best part of living in the apocalypse, it seems.)—Ed.

HE WOKE UP.

He smelt the coffee.

The sunlight was streaming through the hole in the wall. Once the hole had been a window, but the glass had been blown out years ago, the frame smashed to pieces. Now it was just a rough, gaping mouth, bricks at the edge coming loose, bricks scattered and broken on the dusty, dirty floor.

He rolled on his side, off the piles of old newspapers, onto his belly. He crawled over to the wall. His nostrils twitched. The smell of the coffee was coming from outside, the other side of the hole.

When he got to the wall he stopped, lay flat and listened. The occasional rattle of a machine gun, thump of a mortar but distant, far off. There was no sound from the street behind the wall. He pulled himself onto his knees and very slowly raised his head, till his eyes were level with the ragged edge of the hole and he could see outside.

He scanned the street quickly, the brutal, relentless

sunlight making it easy for him to pick out every detail. Single-storey brick buildings, windows blown out. Some with crude corrugated iron roofs, some just walls, empty to the sky, in ruins. Rubble, rubbish, old tin cans, dirty plastic cartons scattered across the broken pavements. The remains of a burnt-out car, rusting in the sunlight. A steel pole with a smashed lamp, felled like a tree, sprawled from the pavement diagonally across the dried, hard, dark brown mud of the road. No birds, no movement, no signs of anything living. Silence.

Suddenly he spotted a flicker of light in the building directly across the road: a tiny orange flame. His eyes focused and he saw it: a flame on a tiny gas cylinder, a simple frame supporting a tiny brown pan. The cylinder was half hidden in the shadow of the doorway but it was there. And then, next to the cylinder, a boot, flat on the floor. The boot tapped. The smell again: coffee.

He gripped the handle of the knife in his belt. He focused for a moment, calming himself, breathing slowly.

He jumped through the hole and into the street. The sunlight hit him, the edge of the light. He raced across the mud, taking big strides, into the doorway, turned to face the wall, and with his right hand plunged the knife up into the chest of the man, standing, back against the wall.

The man stared at him and made a strangled, choking noise. The knife had struck directly into the space between the ribs, into the heart. The man waved his arms in an impotent, jerky, flapping movement. He twisted the knife and jerked it out. The man fell forward, away from the cylinder, and sprawled face down on the floor.

In the shadow he surveyed the objects on the floor of the room, eyes darting, quickly. A back pack, a machete, rope curled round the handle, out of reach. A small brown battered saucepan filled with coffee, simmering on the frame of the gas cylinder. He switched off the gas and then kicked the pan on the floor, the coffee spilling, spreading slowly over the cracked floor, mixing with the blood from the body. It was a waste, but he had to move. He peered inside the backpack, then grabbed it by one of its straps. He slid his knife into his belt, picked up the hot gas cylinder by its frame and then dropped it into the backpack. He clutched the backpack to his chest, folding his arms around it. Then he sprinted back across the street, and jumped back into the room.

For a long time, he sat in a corner, the corner furthest from the street, his back against the wall, next to the piles of newspapers, watching, listening, alert. He had a view of both the hole in the wall and the door in the corner that lead into the back room. The gun fire was like the soft patter of rain in the distance.

He relaxed. He opened the backpack. He took out the four plastic, rectangular containers. Three packed with ground coffee, one packed with coffee beans. The beans were the real prize, so rare, so precious. He picked up one of the containers and turned it in his hands, taking care not to open it, examining the beans through the transparent plastic. He could see no rotten or bad beans, they looked clean, dry, perfect. He could see how good they were, tightly packed into the box. With great care he put the container of beans back in the backpack. Then he examined one of the boxes of ground coffee. He lifted the lid at one corner, pushed in the tip of his finger and tasted it gently on his tongue. High quality, probably made from the beans. He put the box of ground coffee on the floor.

He pulled two bricks out of the wall. Behind them was a small hole where he had hidden his percolator, and his tin cup. He unscrewed the base section of the percolator, pulled out the metal filter and lay it aside. He had a leather gourd half full of water, lying next to the newspapers. He picked the gourd up with his right hand. Holding the base in his left hand, carefully, slowly he poured water into the base. Water was scarce; he might not find more clean water for days.

He took some pinches of ground coffee from the box, then dropped them into the metal filter until it was half full. He put the filter on top of the base, and screwed the main metal section back on. He placed the percolator reverently on top of the frame of the cylinder. He turned on the gas, and clicked the flint with his thumb. The flame lit first time. He sat back and waited for the coffee to bubble up.

When it was ready he poured the hot black water into the tin cup. He let it cool, then took a sip. It tasted good, dark, bitter.

He could feel himself coming down from the rush of the kill. The coffee would help him keep his edge.

The percolator and tin cup had been given to him by his father. One of his "gifts" to him, his father had said. Like teaching him to read. In the long evenings, when they weren't moving, scavenging or fighting strangers on the road, his father would tell him stories and teach him the alphabet, using stones to draw the letters on walls or sticks to trace them in the ground. The percolator had been a better gift than the reading.

As he drank the coffee, sip by slow sip, he took a handful of the rotten newspapers and idly pulled and pushed them across the floor by his feet. They fell to pieces quickly. Dusty, fading words. A date in a headline in large type. What was it? He couldn't make it out. It didn't matter.

The calendar had been torn to pieces. His father said that, on the night before they ran into the ambush. They butchered his father, left his gutted corpse on the road. He had escaped, running into the dark. People couldn't agree what day it was, his father had said. Now people lived and died by the rhythm of the seasons, the heat, the cold.

He remembered the times, as the pitiless sun dropped below the horizon and they shared a precious tin cup of coffee, his father had told him stories. Stories of boiling seas, of flocks of birds falling out of the sky, dead weight. Stories of the corpses of animals piled up in fields where grass was the colour of sand, the acrid stench of pyres of meat, burning, stinking. Stories of the white castle made of the hard shards that littered the landscape, brittle, indestructible. Stories of the gods, face covered and black, who tore up the books, made the machines and all their twinkling lights and noise go silent. Not all at once, but off and on in a steady procession across the cities until all the machines everywhere fell silent, men and women pleading with them, crying, hitting them, smashing them in a futile effort to bring them back to life. His father would chuckle and say things were better now. A man could fight and win and take what he wanted.

He could get a good trade for this haul of coffee. Whores, plenty of food and water. But what he really needed was a gun. Guns were rare and expensive. With some haggling and threats he might be able to trade the coffee for a gun. But not here. This place was ruins, no one left but gangs and thieves. After dark he would hit the road, move east. Maybe the next place might have a market where he could trade.

He finished the coffee and put the tin cup down on the floor. He sat for a moment.

To his left, from the doorway, he heard a sound.

He reached for his knife.

HOW DO THEY LIKE IT?
by Ray Prew

Do you feel like an outcast, living on the periphery of society?
If so, this one's for you, babe.—Ed.

HI, MY NAME IS Brad Bostwick, and I have quite a story to tell you. You've probably seen me and passed me by without a second look. I'm the homeless guy you wouldn't give spare change to. Remember me now? No? Well, I'm not surprised. Most people overlook those in my situation. At least, they used to.

That was before the pulse, the electromagnetic pulse that knocked out power systems around the world, along with all forms of electronics, even things that run on batteries. In that brief moment, all over the planet, mankind was thrown back to the 1700s. All technology upon the earth ceased to work.

It started with someone attacking the United States and our responding in kind. Thereafter, nothing worked anymore. Mass communication, lights (including flashlights), railways, planes, all of it stopped working.

No one had jobs to go to as nothing worked, and aside from walking, they had no way to get there. Food stores had no way to preserve perishable food and couldn't ring up sales. Cash registers couldn't work without electricity.

Hungry mobs raided markets for whatever they could find. Within a month, most people were reduced to my situation—no money, no food, no way to get either. It was amusing to watch the fat cat businessman, chauffeured to work every day, rummaging through dumpsters for anything edible.

I can survive like this; I've been doing it for years now. Others had a hard time adapting. Some parts of the country have it a bit better; they hunt, fish, or grow vegetables. The major cities, however, are falling apart.

In the 1700 and 1800's people could hunt or fish to feed themselves, but the population has grown so large it will soon deplete the lakes and streams and hunt small game to extinction.

Ah, the domino effect. Usually, it refers one persons' life going to hell; now it applies to mankind as a species. We may never recover from this—to make it worse, winter is coming.

Like I said, most people looked down their nose at me, or called me a bum, but they're in my situation now. They have no money, no food, and, in some cases, no homes. I wonder, how do they like it? I'm used to living like this, sleeping in alleyways and scrounging meals. It's a bit more challenging now, but nothing I can't handle.

Where I once could go to soup kitchens or food banks to

get food, only occasionally having to catch cats and raccoons and such for food, now I hunt daily for my dinner. I wonder how well the people who spared me no change, or even a kind word, will like making a meal of the family pet?

Society has deteriorated at a steady pace. The future looks grim. The police protect only their homes and families.

Most people steal food and clothes from each other. Money has less and less meaning. Remember how New Orleans fell apart after Katrina? That was a day at the beach compared to this.

Several months before this began, I found an underground cave in a small thatch of woods. I've camouflaged the opening to render it invisible. I sit back and watch those that disregarded me fall apart. They have no money, no food, and no homes. How do they like it?

I may have eaten cats and squirrels, but I've never eaten a person. I fear, however, that it is coming soon.

The street gangs that were once a small threat took over the small towns. Fortunately, ours was deep in a fierce gang's territory, so we never saw much turf war.

They actually kept the streets safe. Once they cemented their control of a town, they put all the drugs and prostitution behind closed doors. They still had complete control, except now drug and sex services were easily available, just not waved in the public's face. Thieves and those preying on the elderly were dealt with swiftly and effectively.

One poor bastard was caught stealing a bag of apples from an old lady, knocking her down in the process. This man was publicly skinned for his crime.

He was brought out—naked, strapped to a table—before the crowd. His crime was announced to the crowd. They began to peel every inch of skin off him. Every time he passed out from the pain, they revived him and reminded him why this was happening. The skinning would continue.

Many in the crowd—myself included—vomited at the sight of such cruelty, but the gang got their message across. Four hours later, the poor wretch on the table didn't have a stretch of skin left on his body. After this, he was vigorously rubbed with sandpaper; he screamed and howled. He was then, still alive and conscious, given to a gang of dogs.

Many people objected to this lawlessness, and some were killed publicly as an example of who was now in charge. The gang had taken over our town. There was no one to stop them.

Fortunate for me, they preyed only on those with something to take. Fools! Money and jewels had no meaning anymore.

Parts of the city are on fire. Without electricity, there is no way to pump water. Anyway, the fire trucks no longer run.

This was not the worst of it. For me, that would be the unburied dead. People who had died lay in the street.

Like the rest of society, the undertakers and

gravediggers protected their own homes. Since they trained on modern equipment, they didn't know how to do their jobs without certain devices. Money having lost its value, there was no way for them to get paid for their work, so they simply did nothing.

The dead lie on sidewalks for the rats and dogs. When a family member dies, the others move the deceased outdoors. They have no other choice. No one collects the bodies anymore. None of the undertakers have horses, let alone carriages or wagons.

I guess you don't believe that. Well, riddle me this: Would you work for free—or on a barter system—at a job like that? Preparing the dead, in some cases well-rotted dead, for burial, then convincing a gravedigger to work by shovel alone? And not get paid? The world is becoming medieval.

People stopped helping each other and started preying on each other instead. Despite the gang's justice, people steal from whomever they can. And they call me a bum! They who once walked proudly now rejoice to find a half-eaten apple.

The saddest of it all is watching children catching rats to eat. What kind of a world will they inherent? What kind of a world will they create? The world as we knew it is gone forever; the effects of the pulse may last hundreds of years. Think about it, no electricity for centuries, not even batteries. What kind of world will emerge from this?

Einstein was right. He said he didn't know how the next

war would be fought, but the one after that would be fought with sticks and stones.

Even the simplest of conveniences are gone; those fortunate enough to have a back yard are able to dig outhouses. Those without must crap in an ally, squatting behind a dumpster overflowing with trash. And I wonder, how do they like it? How do they like not having a home, or food, or choices? I may have been homeless before the pulse, no more than a beggar, but I had my self-respect. Some of these people have gone to hell.

As I said, winters coming, and I have firewood stored in my cave. What will the others do? The survivalists of the early 80s who thought they were preparing for the apocalypse couldn't have prepared for this. It happened a little over three months. The ironic part is: If people had learned to work and play well with each other as nations, we wouldn't have to feed on each other now.

The once proud and judgmental now rummage through debris for rats to eat, and all I can wonder is, how do they like it? The high point of my week happened yesterday. A certain man used to walk by me every day on his way to work. This man never gave me spare change—instead made cruel remarks about my being homeless. He approached me and begged my help in learning to survive in this new world. I told him to get a job. The look on his face was priceless. I guess there is something in Karma, after all.

When the pulse knocked out the electricity, it also killed civility, kindness, and compassion. In the three months since then, I've seen people kill over a can of beans. Within another three months, they'll resort to cannibalism. Hungry people do squirrely things to feed their families.

I, who once was overlooked and made to feel like an outcast, now have lots of company, people with no food, money, or hope. And all I can think is, how do they like it? How do they like living like me?

After the pulse, the only contact our town had with distant places was through riders on horseback passing through looking for family members. At first, we hoped the government would send troops to maintain order. However, the few reports we heard indicated that the military was trying to turn us into a police state. There was nothing left anymore, no law, no order, and no government. Anarchy is too soft a word for what is happening.

Among the more unsettling stories we heard included native American Indians attempting to reclaim their lands. Good luck, white man, getting the land back a second time. We heard that large groups of South Americans were streaming over the border, armed with knives and clubs. They were intent on reclaiming Texas in the name of Mexico.

Prisoners in state and federal prisons took advantage of the disruption to stage mass escapes. Therefore, there are roving bands of convicts preying on anyone foolish enough to travel. America, along with all the other nations, is finished. Mankind has fallen into barbarism.

I knew it was all over when I watched a preacher banging on a bell with a rock to summon the faithful to prayer service. He was attacked by a gang of young men—they beat him to a pulp and stripped him of his clothing. They left him bleeding, lying on the ground in his underwear.

Maybe you think this is fiction; maybe you think it's prophecy. If everything you knew went to hell in three short months, what would you do to feed your family and survive?

GHOST WOMAN
by Roxanne Dent

*Sometimes the best post-apocalypse stories contain an element
of Science Fiction. Look no further if that's your thing.—Ed.*

THE MANHOLE COVER ON West Twenty-Eighth Street
squeaked as I lifted it. I climbed out and studied the bleak,
snowy landscape. My watch read eight in the morning, but
there was little difference between night and day.

Hu, the raven I rescued, and named after one of the two
birds who sat on Odin's shoulders, flew out, and took off
screeching.

It was the middle of July, but a freezing wind blew the
lingering winter snow into three-foot drifts. The twenty-
degree weather made the scar on the right side of my face
ache. I pulled my gaiter up, removed a large backpack with
an extra jacket, boots, and plastic explosives, and kicked the
manhole cover into place.

My down-filled parka with the fur-lined hood, was
water resistant. I shifted my backpack, and pulled on my
thermal gloves, insulated with heat packs. Strapped to my
waist, was a dagger with an obsidian handle. Slung around
my body was a sonic laser and a smart rifle.

My name is Ariel. I'm a new breed of human. The Aliens call me Ghost Woman and fear me.

When I was eleven, religious and ethnic terrorism, greed and economic collapse, led to war breaking out all over the world. Despite the ban on nuclear, chemical and biological weapons, their use spread across the globe.

Steel skyscrapers and technological wonders turned to rubble, or disappeared beneath gigantic tidal waves, in the aftermath of what the military optimistically promised, would be a limited war. The rest became hollowed out cement and brick caves, whipped by radioactive, solar winds, and haunted by the ghosts of its dead occupants.

No one noticed the tears in space, which ushered in a race of Reptoid aliens called Saurinians. They arrived in their triangular, black crafts from another dimension, looking for slaves, gold and other metals. Eight and nine feet tall, with huge heads, their skin was covered in bright green scales. Their oval, black eyes were hypnotic and could scan great distances. Through evolution, they had language and no longer sported a tail. It was a futuristic, Jurassic Park nightmare, no one was prepared for.

The few war ships left in our arsenals, exploded like matchsticks. We were defeated by a superior technology. Survivors surrendered, hoping for mercy. The strong were sent to the mines to work, until they dropped from exhaustion, beatings or starvation. The dead were frozen and sent to the alien home world as food.

After my parents' deaths, I came to live with my aunt, Dr. Lauren Mason in an underground laboratory. She experimented on me in a desperate attempt to alter the human race to better battle the aliens, and our toxic environment.

Laser splicing of genes, mixed with alien DNA, transfusions of treated blood and nanotechnology, were pumped into me. The combinations made me violently ill. I came close to death more than once. Being young and blessed with an unusually strong immune system, saved my life. I eventually recovered. Others were not so fortunate. Some had to be put down. Others refused to participate in the experiments.

Like the scurrying vermin who adjusted to the poisons in the water and atmosphere, my body morphed into something no longer human. My strength and sight were magnified ten times, my movements were quicksilver.

No longer vulnerable to radiation sickness, I discovered my wounds healed in minutes but to my horror, whenever I became angry, my eyes burst into silver fire. I grew fangs. Although I ingest food, not blood, I still think of myself as a monster. So, did others of my kind.

I watched as a pack of rats turned on one of their own, a smaller one who only had three legs. Tearing it apart, they ate it. Life is harsh. Those who are different suffer.

The snow made a swooshing sound as it blew in my face. I remembered the cruel whispers once I healed enough to rejoin the others.

"She carries their blood. Maybe she's a spy."

"Or a vampire."

"Or a robot. She never smiles. She's not human."

I refused to let the remarks get to me until I met Rick, twenty-one, two years older than me. All the girls had a crush on him, including me. He ignored the comments about me and sought me out. I was suspicious at first, but we talked about life before the war, the alien's arrival, books we read, shows we watched and food we missed. Our friendship slowly turned into something deeper.

A stealthy shuffle to my right, alerted me to present danger. One of the sub-humans, the light of madness in his eyes, held a rock in his raised hand, ready to bash me over the head. He wanted to drag me to his lair and eat my flesh while it was still warm. I lifted my weapon and shot him between the eyes, worried the sound would draw the aliens. He fell over and didn't move. On a bad day, I would have thought him lucky.

As I continued my trek, I head scurrying creatures scrabble out of hiding to devour the tainted remains. I didn't look back.

My own dark day was the scouting mission with Rick and eight others. We were ambushed by a party of ten

Saurinians They slaughtered half our members before we knew what hit us.

Whether from panic or rage, oblivious of danger, I felt a savage ferocity take over. Screaming at the top of my lungs, I took out half their number. The rest of our team did the rest. Their leader, a massive beast remained. I leapt on his back, dug my fangs into his thick neck, and sucked deep. The blood was green, thin and burned going down. I gagged but held on, until his corpse was drained.

As I fed, something unexpected happened. I could understand fragments of the dying alien's mind as I drank, and learned the location of their ships and search parties. Thrilled, I hacked off his head with my dagger. When I looked up, Rick and the remaining members of our party, stared at me in horror.

I was covered in green, iridescent blood. My eyes flashed molten silver, my bloody fangs clearly visible. I held the decapitated head by its hair in one hand, the bodies of the other aliens were torn apart all around me. As my blood cooled, I saw revulsion on his face. It was a knife in the heart. We never spoke again. Sometimes, as I fall asleep, I can still hear the blood drip from the Saurinian's severed head onto my boots, as Rick and the others stare.

When my aunt died from a radiation sickness, a month later, I was bitter. I left the safety of the bunker. Rick didn't try to stop me.

Loneliness finally drove me back a year later. In my absence, the Saurinians discovered the location. They set the facility on fire when they left. No one was left alive.

Communication with other groups still fighting for earth, was cut off early on. We'd continued to hope some survived, but the lines were dead long before I left the bunker. Despite rejection by my own people, revenge consumed me. I began my own private campaign of quick and dirty attacks. The Saurinians didn't knew when I would strike, or where. They couldn't capture me. I became Ghost Woman. That was three years ago.

Hu returned, giving off a series of whistles, his long, wedge shaped tail making a whipping sound as he landed on my arm. I smiled and patted his silky head. Over time, I studied the raven's complex language of clicks, whistles, rattles and bell notes, correctly interpreting affection, desire to play and enemies nearby. Having lost his family, Hu adopted me as his own, exhibiting a keen intelligence and ability to decipher some of my commands.

I knew from previous missions, most of the alien ships in North America already departed for their home world, having decimated what remained of the earth's resources, or to rape and plunder other planets. If there were any humans left on earth who hadn't succumbed to radiation sickness, starvation or slavery, I was unaware of it. I battled bouts of grief and depression. Killing aliens became the only thing that kept me alive.

Three days ago, I dragged one of the aliens off and slowly drank his blood, my saliva holding him fast, preventing struggle. I learned about a captured human male. I felt a surge of hope. Perhaps there were more. I was determined to rescue him. He was being held uptown in Central Park. I started out, but a sudden ice storm trapped us underground until today.

A party of twenty lizards held the prisoner. It was too few for a war ship, and too many for a reconnaissance mission, or a slave ship. The question nagged at me. Why hadn't they killed him, or shipped him to one of the mines? It slowly dawned on me. The bastards set a trap for me, using the human as bait. I smiled. I wouldn't be that easy to capture. Over the years, I collected a warehouse of weapons and stashed them all over the city. I took the time to arm myself with the best before starting out.

In addition to the plastic explosives and a dagger, slung over my shoulders, were two guns. One was a lightweight, sonic laser that recharged itself. It destroyed the internal organs and central nervous systems of its targets. The other was a sel-aiming rifle that allowed me to hit targets nine hundred metres away. I didn't pack night goggles. Once the sun went down, there were ice storms. Temperature dipped to fifty below. I was well armed but knew the odds were against me.

Hu flew ahead. As my scout, he looked forward to hunting the lizards. I carefully avoided sink holes, unexploded bombs and crumbling debris. My friend returned and flew around my head chittering a warning. I glanced back in the direction he came from, and spotted two bald mutants. The pale flesh on their faces were botchy with oozing, red pustules. Slung over their shoulders were dead carcasses of rats. They were gutted down the middle, and strung on what once was a curtain rod.

Dressed in rags, bits of raccoon, skunk and wolf fur, they kept their distance, anxious to reach shelter and eat their kill.

"If they don't bother us, we won't bother them," I muttered. The mutants disappeared out of sight. Hu flew off.

~ ~ ~

Fifteen minutes later, I started to sweat, as the temperature began to rise. It would never reach sixty. By noon, it would start to plummet. I spotted a woman's bald head, half buried in the snow. As I came closer, I saw it was only a broken mannequin from what remained of Macy's department store.

A memory took me by surprise. It was the Christmas before the outbreak of war, and the aliens' arrival. It was snowing heavily. My mother and I stood in front of Macy's gaily decorated windows. We watched as mechanical elves helped Santa wrap presents. Christmas carols played in the background. That innocent time was lost to me, like the day magic died in the world, and we embraced technology. Such a deep sense of loss could never be healed. I felt it in my bones.

Hu shrieked a warning. I crawled up to the top of a small hill and peered over.

At the bottom, icicles were hanging from a rusty pipe near an old, broken sewer. The temperature had warmed up enough to melt a few of the icicles, forming a puddle in the snow. Near it, a nest of fifteen reddish-brown roaches a foot high, were hunched over what remained of one of their own eating. Their mouths moved from side to side as they swallowed. Two of them drank water.

The raven's cry and my stealthy movements, stirred the hair on the roach's legs which quivered, alerting them to danger. No longer small and fearful of predators, they looked up. The yellow band around their necks was clearly visible, as their oval, black eyes scoped out the area and spotted me. Without hesitation, they raced at lightning speed on six, hairy legs toward me, making loud, clicking sounds.

"Crap!" I muttered. I hated roaches, especially mutants. Raising my laser, I fired at the two closest, decapitating one and blowing off the legs of the other. The headless one ran around in circles. Hu flew down and finished off the one without legs lying defenseless on his back. The rest of the bugs rushed me knocking me over.

"Get off me," I shrieked, firing into the skittering roaches with the laser. Wounded, their white, sticky blood stank almost as bad as that of reptiles. The bites stung. I could feel the flesh on my face swell up. The roaches were all over me, smothering me. I tripped and fell back, the laser flew out of my hand.

I reached for my rifle, but their blood was like glue, pinning me to the ground. I managed to free one hand and pulled out the dagger. I slashed, stabbed and wedged my knife between the roaches' hard shell. It wasn't easy to penetrate. I let fly curses that would have shocked my mother. Hu dug his claws in and helped to rip off the bugs' outer armor. With a swift motion, he pecked out their eyes and bit off their legs.

I pulled myself free and lunged for my laser. I took out two more, before the last of them skittered away. The survivors flattened their bodies and slipped down broken, hollow drains, into empty buildings, or behind slabs of cement and bricks. I finished off the wounded before Hu got to them. Shuddering, I turned away as he gulped down a few victory morsels. After a few minutes, I announced, "Time to go."

As I got within a half mile of the site, I could hear the aliens give orders in their own harsh tongue, their deep voices audible, even from a distance. I silently made my way through patches of ice, snow, weeds, and rocks, alert for traps. I would have been blown to bits if my expanded senses hadn't detected a switch buried near the surface, that would have set off an explosion the moment I stepped on it. Coming to a set of rocks, I slipped off my backpack, lifted one of the larger boulders and hid the backpack underneath.

Hu returned and flew around me urging me to hurry.

I put out my arm. He flew over and landed. He tossed his black head back and forth staring at me with his three, black eyes, as he shifted on skinny legs.

"Stay," I commanded.

Hu stuck his black head in my face, as if he tried to read my lips.

"Stay," I repeated.

Hu flew up to the top of a stump, where he rustled his black feathers and glared at me. He wasn't happy. He showed his displeasure, by making a series of clicking sounds. I put a finger to my lips and he stopped.

"Stay, I ordered. Hu was my only friend. I couldn't risk losing him.

As the voices got louder, I flattened myself on the ground and crawled closer.

Two Saurinians guarded the prisoner. He was Asian in his early twenties with shoulder-length black hair, high cheekbones and dark eyes. Thin, his jacket was off and he was shivering with the cold. Tied to a pole in front of the ship, his face had a few bruises, but he didn't appear to have any serious wounds.

One of the guards added wood to a fire and two checked the ship. I figured the rest would be inside the ship or outside, looking for me.

The longer I waited, the more danger I was in. It was time to act. I stood up and marched into their midst, turning my weapon on the two guards. I dove for the ground, rolled over and fired repeatedly, taking out another three who burst out of the ship.

Their screams were short-lived. They dropped their weapons as their blood boiled inside, exploding out of every orifice. Internal organs turned to chopped meat, as they collapsed. Charred flesh and green blood stained the slush around the ship.

The human shouted a warning but not in time. A blast from behind knocked me out cold.

~ ~ ~

When I woke up, my head pounded. I was in a capsule inside the hold of the Saurinians' ship, bound by metal rings around my wrists and ankles.

As my vision cleared, I realized one of the lizards was standing in front of me. He had to be nine feet tall, with a scaly, dark green body, a large head and huge, black, oval eyes.

His pupils telescoped, and his black eyes burned with hate. I recognized the leviathan at once. It was Zar-El, a Commander who could speak our language. He was the only one who ever escaped, once I sank my fangs into his neck and started to drink his blood. He wore a tracking devise and his followers successfully located him. I barely escaped with my life.

"Soon, human, you will be on our world, stripped of your clothes and locked in a cage, exhibited for my people to stare at. When they lose interest, I have requested your flesh for a fine meal." The alien's lips drew back exhibiting long, razor-like teeth in what I took to be a grin before stalking off.

I strained against the metal cuffs and pressed my body forward as far as it would go, but even my strength couldn't free me. I took a deep breath. Ingenuity and planning would.

The other prisoner watched the exchange from a similar prison to my left. He looked fit enough to fight. I killed five. That left fifteen against two. I'd been in worse situations, but we needed to escape our shackles before the ship took off.

I elongated and twisted my body as far as it would go. I let rage take me over and felt no pain. As I bent my head I dug my fangs into the flesh of my own shoulder.

The man stared. "What are you doing?"

When I looked up, my mouth was bloody. I held a tiny weapon in my teeth, three inches long. The night before, I planted it in my arm in case of capture. It was as thin as a needle, with a round, steel tip. It could cut through any metal, human or alien.

Directing the tip at my wrists I slowly pressed down on

it with my teeth. A red light shot out. It cut through the steel band as though it were paper. Gently, I let up on the pressure. I didn't want to slice my wrist off. Once my hand was free, I grabbed the weapon and sliced through the rest of the rings before turning it on the capsule itself.

Feeling self-conscious I avoided the prisoner's eyes as I sliced through his capsule, cutting a gap big enough for him to escape as soon as I released him from restraints.

"You're real. I thought Ghost Woman was a myth."

"My name is Ariel," I growled.

"Percy."

As I freed him, I heard heavy steps coming closer. I leapt onto the top of the cargo and crouched low.

Two guards entered the room, saw the empty capsules and spotted Percy. Before they drew their weapons, or could shout, I dropped on top of them knocking them both to the floor.

Baring my fangs, I ripped out one throat as Percy joined me. He pulled out the other alien's knife and buried the blade in his heart. For a guy with a name like Percy, he fought well.

As I stood up, my fangs retracted. I wiped my bloody face and glanced at Percy ashamed, steeling myself, sure I would see disgust. He looked impressed.

"The stories about you are true," he said.

I snarled, "I'm not a fucking vampire or one of them."

"You're awesome."

Surprised and pleased, I felt myself flush at the compliment. To hide my emotion, I handed him one of the dead alien's weapons, retrieving my own. I used my laser to create an opening in the ship's exterior wall. As we began to run, we heard the Saurinians' shouts of alarm.

I placed my weapon on detonate and fired at the ship's engine. It exploded into an instant fireball.

One of the creatures staggered out screaming, his back in flames. Percy aimed his weapon at him and the alien exploded. Bits of charred, green flesh floated to the ground.

Shots whizzed past us. Percy cried out and collapsed. Blood gushed from his thigh. Rolling behind a rock, he tied his belt around the leg to try and stop the flow.

More shots rang out.

I felt a burning pain on my left side, and whipped around. A second shot slammed into my chest. Blood poured through my clothes. It felt like a heavy weight was pressing down on me. I could barely breathe. Strength seeped out of me. My solar disintegrator fell out of my hand. In agony, I made a lunge for it. Zar-El rushed me. With one kick, he sent it out of my reach.

Sure of his kill, he knocked me flat, before he stepped on my neck and roared in victory.

I grabbed his leg and yanked hard. He staggered. I leapt up. Although I tried, I couldn't get close enough to sink my fangs into his bulging neck.

Zar-El aimed a savage kick at the wound in my chest and connected. I cried out and fell to my knees. He snatched my hair and hauled me to my feet. With his weapon pointed at my head, he whispered, "This time, you die."

Hu dropped from the sky and flew, screeching into battle.

Startled, Zar-El looked up. Hu drove his long, black beak straight into one, black eye, ripped it out, and flew off with it. Zar-El screamed and blindly shot at Hu. He missed.

I twisted free, grabbed my weapon, and shot the lizard bastard six times in rapid succession. I watched with pleasure as his massive body bounced, until he was covered in green blood and smoke, and lay still.

I limped over to Percy, whose leg was soaked with blood. He was barely conscious.

As I knelt beside him, he tried to speak. His voice was so weak I had to lean closer.

"Others like us. Not far."

"Don't try to talk," I said gently. I undid the belt that bound his leg and tore the material apart. He groaned.

"This will hurt," I said as I licked his oozing thigh wound. He screamed and lost consciousness. I sealed the artery and outer flesh with my saliva. The wound closed-up, but he lay still.

A freezing wind blew my hood back. I shivered. My own wounds had closed and begun to heal. My strength returned.

The Saurinians would be furious at the massacre, and loss of their ship. They would return, armed with the latest in surveillance, trackers and heat-seeking missiles. I needed to keep a low profile and keep moving. Percy lost a lot of blood, but he would live, if I could get him back to a warm, dry place before the ice storms hit.

Hu returned, and whistled nervously. I glanced up at the dark, grey sky. It was time to go. I took off my jacket and wrapped Percy in it. The extra clothes I buried weren't far. The temperature had already dropped twenty degrees and it started to snow. The weather would steadily decline and be five below by the time we reached safety. I gently placed Percy's unconscious body over my shoulder.

As I moved off, I thought about what he said before he lost consciousness. There were others. I wasn't alone. I had misgivings about my reception, but my heart grew lighter, as I pushed through the thick flakes of falling snow, which quickly covered my tracks.

TAKE ME TO YOUR FUCKING LEADER!
by Olin Wish

What's not to love with a name like that? This one is very entertaining (and not as profane as you might guess from its title.)—Ed.

"WELL, HOWDY, YA'LL!" Sara said to the loose conglomeration of non-biodegradable doll heads. The alien, in turn, regarded the naked mechanism gone to rust with something akin to a mix of curiosity and wonderment. It had traveled a long way on inferior legs made from empty plastic water bottles, recycled radiator hoses, and lawn gnomes all magnetized into some semblance of uniformity. And, before that, an intergalactic spaceship ride that gave new meaning to the archaic and infrequently used term "jet lag". If the creature had a body upon which to inflict self-harm, instead of just a consciousness capable of telekinetic manipulations, it would have slit its own wrists long ago.

That was how pointless, how frustrating, the search for intelligent life on this planet had been. And now this. "Ya'll speak Texan?" the helper bot declared.

Using a plasma screen it had requisitioned from an

ancient junkyard, the alien went for its go-to response. A laugh track from a 1950's sitcom. Canned laughter from a species that by all accounts had gone extinct nearly three hundred years before the alien's arrival. Don't blow this! it thought. If you scare it away, you might not see another for many years.

One of the grand disadvantages of being pure consciousness was the loneliness the alien felt, having lived here, scouring the land and sea for life and coming up empty. The polyhedron helper-bot with its many tarnished surfaces regarded the alien blankly. The alien was shocked and appalled by the reflection of its own deteriorated state in the mechanism's once mirror surfaces. I'd be frightened of me too, it thought. The alien had watched enough pirated American television to know what it was attempting to do fell well outside standard social convention.

Without a mouth and with no way to talk to the helper-bot through thought, which was customary where it was from, the alien was reduced to trying to get its point across by means of hastily-edited snippets of old TV shows. The ones it loved so dearly. Ones about alien invasion in a two-tone world where the men smoked profusely and the women shrieked like startled birds. There were no birds here anymore. But there was an appalling abundance of reptiles. None with the wit necessary to share ideas. Not yet anyway, the alien amended. In a few million years who knew what philosophical feats the bearded lizard might be capable of?

That is, if it didn't manage first to hang itself into extinction on the many plastic rings made for holding six-packs together as it was in the habit of doing. "Ya'll look tired," Sara said amiably. It came so suddenly it startled the alien deep introspection, which, lately, and more often than not, was its preferred mode of existence. "Why don't you come back to the house? Get you a glass of lemonade," Sara persisted. "Ya'll don't wanna be out here after dark. Rogues in the woods be liable to eat'cha up."

By rogues, Sara was of course talking about the ones whose circuitry had gone haywire in the intervening years. Helper-bots who had once started life as up-cyclers or bed companions had gone mad without humans. Some, like the garbage trucks that had tank tread for traversing the toxic mire and accusing spotlight eyes, had become homicidal, even cannibalistic, without human intervention. The mere sight of the alien, with its up-cycled bicycle frames, rusty bird cages, and porta-potties, was enough to incite the devils to anger. With their long, ropey strands of moss which served for hair, hunched shoulders, bound up with inner turmoil and perpetual rictus—

The alien had been forced to reconstruct itself several dozen times in its long history on this world after coming face-to-face with such as these. And while they qualified, in many respects, as intelligent, communication was absolutely out of the question. The Moorish rogues were incapable of empathy, were driven by a singular mad purpose. To kill. To up-cycle. To obey a dead directive. The plasma screen flickered, alight with a handful of living pixels, the others cold and featureless. It was a B-production movie. One of the alien's favorites cast out long ago when the planet was still a vibrant little jewel.

An alien, looking more like a trash compactor, with a dwarf actor inside, descends a silver ramp at a hobble at a set in Hollywood. Through scavenged car stereo speakers, crackling with static, the long-dead actor drones, "Take me to your leader." It's monotone and corny. But the sentiment is real. The loose conglomeration of doll heads, hub caps, and tennis shoes had used this particular film clip more times than it cared to remember in hopes of establishing meaningful dialect with the remnant survivors. For once, the alien feels like this hope might not be in vain.

When Sara hesitates at the cusp of the forest, the alien initiates its old tried and true fallback: Canned laughter. The staticy noise is like a partially dissolved suspension and seems to pacify the servant. It continued on at a brisk pace across a field of brown dirt craters. Ancient timber, uprooted by the explosions, create a buffer between the forest and the house, which is only half a house. The eastern facing wall is a gaping orifice bristling with splinters and stains from carbon residue many times washed during the rainy season.

"Ya'll look like you could use a bite to eat too," Sara says in a southern belle drawl. "How's a ham on rye with a slice of Swiss, a dill pickle, and a cup of tomato bisque sound? Good I hope. Because that's what we're having!" The laugh the mechanism produced was nothing like the canned variety intermixed with uproarious applause the alien was used to. This was of the sweeter, song-bird variety the old masters found so quaint and charming. The alien made a point of sampling the vast collection of captured sound bites for something like it. An old moth-eaten anime short came closest, but was too corrupted by penile enhancement spam to be of any use.

Instead, the alien responded in kind with, "Take me to your leader," as spoken by a trash compactor. "Don't you worry bout that none, sugar," the helper-bot insisted. "I'll take you to meet the misses, first thing. She'll give you a great big dose of southern hospitality, I reckon." For a wonder, the house had not burned to its foundation. Though its roof was badly weather damaged, collapsing in places, and the aforementioned wall was missing, the structure the alien inched toward like a slug on a hot skillet was in surprisingly good shape.

On the hard-packed dirt beside a well were human remains. The helper-bot clicked an imaginary tongue as it passed. "That there's old Mr. Hobbs," Sara said, shaking what served for a head reproachfully. "Sleeping on the job again.

You wouldn't believe me if I told you how long ago I sent him out for a pail of water." Scavengers, feral dogs perhaps, had removed the skeleton's lower half. The button-up shirt it still wore hung in tatters; a rag fluttering in a gentle breeze.

The skull was polished so gleaming white by dust and wind that had the alien eyes, it would have had to divert them from the glare of the sun on its surface. "Just you wait," Sara continued, "See if he don't come runnin' when I ring the dinner bell." The alien couldn't believe its luck. The only human remains it had been able to find that hadn't been upcycled by savage rogues into nutrient-rich mulch was a pinkie finger curled around the steering wheel of a late model sedan.

When the alien had revived her, the human had gasped, clutching feebly at the towering wall of junk before dying again. A painstaking autopsy, using salad tongs and an ice cream scoop, had proven inconclusive. She had remained conscious for less than thirty seconds, after which, her heart had continued beating for nearly three full minutes. Brain death occurred in under ten minutes with no visible explanation as to why. Why hadn't it worked? Why did these creatures stubbornly insist on staying dead? Maybe if they knew how lonely it made the alien they might reconsider, the alien thought.

It wondered if Sara felt the same way about her deceased master, Mr. Hobbs, but had no way of asking her.

Inside, the house was scoured clean. Exposure to the elements was no match for Sara's attention to detail. Dust that blew in from the east barely had a chance to settle before being sucked up and redeposited outside. Evidence from where a family of barn owls had once slept high in the rafters were sprinkled on the water-damaged hardwood floor. Sara dutifully cleaned up their feces, but was unable to hide the stain.

At one time, she might have been able to send for better industrial sanitizer. But seeing how long it was taking Mr. Hobbs to return with the water, the alien suspected the odds of that ever happening unlikely. "You wait here, now," Sara said, "I'll be right back with your refreshments."

One time, in the Marianas Trench, the alien had bechanced a fish like something out of the devil's nightmares. It had become so excited it nearly lost cohesion of the fishing nets, ship wreckage, and oil drums that made up its physical manifestation. It equalized quickly though and tried making small talk using an "I Love Lucy" re-run it kept dry inside a bubble of displaced salt water. Its desire to make friends had somehow been lost in translation though. The fish had darted into the inky blackness never to be seen nor heard from again. That had been the closest the alien had ever come to meaningful, productive discourse until now.

The plasma screen flickered, and two-thirds of Ricky Ricardo yelled out something unintelligible out across the wrecked house from the treble speakers from a 1994 Honda Civic. Sara returned to the main hall at what amounted to a canter for the polyhedron helper-bot. "Did you say something, sugar?" The trash heap attempted a polite response, but fell short. This time, the canned applause came off condescending. Do you dream? It so wanted to ask. If Sara dreamed then there was a real chance they could communicate on some fundamental level.

She would at least be made aware of the alien's true intentions for being here. "Forgive me," Sara said. She rolled hesitantly toward the refuse. This is it, the alien thought. The part where she gets scared and swims off in a hurry. Only, this wasn't the ocean. Things on land did things different. The alien prepared itself for another attack. Perhaps this time it would simply give up and refuse to reassemble.

This was a dead place, full of awful things made worse by the things the dead left behind to replace themselves. "Seems we're fresh out of ham on rye. Same with the lemonade, I'm afraid. Soon as Mr. Hobbs returns with the water I can see about making tea. Do you take sugar and milk in yours, Mr.—"

"Dillinger," the plasma pixels coalesced and croaked, "John Dillinger."

The film, starring Lawrence Tierney in one of his earlier roles, had gone largely unnoticed by critics the world over. It was, however, heralded by aliens, as a prize example of

American cinema. "Well then, Mr. Dillinger," Sara replied crisply, "shall we see about the misses then, anyway?" It was a question that brooked no response. The alien offered none. Only followed at a snail's crawl as Sara tumbled down the hall into the darkened interior beyond the deteriorating staircase.

The alien was so relieved she hadn't insisted on escorting it upstairs it might have sighed. The weight of its sun-bleached crumbling plastic was immense. In a dark room, beyond a door that creaked, the alien saw the misses through a sliver of sunlight. She lay in a bed, mostly springs, draped in a white sheet as thin and delicate as wood ash. Plastic tubing, once connected to the misses' veins, and also to her urinary tract, now lay coiled feebly in the bones of her inner elbow and also between her femurs.

The alien scarcely believed what it saw. An intact skeleton, artfully preserved by Sara and her obsessive cleaning. "Mr. Dillinger," Sara began, "allow me to introduce you to the lady of the house, Ms. Hobbs." Wooden shutters prevented some of the dust and most of the sunlight from infiltrating Ms. Hobbs' sick room. In one swift motion, Sara undid the shutters so that her guest might greet the lady proper.

"She ain't been herself of late," Sara admitted, "but ain't nothing a little of Aunt Sara's world-famous chicken soup can't cure." The alien wanted to tell Sara it was prepared to do for the misses what even she and her chicken soup could not. "What I'm about to do might scare you," a doctor in a white coat in two-tone said, appearing on the screen. "I want you to relax and take a deep breath."

The alien feared that the moment it reached for the misses, Sara would interpret it as a sign of aggression. The alien hadn't seen Sara fight, but if her efficiency in the kitchen and elsewhere were any sort of indicator, it suspected she could make quick work of an old junk heap. She had managed this long, keeping away the rouge upcycles, the riffraff, the upstart psychopaths, without any explanation. If the alien grew too presumptuous, too forward, it suspected Sara would reveal how she had done it in no time flat.

The alien would learn to his peril what sort of momma bear default setting Mr. and Ms. Hobbs had installed in the police polyhedron. Thin ice, the alien thought. You're already dancing on it. So might as well put on your tap shoes. It reached out an appendage comprised primarily of fossilized dirty diapers. Sara stiffened opposite the open window. This is it, the alien thought. As soon as I touch the bones the fight will be on. It cringed at the thought of having to assemble from the whirlwind of scattered toys and garbage bagged lawn clippings. But felt it had come too far to go back now.

Applause filled the room, echoing in the din of silence. Ms. Hobbs gasped as soon as the last stitch of flesh was returned to her. Great, the alien thought. Here we go again. It sighed inwardly, resigned to the fact it would never find a companion here worth having. The bones, restored to a woman in her prime, clawed at the IV pole beyond her bed railing, toppling it. The sound it made crashing down seemed to awaken Sara from an improbable dream. "I know just what to do!" She hollered. "Just you wait, Ms. Hobbs. We'll get you all fixed up!"

She rushed from the room and returned from down the hall with a push cart and a tall green cylindrical tank. Ms. Hobbs stared with bug eyes at the cylinder. She had crawled most of the way across the room and had just about abandoned hope. The alien had seen it before. The resignation for death. It knew that look. At sight of Sara with the pushcart, Ms. Hobb's limbs were revitalized. She clawed frantically at the clear plastic face mask. Before it was even in place, Sara turned a valve, releasing a hiss that startled the alien, once more, from its bright internal commentary.

This time, as Ms. Hobbs gasped, fogging the clear plastic, she seemed to be doing better. Her shoulders heaved and she stared, disoriented, into a corner of the room the sunlight hadn't reached. "Oh, praise Jesus!" The helper-bot howled and would have wept if the humans had thought to gift her with the ability. "It's a miracle!" Wild applause, canned laugh tracks, and flickering erratic images emanated from and graced the mostly broken plasma screen. At last! the alien thought. Success! One with the fortitude to stay alive where all others hadn't.

"I can't—"

Ms. Hobbs moaned.

"I can't," she repeated, lungs billowing. Such curious fixtures, the alien reflected. How they balloon full of gaseous material and then deflate again. Over and over again to initiate metabolic processes. Nearly ten percent of this species DNA consisted of the leftovers from ancient viruses. Perhaps the organs were a lingering hold over, like the appendix, with no real practical application. Heck, even the mitochondria functioned as something else originally. A single celled organism that evolved to serve as critical energy producers in these critters.

All this the alien knew from watching public access television and from a water damaged text book recovered from the ruins of a place of learning. The hardest part had been teaching itself the most common of the many subcategories of dialects these creatures used by pushing wind past flaps of skin called the larynx. The resultant resonance had meaning, was assigned value, the alien learned early on. It wasn't quite sure what "Texan" was, but for the most part it understood Sara just fine. A branch of English, it assumed. Or perhaps a precursor, like Latin. A deteriorated form, scarcely used.

Once it picked up the habit of watching shows, piecing out irregularities and inconsistencies was a snap.

"I can't—"

Ms. Hobbs tried again. She had yet to become aware of the alien's presence looming over her like some angelic midden heap, some petroleum-based, mountainous lifeform who wished her glad tidings. The alien knew what "I can't" meant. To negate, to declare an unwillingness. The contraction of the words cannot. But was confused by her reluctance to elaborate. In a desperate bid to garner attention from the naked human, the alien began peppering her with sound bites of the word "fuck" gathered from many thousands of sampled American movies.

In the old form, fuck implied urgency. A seriousness of task this occasion warranted. "I can't breathe!" Ms. Hobbs shrieked into the face mask, ignoring the alien. Now the alien was thoroughly confused. What little it knew of human physiology was limited to a seventh-grade life sciences text book. But even it was not so clueless as to not understand the relationship between the former dominant species and their precious oxygen.

What came out of the face mask in a hurry was an almost hundred percent pure form of the gaseous element and yet still she struggled. Confused, the alien tried sampling the surrounding atmosphere for clues. Comprised primarily of nitrogen at 81.6%, oxygen was the third most abundant gas at 2.53%, narrowly losing the second-place spot to nitrous oxide at 7.8%. The rest were of such small concentration as to barely be a concern. Methane remained steady at 4%, carbon dioxide 2.4%, Argon 1.3%, and ozone 0.37%. But the alien knew one of these gases had to be responsible for her violent and less than friendly reaction.

She retched, but because her stomach was empty nothing came out. Her bowels clinched, but for the same reason, produced no flatulence. "It burns!" Ms. Hobbs wailed. "Oh God, it burns!"

"What do we do?" Sara asked the collection of moth-eaten granny panties and feminine hygiene products, for once sounding like a small child instead of the take-charge head of household the alien initially mistook her for. Her scared words and uncertain tone attracted Ms. Hobb's attention, who turned to look at her. "Sara!" the young woman said. "Oh, thank God! Please! Help me!"

"What do you need, Ms. Hobbs?" Sara asked, falling forward on her many surfaces towards the woman. Sara made the "S" in Ms. into a long "Z" sound which the alien found intriguing. Another peculiarity of the Texan dialect? "Anything," Sara said, just short of being groped at by Ms. Hobbs' talon fingers. "Just you say the word."

"More!"

Sara opened the valve all the way. A huge roar ensued as oxygen flooded the face mask. This can't go on much longer, the alien thought. Better get from her the information I need and be done with it. Again, a black and white image of

Lawrence Tierney as John Dillinger flicked across the upcycled plasma. Then it was Clark Gable in a cowboy hat. "Howdy, ma'am," the image said. Ms. Hobbs' head whipped around to face the pile of junk occupying an entire corner of her sick room.

"Ms. Hobbs," Sara said with a long "Z", "This here's Mr. John Dillinger. He came here to help us. Ain't that right, Mr. Dillinger?" By now, the alien would have thought Sara had learned not to ask of it direction questions. But he gave her a round of applause anyway, if only to confirm her suspicions, intermixed with a few more swear words to drive the point home. Panting on her hands and knees on the floor at the foot of the bed, Ms. Hobbs turned once more to regard the towering, yet surprisingly sterile, mound of garbage. As soon as it had her full attention, the alien played the grainy clip of the cumbersome space ambassador with the dead little person inside descending the ramp from the yawning opening in its spaceship.

"Take me to your leader."

Hobbs regarded the failing television screen with something across between horror and fascination. How long had it been since she had bore witness to one of the great American classics? The alien wondered.

DEAD WRONG
by Vonnie Winslow Crist

Here's another zombie story for you deadheads out there, meshed with another popular genre.—Ed.

TO THE UNDEAD, WE'RE nothing but a snack, thought Allie "Mac" MacDougal.

It was a reality harsher than the battles Mac fought in while in the Army, or anything she saw when she patrolled the Philadelphia streets as a beat cop. But when the outbreak started, she knew she had the skills needed to deal with the dead. She gave up her teaching position at the police academy and volunteered to train rookies to work the front line. Though some days, after dealing with rotting flesh, maggots, and sprays of bone and blood from reanimated corpses, retirement looked good.

MacDougal glanced at the rookie—he was sitting next to her in the car. An Emergency Urban Outbreak Control, Department of Thaumaturgical and Tactical Response mandate forced the academy to churn out recruits at a quick pace. He was a product of this accelerated training.

It was up to Mac to make sure he understood that one misstep could lead to a newly-minted DOT&TR Special

Forces officer would become worm-fodder. Good news was, they didn't have to Mirandize or handle their suspects with kid gloves. Their only goal was the death of the dead, with minimal loss of human life.

She glanced at the rookie again. They seemed to get younger with each passing month. What kind of world was her generation leaving to these kids barely out of their teens? At least, she hoped he was out of his teens.

As if he'd heard her thoughts, he turned toward her. "Don't worry, Mac. I'm not scared of the undead."

"You should be," she replied as she pulled their car into the Forever Rest Cemetery's parking lot and turned off the headlights. Being too self-assured could cost you your life in this new world, where crime syndicates employed necromancers to keep law enforcement busy protecting the public from the reanimated dead while the criminal sector stole, maimed, and murdered without mercy.

"The DOT&TR has charged me with training rookies to use magic and weapons to kill the dead after they return," began Mac.

The new officer appeared to tune her out as he released his seatbelt and looked eagerly through the squad car's windshield.

"Take a deep breath, focus on me, and listen," she said. "You'd be surprised to know how many don't make it through their first day because they're book-smart but inexperienced."

"I'm ready," he said.

She hoped that was true.

"Cemetery fence is down."

"That's why we're here, Taylor." She wished his last name didn't sound like a first name. She'd stopped using first names after returning to the street. "Had the threat been contained, a squad of academy recruits would deal with it."

Taylor nodded as he climbed out of the vehicle and double-checked his protective gear and weapons.

Before exiting the car, Mac checked its computer screen. "According to department records, there are twenty-six dead loose. We'll start at the graveyard, and then work our way out from there. The undead usually travel in packs. It's the stragglers that are a problem," she explained.

"I guess we're lucky it's a tiny cemetery, so there weren't many bodies to reanimate," said Taylor. "Can you imagine if there were acres of graves?"

"I don't have to imagine. I've been dispatched to locations where the undead outnumbered DOT&TR officers by the hundreds. The corpses tore through the living and kept coming." She paused, remembering fallen friends. "Stopping them was difficult. And no matter their station, a person is doomed once bitten. Whether colleague or civilian, euthanasia is the standing order."

"I know."

"Taylor, never let your guard down. Not even for a minute."

"Got it," said her new partner.

As soon as they entered the Forever Rest Cemetery, Mac spotted a corpse trying to fight its way out by repeatedly banging into a portion of stone wall. Here was an opportunity for Taylor to get his first kill with minimum danger.

"You take this one."

"Sure," said Taylor.

He extended his left hand, chanted the prescribed incantation, then shot the corpse between its eye sockets. Flailing its arms and opening and closing its jaws, the cadaver dropped to the ground. It took a few seconds for the thing to die. Again.

"Good work," said Mac. "But remember, when dealing with a group, reloading time needs to be taken into consideration. Keeping the largest possible distance between yourself and the undead is. . ."

"No worries. I'm quick." There was excitement in his voice.

"So are they," she warned. Mac knew encounters with packs required greater speed; plus—they'd be messy. The real test was yet to come.

Leaving the carcass for the clean-up crew, they exited the graveyard.

"The undead are drawn to the lights and sounds of

people, so we'll begin searching the neighborhood to the east. Keep your..."

"Eyes open for corpse-sign. And don't depend on your ears, because most of them make little noise."

"Right." His enthusiasm both reassured and worried Mac. There was no room for mistakes.

Mandatory streetlights illuminated the road before them as they followed a trail of corpse-sign. Tracking the dead was easier when there wasn't any rain to wash away the dirt, debris, and body bits which fell from them.

A shrieking car alarm disrupted the quiet.

"That's probably them," said Mac as she and Taylor un-holstered their guns.

Side by side, they ran in the direction of the commotion. When they reached the last building three blocks down, they peered around the edge and saw a pack clawing at a parked minivan. Attracted by the noise and flashing lights, it appeared all of the wandering dead from Forever Rest Cemetery had congregated around the vehicle.

"I hope there's no one alive in there." Taylor sounded worried.

"Must be people inside." She studied her partner. "Kids probably, since they don't know how to turn off the alarm or drive away." Mac had learned to take a head shot without regard for the age at death of the undead. Taylor needed to be prepared to do likewise. "No matter the size or gender, our goal is to put down the dead while avoiding their jaws. We're not heroes."

"You're too cynical. There's always a chance to save people," he responded.

"And you're not cynical enough. We've got to kill them all."

He opened his mouth as if to object.

"At least the ones on the outside of the van," Mac added. "Don't forget, mercy can get you killed."

She took his silence as agreement.

"A bullet through the brain while chanting a lethal spell," she reminded him. "And if there are dead kids, remember, they are corpses, not children."

"I know."

Maybe Mac was worried about nothing. Taylor seemed calm as they stepped from behind the building and walked toward the van. Following protocol, they called forth magic and shot the corpses.

Like marionettes whose strings had been cut, the undead fell.

As she'd anticipated, some of the cadavers were children. Mac took out three of the undead kids, but the fourth managed to shuffle to Taylor's side of the vehicle before she could kill it. She no longer had a clear shot.

"Shoot!" she yelled at her partner from her side of the van.

He didn't fire.

"Dammit, shoot!" Mac took out the last corpse on her side of the vehicle and rushed around the back of the van. She was too late. The undead kid and another corpse were latched onto Taylor. After kicking the larger cadaver off of her partner, she shot it. She hoped Taylor's body armor had protected him from a bite.

As for the dead kid, it had a vice grip. When Mac finally pulled its corpse off of Taylor, she heard bones snapping. There was a loud pop when she killed it.

"Why didn't you shoot?"

Helmet still strapped on, visor and neck-guard in place, Taylor didn't answer as he checked his legs, arms, and chest.

Mac noticed his torn glove first.

"It's just an abrasion," her partner said as he examined the exposed part of his hand.

"Let me have a look."

A bite mark shaped like a half moon marred the edge of his palm. A matching bloody half-moon was visible on the back of his hand. Neither of them spoke as they both raised their visors.

"Maybe, it's not that bad," whispered Taylor as he gazed up at her. "Maybe, because I was using magic. . ."

"That's not how it works."

"I know." He pressed his lips together, but there were no tears. "How long do I have before I turn?"

"It varies." Mac didn't have the heart to tell him he only had minutes.

"Will it hurt?"

"I don't think so." She'd witnessed enough of the living to dead to reanimated corpse transitions to believe pain wasn't part of the process.

"What about the children in the van? Are they safe?"

Mac stepped between the vehicle and Taylor. "Their parents will be out here soon to retrieve them. Let's get you back to the car."

"Good idea." He looked at his hand as they walked. "I messed up."

Mac put her arm around his shoulders. "You're not the first." Or the second she could have added. Curse the academy for sending her kindhearted rookies. Only grizzled old women and men should have to face this horror.

It took about five blocks for her partner to collapse. Mac knelt beside him, removed his helmet, and took his hand.

"You buy the ticket, you take the ride—isn't that what they say?" Taylor's eyes were locked on Mac's eyes. He was still fighting the inevitable. "But it's okay, I saved those kids."

"Yeah, you're a hero." No need to tell him both of the children inside the van, caught in the cross-fire, were dead. In a few minutes, she'd go back to the van and make sure they stayed that way.

"It's not your fault." His grip on her hand tightened. "I

just couldn't shoot a kid—not even a dead one."

"I know," said Mac. She also knew, because she could shoot the dead, no matter their age, she'd continue losing partners until the outbreak was over. Assuming it ended before she made a wrong choice.

Still holding his hand, she watched the brightness leave Taylor's eyes. Then, on the silent street beneath dim stars, she raised her gun. When she felt his slack fingers begin to move, her mind screamed, *This is wrong—he's too young.* Mac mumbled an incantation and pulled the trigger.

•

AND TO ALL A GOOD NIGHT!

by Steve Bissonnette

This story is about young people—much like a previous tale in this collection—but it may be the hardest hitting piece in the whole book.—Ed.

IT WAS CHRISTMAS EVE in Commerce, NH; already it was sticky-feeling 95 degrees. Main Street was decorated with Independence Day flags no one had bothered taking down. Dried out Maple trees lurked over asphalt streets. Heat that had built up in the pavement radiated back towards the sky in waves, like fingers reaching up to strangle the morning air. Telephone poles stood vigil over discarded belongings which had once been treasured objects. No longer carrying the currents of human activity, electric wire and telephone cables were useless strands strung from pole to pole.

Every storefront sat empty, most with broken windows and doors creaking open and shut in the breeze. Paint dried and peeled revealing aged clapboards; vinyl siding faded and warped in the heat. Signs advertising ice cold beer faded in the sun alongside shingles hung by attorneys and accountants. The stories they told were ending—fire was coming. Once the flames had finished their work all would be lost to the icy emptiness of an indifferent universe.

Three old-school car salesmen were the only ones in town who weren't hiding somewhere underground. Big Bob Bentley was outside on the car lot his family had owned for three generations. A large man with a booming voice, he seemed tiny in comparison to the looming disaster. His two High-powered salesmen, Jim 'Jalopy' Jackson and Easy Eddie Mountebank, sat inside making small talk. Bob hadn't paid them in months. Even if he had, there was nowhere left to cash the check or spend the money.

"I don't know," Jim said. "I think this is it for me."

"Don't be a quitter, man!" Ed teased, "it ain't over til the sun scorches your shorts."

From his cubicle inside the showroom of *Big Bob's Auto Emporium,* Jim could see the town clock looming over empty streets. "It finally stopped."

"What stopped?" Ed asked.

"The clock, it finally stopped. And look...it stopped exactly at 10:10, like a big ole smile. That's what you would call 'ironic'."

"Yeah maybe," Ed said. "But I think time is just laughing at us."

"What do you mean?"

"It's kind of like a woman that you've ignored forever"

Ed said. "Because you figure she'll always be there. Then you're surprised when she ups and leaves you—and you're left crying like a baby. She's not coming back."

~ ~ ~

Outside on his sales lot, Bob lovingly stroked the curves of his 1959 Cadillac Eldorado Biarritz convertible. In one hand was the softest cloth he could find, in the other a near-empty bottle of car polish. His employees sat inside and watched from their desk.

"What's he doing?" asked Ed.

"What do you think?" Jim answered. "He wants the car to look good."

"For who? The cockroaches?"

Jim was a fan of everything from the 1950's era. He could tell you what songs were popular, who was in office, and which movie stars were lighting up the silver screen. He loved that beautiful old Caddy as much as Bob. "When that beast was built, you could get a gallon of gas for like a quarter."

"It cost more than that," Ed said.

"No, it was about a quarter." Jim replied.

"That's not what I meant. I meant we're paying the cost now."

"Don't start that crap again. They didn't know."

Ed didn't share his coworker's appreciation for America's so-called Golden Age. "Maybe back in the 50's they didn't worry about it, but you can't tell me that somewhere along the way someone didn't figure it out."

"Lighten up. It's not like the world's coming to an end." Jim paused. "Oh yeah, maybe it is."

There was no point in replying to Jim's stupid comment; besides, Ed wasn't in the mood.

Out on the sales lot, Bob continued shining his car as if he were caressing the curves of his lover's skin. He ran his hands along a glistening strip of chrome on the big tail-fin, then fondled his way down the car's backside, around the two bullet-point taillights, before finishing with the car's giant chrome bumper.

"You think the car's going to survive?" Ed asked.

"Doubt it," Jim replied.

"I see what he's trying to do. He's got it way up there on that cement podium, he put a steel roof over the top of everything, and took the tires off; I guess I understand all that. But what's up with leaving the windows down and the top partly open? Isn't that going to let bugs in?"

Jim thought a minute. "I think he figures if the air can circulate through, the car won't get hot enough to melt the interior."

"You know," Ed said. "Nothing's going to save us or that car. I mean, maybe the car will last longer than us—but it's toast."

"If it makes him feel better, I say let him try."

"Try?" Ed still didn't understand. "Why bother?"

Jim pondered what his legacy would be if things were different. "Maybe it's his tombstone."

They sat in silence a few minutes as Bob put the finishing touches on his car. Watching the winter sun burn its low arc along the horizon, Jim thought about what was coming. "You realize Thursday was winter solstice?"

"Yeah. . .so?" Ed replied.

"The days are going to start getting longer now; more sun. . .higher in the sky. . .all that. The ole Earth oven is about to be set on high."

Both men understood what that meant. "Shit," Ed muttered, "thanks for reminding me."

"Reminding you? How could you forget?"

"I guess you could call it a survival skill," Ed replied.

Everyone did what they could to get by, many lived in their basement, or—if they'd been able to afford one—a specially-constructed heat-resistant capsule. Some preppers had been able to build bunkers complete with refrigeration and air conditioning powered by the sun. Jim thought about his neighbors who were holed up in their survival compound. "How long you think the Norris's are going to be able to hold on?"

Ed laughed. "Bet someone breaks into their compound. I hear he has ice cubes in there, imagine that. . .what I wouldn't give for a cold beer right now."

"If someone breaks in, I expect they won't like what happens."

"Whatever! All they're accomplishing up there is making sure they're the last ones to go. Nothing like dying lonely, I suppose."

Jim agreed. "On that note: Merry Christmas, friend."

"Yeah, *Merry* alright! Probably no food convoy again tonight."

Jim shook his head in agreement. "Par for the course, isn't it? I'm starting to think they're going to let us starve."

"I had the same thought; probably some bureaucrat decided to focus resources on more vital areas."

"Well thank God for the survival packets." Jim tried to strike a positive note. "We saved a powdered-ham dinner for tonight. It's kind of a tradition in my family—minus the powdered part."

"We used to watch Christmas specials on TV, and then go to Midnight Mass. Obviously not happening tonight," said Ed. "But if you guys want to come by, we're gonna crank-up the radio and see if we can find any Christmas music."

"Maybe you can find some toilet paper, we ran out last night."

"I might be able to spare a few rolls. If you have some filters for a water recycling system we could make a trade."

Like everyone else in the town, Jim didn't have much of anything left to barter. "Too bad we couldn't bottle up bullshit and trade that for something useful."

"That, my friend, would make us politicians."

"You weren't listening, I said *useful.*"

Ed laughed. "Okay then, it would make us preachers."

"I suppose we could trade a couple rolls of toilet paper for a ticket to heaven," Jim offered.

"I'd give up all my toilet paper for a ticket out of here."

Like everyone else trapped in a scorch-zone, the residents of Commerce, NH could not leave. To prevent chaos, the government did not allow out-of-zone-migration unless the applicant had a vital skill needed elsewhere, or was lucky enough to get accepted into the military. Every month there were fewer areas considered habitable, and allowing mass migration to those places would benefit no one. It was a strictly enforced prohibition; even if you somehow made it past the troops surrounding your zone you would probably be killed by the occupants of the next one.

What little activity was happening in Commerce was happening at night—away from the heat of day. By 10:00 AM it was way past quitting time; the men prepared to go home for the day. Their children were just getting started. They had spent the last week scrounging for treasure in the form of anything they could find to drink. Their loot included alcohol stolen from cubby holes, mouthwash, cleaning supplies, and cough syrup. Some of them managed to steal old prescriptions and various other substances to add to the mix.

If their parents had known what they were up to it's possible that they might have tried to stop them. Or they might have envied their children for making such a bold choice. None of them were headed to college. They would never be able to buy a house, or raise a family. Everything was already decided for them. Denied their opportunity to rebel, they seized upon the one thing they could still control. It felt like a gift, being able to make such a choice, so they resolved to do it on Christmas Eve.

~ ~ ~

On the outskirts of town, a group of teenagers gathered, each carrying with them an assortment of bottles containing whatever liquids they managed to scavenge. The thermometer dial was now touching the 100-Degree mark and the humidity made it hard to breathe. Slowly the group shuffled toward what had been the town beach. Now nothing more than a shallow, bacteria-infested pool of mud, it was the closest thing to a hangout spot they had.

~ ~ ~

Robert Edward Bentley III wanted nothing to do with his father, Bob Bentley. His friends knew not to call him by that name; they called him Reb. But regardless of what name he went by, there was no doubt that Reb was Big Bob's son. In Commerce, and the surrounding area, the Bentley Men were known for their intimidating size and strong personality—Reb was no exception. He was a natural leader among his peers. As the adolescents of the town assembled for their carcinogenic undertaking, he was their Shepherd.

Reb counted how many others had shown up. He noted that a few were missing. "Anyone know if Greg and Judi are still in?"

"I don't think they're coming," answered Jake Deblois, the banker's son. "They're at the library stealing books or something."

"Whatever," Reb answered. "Let's get this party started."

~ ~ ~

By the time Big Bob Bentley made it to his heat shelter, his son wasn't there. "Where's Robert?" he asked his wife.

"Who knows?" she answered. "He took off with friends."

"Should I go look for him?"

"Why? You plan on dragging him back here so he can make us miserable? I'd like to get some sleep. Just let him be."

Bob agreed. "I suppose you're right. Let him have his fun."

Reb and his friends weren't out to have a good time. They'd heard about fun things like going to movies, and cruising Main Street, but that was a world away, and the business at hand was gravely serious.

Jake managed a few words. "I wonder what it was like to sit in an air-conditioned room all day and talk to your friends on the computer?"

It was the kind of thing many of them wondered about,

but no one answered.

Reb took charge of the group. He counted how many had shown up. "Alright, there are 17 of us and 83 sleeping pills—thanks, Johnny. I guess your mom won't be sleeping too good today."

"I left her one," he said.

The group laughed.

From within the group, a girl named Vickie spoke up. "I think we should make sure everyone knows they can change their mind."

"I vote we all go out for ice cream instead," said Jake.

"Yes, that's a wonderful idea," said Reb. "Just as soon as I finish swimming a few laps in my Olympic pool."

Jake smirked. "I guess we have so many choices we don't know what to do."

"Seriously," Reb said. "If you don't want to do this you don't have to. But you should head home now because it's going to be a miserable day out here."

No one left. Reb continued. "We need to make a quick run into town and have some fun at Bob's. You guys get everything mixed together so it'll be ready when we get back."

"We want fun too!" Vickie said.

Reb was a bit surprised he hadn't thought of it already. There was no reason not to do it at the car lot. "Ok, who votes that we move this project to *Big Bob's car lot*?"

Everyone raised their hand.

"Alright," Reb said. "Let's get this shit gathered up and head back to town before it gets any friggin hotter."

Gathering their supplies, the group worked their way back to town, toward the sales lot. Along the way they encountered a shuttered Dairy Queen withering in the late morning sunshine.

"Place is never open when you need it," Reb joked.

"Be a good place to open an ice cream stand," said Jake.

~ ~ ~

Big Bob's Auto Emporium glistened in the sunshine as they approached. From within the group, Jake yelled out "You suppose any of those still run?"

"They've all got a lifetime warranty, my friend," Reb answered. "As long as you die when you're supposed to."

"When are we supposed to die?"

Pointing at the Caddy on its concrete throne, Reb said "I need everyone to get on the front of that car and help me push it off."

"It's got no tires! It probably weighs like a million tons, how we supposed to push it off there?" asked Jake.

"It's heavy. On the count of three don't push just a little—give it everything you got. We gotta get it off the jack stands and over the side."

Jake said, "Won't that void the warranty?"

"I hope it voids my old man," Reb said. "All he cares

about is these stupid cars."

One by one they climbed onto the podium and gathered at the front of the car. Reb's heart beat a little faster as he got close enough to put his hands on the vehicle. He'd imagined himself doing this at least a hundred times, and now here he was, hurting the old man right where it counted! After looking around to confirm that everyone was ready, Reb started to count. "1...2...3!"

The Caddy moved slightly before regaining its balance. Reb repeated the count. "Push like you mean it!"

This time the big car rocked backward, then lurched to the left, over the side of the concrete pillar. As it crashed the children jumped away, first in surprise, then in delight. With a post from the awning poking through the convertible top, and a corner of concrete stabbing through the floorboards, the Cadillac lay precariously on its side.

"You think we can finish rolling this thing over?"

"I doubt it," Reb answered. "But let's try. 1...2...3!"

With surprising ease, the car finished its death roll, landing upside down on top of a vintage Prius parked next to the Caddy's concrete platform. "Damn!" Reb exclaimed, "how cool is that!"

Now bent and leaning slightly to the side, the steel awning offered a mirage of shade. The teens lingered under its promise. The 100 Degree air was damp and heavy, the kind of day where you wish for rain to cool everything down.

But it didn't rain very often, and never enough to make a difference.

Sensing the day's waning, Reb spoke up. "If we're going to do this, we should get started. Let's get everything piled up here and start mixing it all together. Everything but the sleeping pills."

"And the stuff that says PM or 'nighttime'," offered Vickie. "Those are kind of like sleeping pills too."

"Good point," Reb answered. "Let's keep that shit separate."

Dutifully, the participants began pouring their liquids and crushed tablets into two five-gallon pails set in the middle of their concrete altar. Reb counted out the pills again. "We've got 83 sleeping pills and 32 PM pills" he announced.

Vickie said, "If everyone gets four sleeping pills and two PM pills. . .except one of us gets five 5 sleeping pills and no PM pills. . .we can add the rest to the mix and that way everyone gets about the same."

"What a nerd," said someone in the crowd.

"Maybe," said Reb as he did the math in his head, "but I think she's right. Everyone cool with that idea?"

"Who gets the five sleeping pills?" Jake asked.

"Seriously?" Said Reb, "who cares? Between the pills and the cocktail, it doesn't matter. But you can have the five if it makes you feel like a winner. Everybody ok with that?"

Everyone nodded in agreement; Reb began handing out

the pills. He noticed a bottle of Scotch in Jake's hand. "Hold off on that one," he said, "let's pass it around."

Jake took the first taste and nearly spat out the warm drink. "Holy shit! How do they drink this stuff?"

"Well," replied Vickie, "it is technically a poison so. . ."

"Poison? My dad loves this crap."

"It's slow poison. That way you have time to share the joy. Besides, it's not usually served at 100 Degrees."

Undeterred by the taste, everyone took turns sipping the liquor as the rest of the drink was mixed together in the buckets. Once the bottle was empty, the pills handed out, and the drink mixed—it was time.

Looking around at his co-conspirators, Reb sighed. "Anyone wanna sing a Christmas song or something?"

Even in the darkness of the moment, some of the teens managed a chuckle. "Your dad is going to be some pissed about that car," said Vickie.

"I know, it'll probably take him a while to notice that I'm dead," answered Reb. "You guys ready for this?" he asked. Even Jake didn't respond. "I guess that's a dumb question, how could anyone be ready for this? I'm just gonna do it," Reb declared as he took the first cupful of the concoction.

Following his lead, the rest of the group began swallowing their pills and washing it down with the drink they had made. "No one is exploding," Vickie joked nervously as she swallowed her pills.

Jake went last. Once it was his turn, he dipped his cup into a bucket, raised it up, and declared, "Merry Christmas to all, and to all a goodnight!"

~ ~ ~

As the day came to an end, some of the parents had begun to wonder why their children hadn't returned home. They found the answer after sunset. Commerce no longer had an emergency response system, just two EMT's with no supplies. One of them was Jim Jackson. He stood looking around at the car lot and counted 17 people dead or dying, and he noticed the beautiful old Caddy now laying on top of the Prius. "Damn tragedy," he mumbled to his partner, Jill. "What should we do?"

Jill didn't have an answer. Looking around, she saw 17 children—she had known most of them since birth. She tried not to let the tears show. "I don't know; what can we do?"

On the concrete podium where the Caddy used to sit, parents held their children and looked to Jim for some kind of answer. "Let's send someone to Norris's place; maybe he has some meds he can spare."

Jill just stared at him blankly.

"What?" Jim asked.

"Norris is dead. Someone broke into his compound, killed him and his family, and cleaned the place out."

"Why didn't someone tell me?" Jim asked.

"I just heard about it myself. I guess Sarah Edney found

them up there yesterday."

"I'm his neighbor! You'd think someone would have taken a minute to let me know."

"Can we talk about this some other time?" Jill asked. "Three of them are still breathing. I told their parents to keep them propped on their side. What do you want to do?"

"How should I know?"

"Because it's just us—and you're still squad leader; I certainly don't want the job," Jill said. "And I already tried radioing for a Medevac. I got nothing. Either the battery is dead, or they just don't want to answer."

"They've left us here to die."

Vickie's mother cradled her still-breathing daughter in her arms and wailed. "What are you going to do? Can't you help her?"

Never in his life had Jim felt so powerless. This was a responsibility he didn't want, and one he couldn't manage. Without looking directly at any of the parents he offered what advice he could. "Folks," he said, "I'm very sorry; I truly am. I know most of these kids. . .and I know most of you."

"Help us!" one of the parents yelled out.

"There is nothing I can do," he answered. It sounded to him like someone else standing there, trying to take charge of the mess. "If your child is still breathing the only thing you can do is bring them home, make them as comfortable as you can. Keep them on their side, make sure their vomit doesn't go back down their throat."

"That's it? That's all you got?" snapped Jake's dad through his tears.

"That's all I got. That's all any of us got," Jim answered. "I'm sorry; this is a terrible mess. I have to go tell Bob about his son, and his car. If someone could round up as many people as possible while I'm gone—well, that would be helpful. And have them bring shovels."

"Shovels?" asked Vickie's mother. "What for?"

No sooner had she asked the question than she realized why no one was going to answer.

~ ~ ~

It was Christmas morning in the town of Commerce, NH; the sun was rising and already it was 96 Degrees. A warm breeze was blowing over fourteen newly dug unmarked graves in the churchyard. There would be three more by New Years.

Bob Bentley stood alone on his car lot, staring at his beloved automobile. He could think of no way to salvage it. All that work had been for nothing.

Well, I guess that's all she wrote, he thought to himself before going into his office and pouring a drink from his well-hidden stash. Raising his glass to the now empty concrete podium he offered a final tribute, "It was beautiful while it lasted."

ENDGAMES AND EPILOGUES
by G. Allen Cook

This excellent, amazing, superlative—oh, wait. This one is mine.
It's the last story in the book for good reason: You can't skip
over it to the next one. The title is not coincidental.—Ed.

THE LAST OF MY family died in the night. I heard a barking cough, feet tripping about the upstairs rooms, and the terminal thud of a falling body.

I leave the corpses where they slump because there's nothing to be done about them. In truth, I've graver concerns—food and water, for instance. Though likely the most dangerous thing to do, I decide to leave the house.

Gathering my courage, I push into the garage through a side door left ajar. Two cars; one body dead in the driver's seat. I ignore the gruesome image and exit the carport— thankful the bay door was left open. I am outside and see for myself a waking nightmare.

No one walks the street or drives automobiles. Grass stands taller than I've ever seen it, the houses and cars on our block filthy with dirt and detritus.

Which way to go? Leaving it to chance, I plod left, toward

town. I know the owner of the deli is undoubtedly dead, but perhaps an unused crawlspace will gain me entrance. It's a gamble—but I'm hungry.

Two blocks later I realize I'm not alone. The unshorn grass rustles beside me, and I hear my tracker's breath. I always carry blades, of course, but flashing them too soon could incite an otherwise mundane encounter. Hedging my bets, I stop and turn in the road, telling whoever it is to show themselves.

A feminine form eases from the verdure. Inside, I wince.

It's the girl from next door, the gossipy minx everyone in the neighborhood tries—tried—to avoid. She's disheveled and looks only half herself. August is her name. Despite her slanderous nature, I've always admired her bosky eyes. The green has faded to gray, however, and they appear haunted.

I call her by name. For a moment she seems poised to flee, but I assure her I'm no threat. With cautious step she approaches me.

"Laszlo," she says.

"August," I repeat. "You look hungry."

"You have a gift for understatement." Those once-exquisite eyes narrow with suspicion. "You appear half-starved yourself."

I force a chuckle. "You needn't look at me as if I'm going to gobble you up. You can trust me."

"There's little trust left to go around. Anyway, I've seen

bones and bodies in the street. Someone's eating survivors."

"Probably wolves down from the mountain," I reply, tempering my voice against the cold unease of encountering a feral pack. "I'm going into town. You're welcome to accompany me."

"Why?" she says, a bit too quickly.

"Because you were following me anyway. Two can travel as safely as one. Might as well make a show of it, no? Let those canine bastards see we're not afraid."

"I am afraid," she cries. "You're the first living thing I've seen in days. What's happening?"

I tell her I don't know, which is true. I assure her we'll be fine and resume my excursion, leaving her with the decision to come on or go back. It is not long before she catches me up.

"Everyone in my home is dead," she says. "Adults. Children. Even the goldfish."

"Are you sure they died a natural death?" I ask in half-jest. "The goldfish, I mean. I understand they are a delicacy."

My joke shocks her for only a moment—it isn't long before she's prattling again.

"One by one they died. Choked to death. What accounts for it? Are we immune, or will we die too? Does it hurt to die, do you think? I've seen dead horses—and cows."

We barely make a block before I regret inviting her on my excursion. August dilates upon infinite topics, jangling my nerves, making my head swim. It's a blessing when we come upon the town.

Or it would be had the town still been there.

A few buildings remain on their foundation, but their windows are broken, the shelves within bare. Most of the structures are nothing more than smoldering cinders— either struck by lightning or purposefully set ablaze.

August makes a sad choking sound. I could console her, but she might misconstrue my intention. Leaving her to weep, I explore the damage. It's mostly rubble, but a charred hand extends from the wreckage, persuading me that lightning had nothing to do with it.

All surviving markets stand empty, clothing stores ransacked. The supplementary shops smoke and glow with hot coals. There is nothing here to gain.

August has pulled herself together by the time I return. She knows as well as I that the town is lost.

"What do we do?" Her voice wavers. Unable to brook another meltdown, I move us on, leaving the ruins behind us.

The day is bright, but quiet. This gives us the advantage over those who might overtake us by surprise. Stealth, however, is *not* our strong suit. August weaves a loud tapestry of one-sided conversation, laborious objections, and general whinging and whining. I am close to demanding silence when I see something in the street ahead.

Upon closer examination, we find a badly-beaten body, obviously dead. A terrible sight, I suggest we move on. Before

I take a step, August screams, and I'm seized from behind, a clutch of blades presses to my throat.

"Who are you?" rasps a voice. "Where you from? Where you going? Got any food?"

"Which question should I answer first?" I say, trying to sound nonplussed. "What was the first one again?"

The blades dig into my neck. If my captor presses any harder, he'll open a vein.

"Don't recognize either of you," he says. "What are you doing on the road in the middle of the day?"

"Going for a walk," I reply. "Sorry we bothered you, but we thought you were. . .unwell."

"Yeah, I know how unwell I look." The blades come away from my neck. I see the "dead" fellow standing before me, rubbing a swollen jaw. "Bastards. Let me get within arm's reach of any of them! I'll make a choke collar out of their eyeballs."

"They who?" August asks, keeping a noticeable distance from the stranger.

"I was on my way to Bay County. Not but two miles from here. I was resting during the heat of the day—you know how damn hot it gets. That's when they ambushed me."

"Who?"

"Wolves. Five of 'em. I was distracted lookin' for some shade, and then—"

He does not finish, for August sets up a terrible racket at

the mention of wolves. Spitting a bloody tooth onto the tarmac, the stranger tells me to stifle the girl lest the pack return to finish the job.

"I'm scared," August wails. "I don't want to die!"

"Then hush up," roars the stranger. "You'll attract every starving predator within five miles with all that noise. Now, I don't know you folks," he continues, "but I'd wager you'd walk a bit further for a meal. You're welcome to come to Bay County. Don't have much—but what there is I'll share."

"Thank you for your generosity," I say. "Can you make two miles in your condition?"

He harrumphs. "Pay no mind to these papercuts. I can make two miles in my sleep. We'll spend the night indoors, away from wol. . .er, out of the chill."

"Thanks, again. I'm Laszlo. This is August."

"Ah," the stranger says, running an appreciative glance her way. "August. One of the more volatile, if not pretty, months of the year. Well, press on. Bay County won't come to us.

"Oh, by the way," he adds, his golden eyes flashing, "my name is Otto. Chop, chop!"

~ ~ ~

Otto spoke true when he said Bay County lay two miles to the East—but neglected to tell us one needs birdwings to reach it before nightfall.

Keeping clear of the road, traversing field and farmland

grown over with weeds, we make our way slowly, our senses alert for the itinerate wolfpack. August chatters glibly; Otto harrumphs and checks the landscape, making excuses each time we pull up lost. With each hour my nerves clangor more and more, but I say nothing untoward to either companion.

There is, however, a tense moment at sundown. Noticing we're not as far along as we should be, Otto snaps at August, tells her to hold her tongue so that he might concentrate. She blubbers and blathers about becoming a predacious supper due to his negligence. By the time I feel obligated to intercede, a hulking shape looms in the gloaming: a tottering barn, dark and long since abandoned.

Making for its southern wall, Otto gains us entrance by way of several loose planks. The inside stifles with the ancient odor of hay and horses; rope and rusted tools hang in the darkness above us. As I hasten to inspect our surroundings, Otto sets about collecting vegetables sprouting wild in the otherwise wasted barn. I've had choicer meals, but—after our trek across the countryside—even the shriveled carrots and potatoes taste wonderful.

Of water there appears to be no trace, but Otto does not disappoint us. Within an enormous horse trough float the dregs of an absent steed's drink. Pushing at the slime from above forces clear water to filter through small cracks beneath the trough's wooden basin—each of us drinks from it. It's not that bad, considering.

Though usually awake through the early-morning hours, I am exhausted by moonrise. The day's heat begins to chill, so I find an unused corner and burrow beneath the hay. The others make their own accommodations, and there is one more exchange before the barn settles into silence.

"A longer day I've never known," says Otto. "I don't suppose, fair August, you'd be in favor of a quick rut to help bring on slumber?"

"Not hardly," she replies, but I feel her eyes shift to me. It is with something like relief that I fall asleep, putting this tiresome day behind me.

~ ~ ~

It seems only moments pass before I'm shaken awake. I'm surprised to see daylight streaming through the barn slats. Pulling myself from the comfort of my pallet, I note August standing before me, a frightened expression on her face.

"He's gone," she says, her voice quivering. "Must've left in the night. Probably out betraying us to those wolves."

"Doubtful." I rouse myself, stretching, wondering if any of last night's vegetables remain for breakfast. "He's just stepped outside to make his toilet, I should think."

"I don't trust him, Laszlo. He's brusque and common and offers nothing we can't find on our own."

"Oh? He led us here, didn't he? Fed and watered us. He seems resourceful enough, in spite of a certain indelicacy.

And I doubt he'll have further dealings with wolves—not after what they did to him yesterday."

"You are confident with his leadership?"

I laugh, trying to disarm the girl's angst. "I wouldn't exactly call him leader; but even at that I would put up no struggle if he insisted I did. We've come further since meeting him than we have in the past month. So he propositioned you last night—let's not confuse decency with industry."

August's eyes goggle with humiliation. "You heard that?"

"It would've been difficult not to. Let's step outside and find our host. He can't be far."

~ ~ ~

We squeeze past the loose boards and out into a morning redolent with summer scent. Taking care to step quietly, August and I inspect the grounds for any clue to Otto's whereabouts. After a fruitless search across the farmyard I begin to think our benefactor dissolved with the forenoon fog.

Before I can share my concerns August nods toward a nearby hedge. We peek around it and find a cow pasture. The cows are there—dead, their throats torn open. I count twelve corpses, all bloated to the point of eruption.

"They've been dead some time," I say. "But they didn't die like everyone else. They were killed."

"Killed by whom?" asks August in a small, shaking voice.

"The Beta Wolves," someone behind us replies. We

turn—there stands Otto, blood trilling from fresh wounds on his body. "They are also known as the Last Auguries," he continues, "and Hell's Harbingers. In the end it matters little who they are, what they are called. They represent the coming endgame, an epilogue to all life."

"All life on Earth?" I ask.

"All life throughout the Cosmos. Advanced life; lower life; life at the atomic level. Wiped out. Gone. Forever. This is their sole task, and they have come to begin their work."

"And they did that to you?" August motions to Otto's injuries. "Why?"

"I don't pretend to understand their motives, fair August. I am a simple messenger and enjoy no privilege— except I die last, which is not as pleasant as it sounds. Announcing the death of those around me. . .watching them die very badly in the jaws of the Beta Wolves. No, not pleasant at all. And in the end what will I be? Alone. The last living thing beneath the sky to draw breath. And then the gnashing of teeth—the rending of claws. Farewell, Otto. Farewell, all."

"That gruff voice was an act," August cries. "You've been putting on this whole time—to lure us here."

"But why?" I ask. "This seems a lot of trouble for just the two of us. Couldn't 'Hell's Harbingers' smite us from a distance? Mutter a spell and obliterate us in our homes? Why bring us here, feed us, make us comfortable for the night? For what ultimate purpose?"

"Because they willed it." For a moment, Otto manages to look apologetic. "They gave the order, and I obeyed. It was nothing more than that, please believe me."

"What happens now?"

"I've summoned the Beta Wolves. Already," he says, turning his face towards a gathering darkness on the horizon, "they come."

The darkness grows, blotting out the midmorning sun. An incandescent arc of lightning fries the air between us, knocking August, Otto, and myself to the ground.

Above the roar of the storm—echoing across the flatlands of Bay County—I hear the demoniac howling of wolves.

I focus my attention on regaining my feet, noting that Otto has done likewise. Unsheathing my blades, I stagger to him and press them to his throat.

"Call them off," I growl.

"I cannot," Otto replies.

"Call them off or I kill you."

"My life was never yours to take—nor mine to keep."

"What does that mean?"

"Too late." Otto looks skyward, his golden eyes round and full of terror. "They are here."

Before I can reply the heavens open up, hurling more lightning bolts at us. One slices through the air to strike Otto, setting him ablaze, his features sizzling and turning to ash.

Once again, I am thrown to the ground, breath ripped from my chest. This time I lose consciousness, the glowing dust of Otto's body scattering on the wind the last thing I see.

~ ~ ~

I awaken some time later in a field damp with rainwater. The storm is over, the afternoon cool and fresh. It takes tremendous effort to pull myself upright. When I manage it I notice I'm not alone.

Sitting in the grass beside me is an enormous wolf. Eyes gleaming, it considers me a moment but makes no move to attack.

"LASZLO," it says, its mouth unmoving. "DO YOU KNOW US?"

I say I do.

"DO WE FRIGHTEN YOU?"

I say no.

"WHY NOT?"

"Otto explained who you are. He did not, however, say why you wanted him dead after serving you."

"OTTO WAS NEVER MARKED FOR LIFE," says the wolf. "BUT LIFE IS SOMETHING WE NOW OFFER YOU."

"Why me?"

"BECAUSE WE WISH IT."

"Again—why?"

"WE FIND THIS MANNER OF COMMUNICATION TIRE-SOME. DO YOU WANT TO TAKE OTTO'S PLACE? ANSWER

NOW SO THAT WE MAY FIND ONE EAGER FOR THE JOB."

"At which point you kill me."

"NATURALLY."

"Where is August?"

"SHE DOES NOT FEATURE IN THIS."

"She's dead then."

"NATURALLY."

I say nothing. August was nothing more than a companion in an otherwise empty world...nonetheless I mourn her.

The wolf stands, scratching its ear with a back paw.

"I GROW IMPATIENT. MAKE YOUR CHOICE."

"I suppose I'd be foolish to decline."

"YOU WOULD."

"Then I accept. What must I do?"

The wolf explains how I am to go before him—them— and prepare those left in the world for oblivion. I do not ask why the Beta Wolves have come, merely agree to the terms despite knowing I, too, am marked for death. Whether tomorrow or a thousand years from now, I too will die.

"GO, THEN," the wolf continues. "WARN THOSE LEFT ON THE EARTH. SPREAD OUR MESSAGE OF DOOM."

With that, the wolf disappears, leaving me alone in the Bay County field.

~ ~ ~

Now I roam the byways and night roads, my eyes and

ears sharp. I've always had superior eyesight—and as for ears none are better. I always find my mark, no matter how well hidden they may be. The job has taken me around the world.

I travel on, the pads on all four feet beaten to leather, but my tail undrooping to the last. I prefer to journey by night, as all cats have done since the world began, which makes taking survivors unawares all the easier. Why the wolves left cats for last, I'll never know...I perform my gruesome duties without fail (despite the crying and begging for mercy).

Men fell first to the wolves, followed by work animals, and then dogs. Again, I don't know why we were left for last, but I have a theory.

Have you ever tried to get rid of a cat? Shoot us, burn us, poison us—we come back. Unfailingly we come back. I think the wolves knew that. As well, they knew this: If you want to truly rid yourself of a cat, get another cat. They call this *fighting fire with fire*.

Otto called the wolves the endgame, an epilogue to all life in the Cosmos. But he was wrong.

I'm your endgame and epilogue.

And before the wolves claim it the world belongs to me.

Never underestimate a cat.

AUTHOR BIOGRAPHIES

HAN ADCOCK

Han Adcock writes short stories, short long stories, and poetry ranging from bizarre to the humorous. His stories appear in Penumbra, Expanded Horizons, *and* Poetic Diversity, *and he edits a new ezine,* Once Upon a Crocodile. *You can find him at* www.facebook.com/wyrdstories, inspirationandlaughs.wordpress.com, *or on Twitter as* @Erringrey

STEVE BISSONNETTE
Steve Bissonnette lives in Northern NH with his wife and two kids. His published work includes articles and regional publications such as Country Folks, Unravel the Gravel, Northern NH Magazine, *and* Kingdom Historical. *He has also written for* VTliving.com. *He studied writing and poetry at Union Institute, Vermont, before switching course and earning a B.S. in Accounting and Finance.*

JUSTIN BLOCH
Justin Block is the author of The Stolen Karma of Nathaniel Valentine *and its upcoming sequel,* The Book of Doors. *He can be found on Twitter* (@JustinBloch) *and Facebook* (facebook.com/StolenKarma.) *He has a wonderful wife who makes everything he writes at last 75% better and a daughter and son who make everything he writers take at least 75% longer.*

VONNIE WINSLOW CRIST

Vonnie Winslow Crist is author of The Enchanted Daggar (Compton Crook Award and Maryland Writers Association Book Award Winner), Murder on Marawa Time, Owl Light, The Greener Forest (eFestival of Books Award Winner), and other books. Her speculative writing appears in Chilling Ghost Stories, Cast of Wonders, Weirdbook, Killing It Softly 2, Defending the Future's Dogs of War, The Great Tome of Fantastic and Wondrous Places, and elsewhere.

ROXANNE DENT

Roxanne Dent, member of New England Horror Writers, Essex Writers and Artists Guild, Fiction Writers Guild, has sold nine novels and dozens of short stories in a variety of genres (including Paranormal Fantasy, Regency, Mystery, Horror and YA). She has also co-authored short stories and plays with her sister, Karen Dent. Killing Secrets, their third short/noir/pulp mystery, will appear in Murder Ink, Vol. 3 (Plaidswede Publishing), due out in February 2018 at the Boston Newspaper Conference. Roxanne has just finished Death of a Hotsy-Totsy Girl, a 1920s novella, and completed a second novel in The Grimaldi Chronicles, a detective fantasy that moves between urban and mythical worlds.

OLIN WISH

Olin Wish is a husband, father of three young children, student, and full-time bread winner. Olin pays the bills at a day job that puts him in close proximity to the criminally insane. Aside from being lost in the woods, he is a regular contributor to multiple on-line and print journals. And he just fucking loves comic books!

G. H. FINN

G. H. Finn is the pen name of someone you are very unlikely to have heard of but who keeps his real identity secret anyway in order to escape the eternal wrath of the ever vengeful, eldritch Elder Gods. Or possibly in the forlorn hope of one day being mistaken for a superhero (it hasn't happened yet).

Having written non-fiction for many years, G. H. Finn decided to start submitting short-stories to publishers in early 2015. He was flabbergasted when the first piece of fiction he had ever submitted was selected for publication. He was even more gobsmacked to discover that he really was going to be paid actual hard cash for the story. At that point he decided that there might be something to this writing lark after all.

HÁKON GUNNARSSON

Hákon Gunnarsson is an Icelandic writer who has done a little bit of everything with words, even though he had intended to become a photographer. Among other things, he has written about cinema and literature. Over the years he has worked in various fields. He has stacked fish, sliced cheese, restacked papers, and watched paint dry, but his dogs will tell you that his main job is walking them.

DAVID HENDERSON

A Game of Tag is David's first foray into the PA genre. Gamer by nature, he has loved the idea of the world after annihilation since first playing games like "Wasteland," "Mad Max," and "Roadwar 2000" on his Commodore 64. He craves stories of loss, survival, struggle, and resolve—stories where the endings remain untidy. Post-apocalyptic fiction fills that craving. We don't know what comes next, but we know it won't come easy.

LUKE KONDOR

Luke Kondor is a writer and filmmaker living and working in the great rainy city of Manchester. He wakes up way too early, drinks way too much coffee, all in the name of getting words on the page. He started writing nonsense on his computer in his early teens and never looked back, and now he's got really sore eyes.

CRYSTAL LEFLAR

Crystal Leflar is not skilled in referring to herself in the third person, but she can be found on Twitter @Crysa_Leflar.

JESSICA MIZELL

Jessica loves, loves, loves to write, and this is her first official publication.

MEGAN MANZANO

Megan Manzano graduated university with a B.A. in English and a minor in philosophy. Her hobbies include reading, writing, blogging, traveling, and binge-watching television.

The genres she writes the most are fantasy and Science Fiction. She has a particular interest in writing pieces that are geared for the emotions or make one question the state of reality. She can be found on https://twitter.com/Megan_Manazano.

JIM O'DONNELL

Author and photographer Jim O'Donnell is fortunate enough to call Taos, New Mexico, his home base. That said, his sometimes-aimless wanderings have taken him to over 40 countries on five continents and are to blame for the five languages he is sure he can stumble through. O'Donnell is the author of Notes for the Aurora Society: 1500 Miles on Foot across Finland and Rise and Go, a collection of short travel stories. O'Donnell is also to blame for numerous articles and short stories, other sordid tales, many brilliant observations, some half-finished novels, a variety of angry letters-to-the-editor and a host of other scribbling. His most recent stories are: The Big Business of Europe's Migration Crisis in SAPIENS, Mesa Verde's Surprising Story in BBC Travel, Aimed at Refugees, Fences Are Threatening European Wildlife in YaleEnvironment360 and New Mexico Zero Carbon 2065in Trend. He was the 2015 Jack Williamson Endowed Chair for Literature at Eastern New Mexico University. Find him at his website Around the World in Eighty Years and support his climate resiliency journalism on Patreon.

RAY PREW

Ray Prew was originally from Rhode Island, but now lives in Florida. He is a graduate of the New England Institute of Technology. Ray has been a blue-collar worker all his life, and started writing as a hobby. He spent nine enjoyable years as a phone psychic. Ray's work has been published in Spinetinglers *magazine (6 times), with one of his stories used in a trivia quiz. Two* Spinetinglers *stories are on* YouTube: *one is called* Some Monsters Are Real, *and the other is a short video called* Ray Prew's Let Me Out. *He has been published in* Blood Moon Rising *(7 times, including 2 poems),* Aphelion *(12 times including 2 poems), as well as several other magazines. He has an anthology book of published and unpublished stories available on* Amazon *called* Delightful Nightmares. *His work has also appeared in* Vicious Circle: Season One *(an anthology put out by Sinister Grin), and one piece in an anthology of vampire poetry,* Vampoetry.

N. J. REYNOLDS

N. J. REYNOLDS did not provide a bio, but allow me to say that he is an author of the highest caliber. Anyone who can compose a post-apocalyptic story about coffee is a truly amazing writer indeed. (Provided by author. —Ed.)

JACK STONE

(I've tried to persuade Jack Stone to provide a bio, but he refuses to do so. The only clue he gives is "Nail Gun." —Ed.)

KAMRON TAYLOR

Kamron Sean Taylor is an avid reader. This is his first dabble into writing. He is married to a loving and supportive wife, Crystal, and has been for the last 22 years. He has three amazing sons, Matthew (21), Logan (18), and Lucas (16), to whom he dedicates this work. "If not for their insistence that I try to do it, it probably wouldn't have been done."

DANIEL WILLCOCKS

Daniel Willcocks is a chart-topping author and podcaster of dark fiction. He is one quarter of digital story studio, Hawk and Cleaver, co-producer of iTunes-busting "The Other Stories" podcast, as well as one of the lead hosts of "The Story Studio podcast." If you're interested in following Dan's work, you can join his VIP Readers Club at www.danielwillcocks.com and get your hands on 3 free stories, including his 2016 #1 horror hit, Sins and Smoke. Or, for anything else Dan is involved in, check out www.hawkandcleaver.com.

EDITOR'S BIOGRAPHY

G. Allen Cook *lives in Northeast Arkansas with his wife and son. Over the past twenty-three years, Cook has written twenty plays and written and composed seven musicals. His short fiction includes* Fat in the Fire, *published in* Robbed of Sleep Vol. 4, Anemone, *published in* Robbed of Sleep Vol. 5 *(both edited by Troy Blackford)*, No Easy Trick, *published in* Ellipses, *edited by Dylan Callens, and many more. He has written for various newspapers and magazines, and he aired on morning radio for a decade. Cook's upcoming projects include a revival of his first musical and an illustrated novel,* Mule-Killer and the Magician, *due out Christmas 2018.*

~ ~ ~

Kathy Cook *holds a* Bachelor of Science in Education *and a* Master's of Science in Library Media. *She has taught junior high and high school English, and is now a middle school librarian. She co-edited* Chaos of Hard Clay *and designed its exteriors.*

~ ~ ~

Jamie Bristol Hampton *created the illustrations. She is a professional artist who "works for food and concert tickets." You can contact her at* Instagram *as* jam.d.ham.

Thank you for purchasing *Chaos of Hard Clay*. The writers hope you enjoyed the various tales within these pages, and the editors hope you come back for the next installment.

Please go to http://gallencook.com/blog-and-buy/ to peruse the growing BANJAXED Books catalogue. We are currently negotiating new titles from authors all over the world, so check back often. If you are a writer, watch for submission notifications.

Until then, thanks for your support and keep purchasing indie-published books. It is impossible to bring out new titles without you.

Happy reading!

—G. Allen Cook

ACKNOWLEDGEMENTS

The publishers wish to thank the following people for their unwavering support of BANJAXED Books.

Stephanie Arnold
Heather Mitchell
Tommy Lane
Vicki Bishop
Jer Allen
Kamron Taylor
Kevin Moslander
Laura B. Hagen
Nicole West
Vickie Dement Kunau
Jessica Mizell
Kyle Vincent
Jamie Pruett Sikes
The Late Debbie Cox Schug
Tina Reed-Brewer
Ron Spence
Joy Robinson
Stony Wyss
Natalie Browder
Stephen Posey
Tim Stone
Nancy Hoke
Neeley Smith
Shawn Barnhill
Glenda McEuen
Missy Stahr Threadgill
Stephanie Cook
The Late Lloyd Cook
Alex Cook

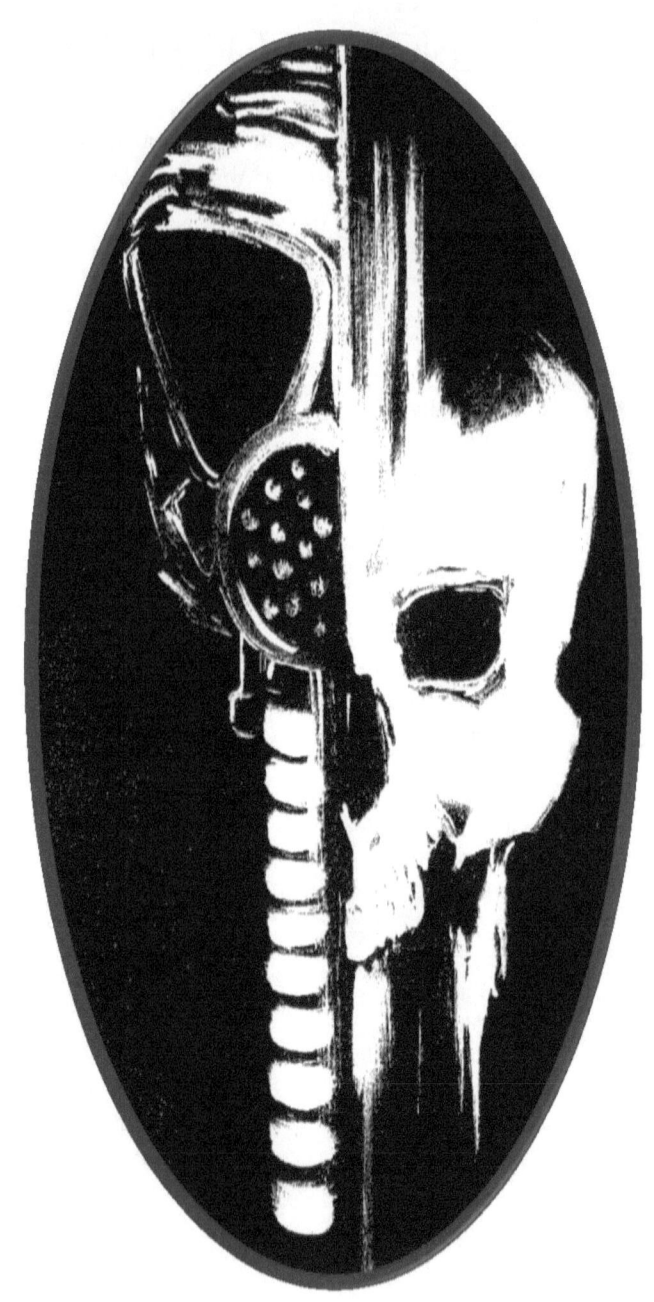